"I've Remembered, Jason," Amanda Told Him with Eloquent Simplicity.

His heart stopped and then started again. He moved her hand to his chest, pressing her palm against the galloping heartbeat there. "All of it?" He wanted to be absolutely certain. "Have you truly remembered how it was?"

"Yes," she breathed in a gentle smile. "Every moment and every second."

"Then tell me, Mandy," he urged.

He eased her down onto the lush meadow grass. She gazed up at his face, remembering the words he had spoken. For so many years she'd sealed them away, keeping them inviolate and fresh in the deepest reaches of her heart. "You said you loved me," she answered.

"Always," he finished, kissing her. "And God help you, Amanda, but you're about to discover just how much . . . "

Dear Reader,

We, the editors of Tapestry Romances, are committed to bringing you two outstanding original romantic historical novels each and every month.

From Kentucky in the 1850s to the court of Louis XIII, from the deck of a pirate ship within sight of Gibraltar to a mining camp high in the Sierra Nevadas, our heroines experience life and love, romance and adventure.

Our aim is to give you the kind of historical romances that you want to read. We would enjoy hearing your thoughts about this book and all future Tapestry Romances. Please write to us at the address below.

The Editors
Tapestry Romances
POCKET BOOKS
1230 Avenue of the Americas
Box TAP
New York, N.Y. 10020

Heart's Echo

Jan McKee

A TAPESTRY BOOK
PUBLISHED BY POCKET BOOKS NEW YORK

Books by Jan McKee

Heart's Echo
Published by TAPESTRY BOOKS

Montana Skies
Published by POCKET BOOKS

An *Original* publication of TAPESTRY BOOKS

A Tapestry Book published by
POCKET BOOKS, a division of Simon & Schuster, Inc.
1230 Avenue of the Americas, New York, N.Y. 10020

ISBN: 0-671-61740-0

First Tapestry Books printing August, 1986

10 9 8 7 6 5 4 3 2 1

POCKET and colophon are registered trademarks
of Simon & Schuster, Inc.

TAPESTRY is a registered trademark of Simon & Schuster, Inc.

Printed in the U.S.A.

*To my parents,
Jim and Ann Baker,
with all my love.*

Heart's Echo

Chapter One

THE STOCKTON, KANSAS, STATION MASTER FIXED A cold stare on the raven-haired visitor who had placed a dusty posterior on the edge of his desk. "Thought you said you were in town to meet the five o'clock train from Kansas City, Thorne," Bert Taylor said with unveiled impatience, stifling the urge to snatch the leaded crystal paperweight from Jason Thorne's work-roughened hands.

"Yeah, that's what I said." The man who had come to fetch the woman and her child, and take them back to the ranch, continued to examine the cut glass, holding it up to the light, seemingly fascinated by the rainbow colors dancing upon the dingy wall. In truth, he was barely aware of his actions.

"Well, it ain't very polite to keep those folks waiting."

The paperweight made a dull thudding noise when it was dropped to the desktop. Glancing up, Jason gave Bert Taylor a tight smile, aware, not for the first time, that his impulsive visit to an old school chum was not at all appreciated.

Bert's expression was just plain unfriendly. The thin mouth beneath the dapper, waxed mustache twitched, silently expressing his opinion of this unexpected social call. Jason might have been concerned if he'd had any welcome to wear out in the first place. Now he was being accused of rudeness, which would add another black mark to the long list already attributed to his unredeemable character. Still, it was preferable to the very real cowardice that was keeping him rooted to the desk. Needling old Bert had served the purpose of killing time while he cooled the heels of admittedly cold feet. Amanda and her little girl were waiting. It was time to face the music.

"Well, I'll be seeing you, Bert," Jason mumbled as he headed for the door. A rueful smile quirked the corners of his mouth when Taylor's exaggerated sigh of relief carried across the room and followed him outside.

As he made his way across the wood platform, Jason acknowledged several familiar faces with a nod of greeting. The more temperate among old acquaintances quickly averted their eyes, while others, less inclined toward restraint, glared with unguarded belligerence. Unfortunately the passage of time and the turn of an enlightened new century had altered little in his hometown. Not the least of which were attitudes formed and cast in the unyielding bias of intolerance and bigotry. The only change Jason perceived was within himself. He simply didn't give a damn anymore.

"I wanna go home! I hate it here!"

Six-year-old Sarah Ames was working herself up to yet another temperamental outburst. To her fatigued mother, the high-pitched wail seemed a bludgeon. Amanda was tired and hot, and more than just a little concerned that there didn't appear to be anyone to meet them, and Sarah's constant tantrums were a strain on Amanda's patience.

Sarah continued to whine and pull at her mother's skirts. Not trusting her voice to carry a civil tone, Amanda looked to the cloudless Kansas sky, counting to ten, while asking for divine guidance to soothe her unhappy little girl. She found little help, but the panoramic azure sky provided a scenic respite from the old weathered station office and uncovered platform. The late afternoon sun on this warm June day seemed additional punishment after the long hours spent in a stuffy train compartment. The shirtwaist beneath Amanda's wilted, gray poplin traveling suit felt uncomfortably damp. Her head was beginning to ache, and the ribbon-banded straw hat afforded little shade.

Where could Aunt Julie be? Was there a problem?

"Mama," Sarah sobbed, demanding her mother's attention. "Can we go home now? This place is ugly. I wanna go home!"

Her daughter's genuine distress tore at Amanda's

heart. She pulled the little girl close and smoothed the golden braids while the cornflower blue eyes—so like her late father's—begged and accused at the same time.

"Sugarplum, this is our home now. I promise you are going to love living on Aunt Julie's ranch. Why, when I was just a little girl like you, visiting the TJ was my favorite way to spend the summer. Now it will be better because we'll be living there all the time."

Sarah frowned and huffily jerked away from her mother's attempt to comfort, shaking her head vigorously. "No, it won't," she said with conviction. Sarah wanted her house, her things, and her friends. She couldn't imagine living anywhere other than Kansas City. Didn't want to imagine it. Her papa would be mad at Mama for selling the house. Papa would have told Mama not to. But Papa was dead and nothing had been the same since. Sarah doubted anything would ever be the same again.

Amanda felt like crying herself. During the last eight weeks she had done and said everything possible to help Sarah adjust to this move. Nothing had worked, and Amanda was growing frustrated with the role of wicked witch. Sarah had always been closer to her father; her papa's best girl. His sudden death had turned a trusting, open, and loving little girl into a withdrawn, petulant brat.

Amanda's thoughts shamed her. Losing her father had been a horrible trauma for her daughter. Sarah had idolized Harry. He'd been her favorite playmate, while Amanda was the disciplinarian, the one always to say no. Unfortunately, Amanda had not realized how spoiled Sarah had become until recently. Of course, it had only been since her father's death that Sarah had come to realize that she couldn't have everything she desired. But her basic nature was sweet and loving. Amanda knew she must be patient and guide the little girl gently. It was just so very difficult at times, especially when Sarah lashed out at her, blaming her for the changes in their lives. It hurt, she admitted. Sometimes she felt cut to the quick.

"I can't imagine what is keeping Aunt Julie," Amanda mumbled aloud.

"See?" Sarah smirked. "She doesn't want us here."

"Sweetheart, that isn't true. She wrote and asked us to come."

Julie Danfield's invitation for two widows to "pool their resources" had been a godsend. Amanda had been very close to losing her mind and the fight to keep a roof over their heads and food on the table. Their meager savings hadn't lasted two months. Everything of value had been sold. If Julie hadn't written, Amanda knew she would soon have thrown herself on her aunt's mercy. Employment was impossible to find without skills or training. And the thought of entrusting Sarah's care to total strangers made her physically ill. Only her pride had kept her from writing Julie Danfield of their true circumstances months ago. But pride, she discovered, did not put bread on the table. Admitting Harry Ames had not been the perfect husband and father she'd always painted him to be in her letters was a small price to pay for the security and haven the TJ offered.

Even now, when one was not supposed to think ill

of the dead, Amanda could not think of Harry without anger. Did a man who loved his family leave them destitute? Handsome, charming Harry had lived every day as if the world were his personal carnival, a celebration, until a heart condition he'd neglected to mention brought his carousel to an abrupt and final stop. Harry Ames had been an immature fifty-five when his weak heart had finally refused to keep pace with his carefree lifestyle. So here they were on a train platform in Kansas, and where in the world was Aunt Julie?

"Mama, why can't we get on the train and go back home?"

"Because, Sarah, we don't have a home to return to." Amanda didn't realize how sharply she had spoken until heads turned, and the golden-haired child at her side began to shriek at the top of her lungs. Amanda regretted the harsh words immediately. She was oblivious to the frowns directed her way by the citizens of this cattle and farming community. All she saw was the hurt she had inflicted on her own daughter.

"I'm sorry, sugarplum," she moaned, kneeling down to gently pull Sarah into her arms. "Trust Mama just a little. We'll be happy here, I promise. You'll soon have new friends—"

She couldn't continue. Not when, in truth, Amanda was very doubtful Sarah would have little more than minimal contact with other children until school started next fall. She remembered well, from her own childhood visits, the isolation of the ranch. Only that last summer, during her sixteenth year, had she enjoyed the companionship of someone near her own age. She could still remember the joy, the sweetness, and the bittersweet pain of that time when she'd stumbled out of childhood to discover—

Amanda pushed the memory away, chiding herself for indulging in the painful nostalgia. Good heavens, it had been years and years since she'd thought of that summer—of Jason. She buried the recollection as quickly as it had risen.

Jason stopped a few feet away from the woman comforting her distraught child. "Amanda," he mouthed silently. He had told himself there would be change, perhaps a matronly plumpness. But the only change he could see after twelve years was that she'd merely become more of what he remembered.

Jason had never entirely forgotten those tawny eyes or the way they could ignite with the brilliance of a flaring match. Neither had he put out of his mind the fire-gold of her hair, now molten red in the glare of the late afternoon sun.

Then, as now, Amanda was not conventionally beautiful. She was vibrant, strikingly lovely, although, if asked, he would have been hard-pressed to say just why. The riotous curls beneath her hat threatened to defy the severe hairstyle. The cheek pressed against her child's hair was peach-tinted and lightly dusted with pale freckles. Her nose was straight and narrow, perfect for her oval face. And her mouth, above a slightly dimpled chin, was generous. When she smiled Jason knew a fully blossomed rose would pale in comparison. She was too tall for daintiness, and her coloring far too flamboyant for the day's standard of beauty. However, in Jason's eyes, there had never been a woman made more perfectly.

Amanda was not quite certain when she became aware of his presence. Although she'd thought his ghost firmly banished, there he was, standing with his thumbs hooked in the pockets of faded dark trousers. Unfortunately, what she first assumed to be a specter of her imagination had too much flesh, blood, and bone to be easily dismissed. The loose-limbed stance, with one knee slightly flexed, was singularly distinctive, and would have brought his image to mind anywhere. Here, in Stockton, Jason Thorne was all too real. And it was the last place on earth she would have expected to encounter him.

Acting on impulse, spurred by a sudden, over-whelming sense of panic, Amanda attempted to save herself, and perhaps even Jason, from this awkward reunion. There wasn't anything rational in her think-ing as she schooled her expression to blankness, letting her eyes sweep past him as she rose to her feet, praying the pretense of not recognizing him would effectively stall any confrontation. *Please,* she silently pleaded, *please play this game and go away until I can come to terms with finding you here.* Surely he could not be eager to hem and haw through attempted polite conversation. It would be embarrassing for them both.

Amanda didn't ask herself why, after twelve years, a husband, and a child, Jason Thorne could still shatter a supposedly mature woman's compo-sure. It was enough that he did. Searching for the whys would come later.

With as much nonchalance as she could muster, she took a firm hold of Sarah's hand. "Come along, Sarah. We'll inquire about finding transportation inside the station."

She would have walked right past him if Jason hadn't stepped forward. "Hello, Mandy," he said, his tone designed to grab attention. Her transparent attempt to consign him to nonexistence rankled, giving him the needed impetus to speak.

Confronted, Amanda could feel her color rise as she feigned first confusion and then surprise. "Jason? My goodness, is it really you? I didn't recognize . . . It's been such a long time." She cleared her throat nervously, feeling utterly ridiculous with her less than sterling performance. She knew, by the grim set of his mouth, that her charade had been anything but successful. Dear heavens, what must he be thinking?

Jason wasn't thinking at all. He was being flooded by emotions and memories, consumed by a biting resentment he'd thought long conquered. The perpetual contempt of Stockton's citizens meant nothing. This woman's deliberate snub hurt like hell, making him acutely aware of the thin blue shirt beneath his old leather vest, and the scuffed boots peeping out beneath the frayed hems of his faded trousers. It had been a very long time since he'd remembered his place in the world—the half-breed, bastard son of a Cherokee whore. Or wasn't it more accurate to say his lack of a place in the world?

Only the knowledge that Amanda had reasons to despise him beyond his questionable bloodlines kept him from lashing out with all the old defenses. "Yes," he finally agreed. "It has been a very long time."

To ease the emotionally charged moment, Jason turned his attention to the little girl clinging to her mother's skirt. "Who do we have here?" he asked lightly, dropping to his haunches to study what might be a very pretty child beneath a face all puckered up in a sulk. "What a sour little puss. Would some sugar sweeten that expression?" From his hip pocket he withdrew and offered a peppermint stick.

Sarah looked at the stranger warily, eyed the candy covetously, and then glanced up at her mother.

"It's all right, Sarah," Amanda reassured her. "This is Mr. Thorne. He's an . . . an old acquaintance. You may accept the candy."

Two things were accomplished by Jason's sudden interest in Sarah: a return of some composure and the promise of temporary, blessed quiet as the stick candy was promptly thrust in the gap of missing teeth.

Jason rose slowly, his eyes traveling upward, studying the figure before him, noting the womanly curves and flesh where once there had been mostly sharp angles. When he reached his full height, which was just shy of six feet, he smiled into Amanda's golden eyes while his thumbs automatically sought the familiar mooring of his pockets.

"Your daughter is lovely, Mandy. Nearly as lovely as her mother. The years have been kind to you."

The husky timbre of his voice and the use of a nickname she'd not heard on any other lips unnerved Amanda more than she wanted to admit. "Thank you," she replied, self-conscious with the flattery, tongue-tied because upon close inspection she could not, in all honesty, return a similar observation.

"You look well," she finally stuttered. He was

only thirty, she knew. Only two years older than herself, yet he looked closer to forty. Beneath the disturbing intensity of his dark green eyes, Amanda studied the tiny age lines threading across the once smooth skin.

Jason read the direction of her thoughts. Life had left its hard knocks and harsh lessons clearly mapped upon his face. They were his own personal testimonials of valor. He'd survived. "You haven't outgrown your freckles," he teased, hoping to ease the tension building between them.

"You've grown into your nose," Amanda spouted without thinking, surprising herself with the spontaneous observation, realizing how intense her study of his face had been.

With his thumb and index finger, Jason pinched the slightly hooked, twice-broken beak, a slow smile spreading across his face. "Yeah. Guess I have at that."

Here was the Jason she remembered. The Pan-like grin, with its devilish appeal, stripped away the protective layers time placed on old memories. Amanda's senses were being beseiged by the mind's ability to recall, in entirety, the images and emotions of the past. The concept of then and now was warped. Amanda was suddenly a young girl again, and Jason was the boy she worshiped to the exclusion of good sense. Her knees went weak, the blood rushed through her veins as if it had been dormant all these years. She felt disoriented, and only a strong instinct for self-preservation enabled her to grasp on to the one thing that could reanchor her to the present.

She turned to Sarah to see the last bit of peppermint slurped through her child's lips. "Good heavens. Look at that face . . . and your hands, Sarah." Digging deep within her reticule, she produced a flowery handkerchief. Then she began to remove the sticky residue from the child's face and hands with an enthusiasm that brought a loud wail of protest.

This motherly task proved effective in restoring the natural order of the world. She no longer felt like a foolish schoolgirl throwing herself wholeheartedly into an ill-fated infatuation with a charming young rogue who could, with a smile, make her bones melt. Jason Thorne was a married man, for heaven's sake. No doubt he had an entire brood of children by now. She already knew one child existed, remembering all too well the reason behind his abrupt flight from Stockton twelve years ago. Again the yesterday feelings attacked. But this time she remembered the humiliation.

Amanda brutally killed these unwanted feelings. The immediate problem was getting away from the Stockton station and to the TJ Ranch before the sun set.

"It's been very nice seeing you again, Jason," she said in a clear tone of dismissal, avoiding his eyes while her own swept the platform in the hope of finding her aunt or a likely candidate for the foreman Julie had mentioned. "Please give my regards to your family." Why didn't Jason take the hint and begin making a polite farewell? Couldn't he see that they were beginning to draw attention from curious onlookers, who had nothing better to do than speculate and draw erroneous conclusions regarding Mr.

Thorne's interest in herself and her child. "Perhaps we'll see each other again sometime soon."

Damn him. Were his boots nailed to the floor? Why was he still standing there with a stupid grin on his face? "You really will have to excuse us, but I must see to arranging transportation to the ranch. My aunt has obviously mistaken our arrival, and I would like to see that Sarah is settled before much later." There. Surely that was plain enough.

"Then we'd better get started, hadn't we?" Jason reached for the small traveling case near Amanda's feet. When she jerked the suitcase out of his hand and said, "I appreciate the offer, but I'm quite sure other arrangements can be made," his smile faded. Eyes suddenly the hue of a dense forest at twilight fixed upon Amanda's face. "Are you trying to get rid of me, Mandy?"

"Of course not," she denied, maintaining a tight grip on the leather case, in spite of his continuing determination to take it from her. "There's just no need for you to inconvenience yourself on our behalf." The tug of war continued with neither of them aware of the childishness evidenced by the silly struggle.

Finally Jason gave a soft snort of laughter. This was ludicrous. "Going home is not an inconvenience, Mandy. I'm your aunt Julie's foreman."

Amanda's eyes flew to his face, filled with startled dismay. "You? When . . . Why didn't Aunt Julie mention this in her letters?"

"Could be she thought you might not come." His expression challenged her to deny or confirm. When she could no longer meet his stare, Jason seized the suitcase. He turned away and started across the platform, leaving her standing with Sarah. She had no other choice but to follow him.

Taking Sarah's hand, Amanda had to hurry to match the swift and unrelenting pace Jason set, anger obvious in his stride. After a few yards of compliance, Sarah suddenly grew rebellious. She began to hang back, often stopping entirely, forcing Amanda to coax and cajole, and then finally give up on gentle persuasion and simply drag the obstinate child along behind her. She was able to catch only a glimpse of the small town of Stockton with its gray stone buildings, the parklike square in the town's center, the American flag waving from a pole attached to the second-story window of the courthouse.

When Sarah reared backward, nearly wrenching her mother's arm from the shoulder, Amanda turned to give her a sharp reprimand, and then ran flush into Jason, who had stopped without warning.

"Stubborn little donkey, isn't she?" he said with a chuckle while steadying the off-balanced woman trapped between himself and a very bratty little girl.

He was so close she could see the late-afternoon shadow of his beard and smell the slightly musky, but not entirely unpleasant odor of old leather. The firm grip of his hands on her arms revealed a tempered strength, vital and energetic, flowing from the slender symmetry of his physique.

Again Amanda reminded herself of the wife and children. It would be pleasant to have another woman her own age in residence. The ranch was so isolated. There would be other children for Sarah to play with and to make the long journey to school with when summer ended. Lucy Blane—funny how the maiden name of Jason's wife was burned in her memory—Lucy Thorne, she corrected, would become a friend.

"My automobile is parked over there," Jason indicated with a slight tilt of his head, his hands falling back to his side.

"Golly!" Sarah exclaimed, taking advantage of her mother's relaxed grip to yank free, surprising both adults by her swift change in mood as she sprinted toward the vehicle.

By the time Jason and Amanda joined her, Sarah had climbed onto the running board, and her fingers, still bearing the residue of sticky peppermint, were leaving smudges and prints everywhere they encountered the shiny green finish.

"It's wonderful," Sarah breathed in astonished admiration, hoisting herself up to lean over and examine the interior of this fascinating invention. "My papa took me home from school in a taxi once," she announced with a hint of smugness. "What kind is it?" Sarah asked as she jumped down and turned big, questioning eyes upon Jason.

"They call it a Model T," Jason explained. Grasping the child's waist, he lifted her up and swung her over the side and gently lowered her onto the cushioned seat behind the steering wheel. "I saw seven of these mechanical monsters chasing one pedestrian the other day, and I decided I was on the wrong end of the sport."

Sarah giggled. Amanda gasped with horror. "You can't be serious? That . . . that's horrible!"

"It was a joke, Mandy. And not a particularly original one. Being a city girl, I'm surprised you haven't heard it before."

"Well, I certainly don't find the picture of some poor man being chased by a mechanical contraption amusing."

"Mama's a scaredy-cat," Sarah taunted with a saucy smile. "She's never been in a taxi 'cause they go so fast. Bet she won't even get in. Maybe we'll just have to go home."

Jason leaned back against his automobile and lifted one foot to rest upon the running board. "I think you're wrong, Pickle-face. You see, I knew your mama before she was a mama. She always had an adventurous spirit and a curious nature. I'll bet *you* that before the summer is over, she'll be driving this *contraption.*" He gave Amanda a broad wink. "Do you want a piece of this wager, Mandy?"

For Amanda, Jason's so very casual reference to her adventurous spirit and curious nature held a hidden, insulting significance. When coupled with the arrogantly bold wink, and his continuing use of an overly familiar nickname, her hackles rose. "I most certainly do not, Mr. Thorne. And I would ask that you remember my name is *Amanda.*"

Jason appeared to be startled, even wounded, by her attitude. He snatched up the suitcase and turned to toss it into the automobile. "Why don't you scramble into the backseat, Sarah," he suggested. "It's getting late."

Responding to the commanding timbre of a male voice, Sarah obeyed without complaint. Irritated that her child would comply so readily, happily, Amanda's tone maintained its ascerbic quality, although her continuing conversation was quite innocuous in content.

"You have a rare talent with children, Jason. Or does practice make perfect? Your wife must think you a virtual paragon." His silence while he escorted her to the passenger side of the car didn't dissuade Amanda's busy tongue. "Just how many children do you and Lucy have? Boys, girls, or both?"

When Amanda had gracefully positioned herself upon the cushioned seat, her skirts adjusted and smoothed, Jason leaned over and rested his forearms against the door. Wayward tendrils of hair lifted off her cheek when his breath forced the words from his throat. "My wife and daughter died of the fever five years ago in Panama. We had only the one child, *Amanda*."

She flinched as if physically slapped, and a pained moan broke the poignant stillness. To lose one's spouse was devastating. The death of a child was incomprehensible. Her hand reached for the knotted fist near her shoulder before he could retreat. "I'm so very, very sorry."

The sincerity of the tears flooding those beautiful golden eyes couldn't be disputed. The angry line of Jason's mouth softened. Very slowly he turned the fist beneath her hand, opening the palm, extending his fingers until they were linked with her own. "I'm sorry, too. For your loss as well." She nodded, accepting his compassion, giving freely in the sharing of grief. After a few moments Jason loudly cleared his throat and broke the silent bond.

Fifteen minutes later, after several aborted starts and some furious cranking of a strange rod attached to the front of the vehicle, the engine finally roared to life. Coming at a dead run, Jason ignored the door to vault himself into the automobile. Sliding down behind the steering column, he quickly began to grind the gears and work the pedals that would propel them forward.

"Hold on tight to your hats, ladies. We're on our way."

Sarah squealed with delight. Amanda squelched a scream of alarm. The automobile lurched, belched black smoke, and then, with a deafening blast resembling the discharge of a shotgun, shot forward.

Jason grinned again. "Marvelous invention, isn't it?"

He was a skilled driver. Or at least that was what Amanda told herself by the time they had traveled several miles of uneven dirt road. She tried not to dwell on the speed of the vehicle while maintaining a tight grip on the doorframe in anticipation of bumps and those occasional deep ruts Jason couldn't seem to entirely avoid. The first time the front tire had dropped into what felt like a bottomless pit, Amanda had slid the entire length of the seat, slamming into Jason's side. "Sorry," he'd apologized. "Believe it or not, I usually manage to miss almost ninety-five percent of those little hazards."

She knew he had meant to be reassuring. But she'd learned to hold on tight. Sarah had curled up on the narrow back cushion and was sleeping soundly, unconcerned about the bumpy ride. Not wanting to distract Jason's concentration, Amanda discouraged conversation, keeping her eyes fixed on the surrounding landscape, and was discovering anew the magic of the Flint Hills.

Wildflowers grew in profusion along the side of the road. The air whipping her hair about her face was filled with their sweetness. A brilliant setting sun hovered at the edge of the horizon, staining the hills a dark purple as they rose upward from the earth, swelling and then falling softly against the prairie: an inland sea of rock and grass, ebbing and flowing for endless miles. Nature's continuity, outlasting generations of man.

Her flesh tingled in response to this desolate beauty. The sky seemed to wrap around her. There was no yesterday, no tomorrow, and the present held the first real peace she'd felt in months. Inhaling deeply, Amanda put all her problems, current or anticipated, aside while her eyes drifted shut, holding the moment. . . .

"Amanda," the velvet voice intruded. She closed her eyes tighter. "Mandy." Her ear tickled and she brought up her hand to scratch the prickling flesh. Something warm and bristly scraped across her wrist before her fingers reached their destination. A puzzled frown crinkled her nose. The deep, throaty chuckle caused her eyelids to snap open. She was staring into fathomless green eyes and a face barely visible in the light of a crescent moon. Confused and disoriented, Amanda was slow to realize the automobile was no longer in motion. It took a few moments longer for her senses to perceive the hard-muscled shoulder beneath her head. "Oh my!" she cried softly in mortification before drawing away, quickly scooting back across the seat.

"You fell asleep some miles back," Jason explained, seemingly unconcerned that he'd been used as a pillow, or mindful of the intimacy and trust

19

implied in the unconscious act. "Necessity guided my steering. I missed them all." Her bewildered expression brought another short burst of laughter. "The ruts. I missed every one of them so you could sleep."

Jason saw her silent nod, felt her withdraw. The woman who had wished him off the Stockton station platform had returned, probably for a long and lengthy visit.

"It's very quiet," she said, looking out toward the barn and the outbuildings of the ranch.

"You shouldn't have come, Amanda."

His statement, out of the blue, said with heated conviction brought her head snapping back. "Why?"

"This isn't the place for you and Sarah now. The ranch isn't as you remember. It's been hard enough with just Julie and me."

"Are you saying you don't want us here; that we'll add to your burdens?"

"No, dammit," he spat roughly. "I'm simply warning you that life here won't be a cakewalk. I don't think you realize—"

"Please, Jason," she begged, cutting him off. "I'm exhausted. No doubt I'll discover soon enough the difficulties you seem determined to tell me. But not tonight. Forgive me if that sounds abrupt and rude. I'm simply not up to hearing a long list of problems right now. It's been a very long day."

He knew the strain and fatigue were genuine, but she needed to be told some things, and he had no guarantees she'd allow him within ten feet of her alone again. "All the days are long around here, Amanda. The bunkhouse has one occupant— namely me."

His voice was very soft as if he regretted hounding on this point. Still Amanda felt her jaw clenching. Would tomorrow not be soon enough? Couldn't she have a single night without harsh realities? "I can appreciate your concern, Jason," she said stiffly. "We'll do our best not to cause additional trouble. I can assure you I'm not afraid of hard work. Perhaps an extra pair of hands will ease, not hinder, your difficult lot."

Jason's eyebrows quirked upward as if skeptical. "Lady, you don't have any idea—" She appeared to flinch, so with a resigned sigh, he backed off. "I'll hold you to that statement you just made. When the day comes that you want to hightail it back to the city and a simpler life, I'll remind you of it."

Amanda wanted to protest his assumption her life had been simple, but she didn't have the energy to argue. Without his assistance, she found the door latch and stepped out. Jason quickly followed her lead, rounding the car to come up beside her, nudging her away when she would have reached for Sarah.

"I'll get her. She's too heavy for you."

"She might be frightened."

It was a reasonable parental concern, but an unnecessary one. Sarah went into Jason's arms without hesitation. It was a gesture of faith, a child's instinctive trusting, and Amanda felt a moment of irrational jealousy before following Jason and Sarah toward the house.

The square, single-story ranch house, fashioned from the native limestone, was every bit as plain and ugly as Amanda remembered. The architecture was without any illusion to grace or beauty. It had been

21

built for shelter in straight, uncompromising lines, much like the Kansas hills surrounding it. However, Amanda knew all the love and warmth she would ever need resided within these austere walls. Suddenly eager, she quickened her pace.

At the door Jason paused. "What I said before . . . I didn't mean you aren't welcome." His eyes were saying more, but before Amanda could decipher their silent message, he'd thrust the door open and was yelling, "Julie! We're home!"

"And about time," came the responding shout. Then Julie Danfield, wiping her hands on a faded calico apron, burst into the narrow hallway and launched herself at her niece.

Chapter Two

JULIE DANFIELD ALMOST CRACKED AMANDA'S RIBS with the enthusiasm she was putting into her welcoming embrace. "I was beginning to think you'd never get here. What happened, Jase? Did that machine of yours break down?"

Jason opened his mouth to reply, but was cut off by the lightning-quick shift in Julie's attention as she turned to reach for Sarah. "Here's that sweet baby."

True to recent form, Sarah screamed at the top of her lungs, kicked out with her left foot, and then proceeded to put a stranglehold on Jason that brought a murderous glint to her mother's eyes.

"Sarah Dianne Ames," Amanda began to scold. She wanted to yank the child out of Jason's arms and pound some manners into her nasty little backside.

Easily interpreting her niece's intent, Julie put herself solidly between mother and child. "Now, now. There's no harm done, Amanda. Poor little tyke must be just plumb frazzled after her day. We'll be the best of friends in no time."

The arm that went about Amanda's shoulders was far too thin, and the once robust complexion had an unhealthy pallor. At least twenty pounds seemed to be missing from Julie's tall frame, and Amanda began to become alarmed about her aunt's appearance. The iron-gray hair was brittle and thinned. The flesh beneath her chin and eyes sagged, evidencing weight loss.

"Look like very hell, don't I?" Julie volunteered, her dark brown eyes snapping with a warm-hearted vigor in sharp contrast to her outward appearance. When Amanda couldn't respond, Julie gave her niece such a hearty shake it was impossible to deny her strength despite the evidence to the contrary. "As bad as that, is it? Lordy, girl, you keep lookin' at me that way and we'll have to get the doc back out here. Jase, will you tell Amanda I'm strong as a horse, and fit as a fiddle? Don't look like she's going to believe anything I say."

"She's strong as a horse, and fit as a fiddle," Jason recited with a cocky grin. "Stubborn as a mule, and twice as mean," he added on his own, the dark eyes earnest and reassuring. "I swear." With his free hand he crossed his heart, validating the oath by raising his right hand in testimony, keeping it suspended near his shoulder until Amanda surrendered her concern with a heavy sigh and a tight smile.

"All right, I'm convinced." She wasn't, but now was hardly the time to make an issue of her doubts. She hugged her aunt again. "But don't try to tell me you haven't been ill, even if you are on the mend now."

Sarah, suddenly curious as to why all adult attention had shifted away from herself, lifted her head from Jason's shoulder. After a quick glance at her mother and the affection being bestowed upon that strange old woman, Sarah expanded her lungs in preparation for another ear-splitting shriek. The arm about her waist tightened, stopping her. Sarah's eyes shot upward to meet Jason's dark gaze holding a silent, yet unmistakable warning.

"You're skating on thin ice, Pickle-face," Jason muttered beneath his breath in a tone meant only for Sarah's ears. When her eyes widened with complete understanding, his straight brows lifted with shrewd perception. There was a brief meeting of minds before he growled, "You little stinker." This precocious little moppet had declared war on her mother. And, whatever the reasons, had found Amanda's vulnerability and went for the jugular at every given opportunity. He bid farewell to peace and quiet before attempting to put this little bundle of trouble down.

"I've known monkeys who had shorter arms," he teased when her fingers locked behind his neck.

Witnessing Jason's struggle, Amanda gave an exasperated groan and marched over to pull Sarah away. "You're behaving like a baby. Now, I want you to say hello to Aunt Julie. You remember her, don't you?" Immediately Amanda regretted reminding Sarah of the circumstances surrounding the only time the child and Julie had met—Harry's funeral. Drawing her daughter close, Amanda gave her a reassuring squeeze. "Please, Sarah."

"Hello," Sarah said grudgingly, her eyes downcast.

"Well, now," Julie beamed, looking quite pleased with Sarah's capitulation. "Don't know about you, but I'm fairly starving. I'll go throw supper on the kitchen table while you all wash up."

Like little chicks following a mother hen, they all lined up and followed Julie Danfield through the dark, seldom-used dining room into the brightly lit kitchen.

Jason pumped water into the chipped porcelain sink while Amanda washed Sarah's hands and then her own. But it was Julie, placing platters of chicken onto a gaily checked cloth covering a rectangular wood table, who noticed the little girl begin to squirm, shifting from one leg to the other, before crossing her legs in a gesture that left little doubt to her difficulty.

"I think our Sarey could stand a short walk out behind the house before we sit down at the table."

Amanda bent down and whispered in Sarah's ear. At the child's enthusiastic nod, Amanda started toward the back door.

"Jase, light that lantern. Not much moon tonight."

Removing the old brass coal-oil lamp from its hook near the door, Jason struck a match and ignited the wick. After slipping the chimney over the flame, he handed Amanda the lantern. "Do you remember the way?"

She nodded. Sarah glanced at her mother, her face clouding with confusion. "Why are we going outside, Mama?"

"Because the . . . the facility is outside, sweetheart. Come with Mama. I'll explain."

"Uh-uh. I don't wanna." The blonde pigtails swung from side to side as Sarah firmly rejected this unimaginable notion. "It's dark out there. Why can't I go potty inside?"

"Honey," Amanda started to soothe, and then she bristled with increasing irritation when Jason stuck his slightly crooked nose into her business once again.

He didn't see the flash of resentment in Amanda's eyes when he knelt down before the child. "We don't have an inside toilet, Sarah. But just a few steps behind the house, down a path, there is a small building. We call it an outhouse. Go with your mother and you'll soon see there's nothing to worry about."

The pigtails ceased their furious motion. Blue eyes were wet with genuine tears. "You go, too," she demanded.

Amanda wanted to groan aloud. Sarah wasn't the only one feeling the need to relieve nature. However, when Sarah clutched herself and bent double, there was little time to dispute Jason's hasty exit—child in tow—from the kitchen. But once inside the narrow outdoor toilet, it was Amanda who dealt with her daughter's rising hysteria.

"Oooh, I don't like it here!" Although her shoes dangled far above the dusty, wooden floor, Sarah lifted her legs straight out and began to kick. "It smells nasty," she wailed, her tiny voice quivering.

When Amanda lifted Sarah off the rustic commode, the little girl refused to allow her feet to touch down, screeching incoherently, "There's patter-rabs, Mama . . . patter-rabs. Don't let it touch me!"

Sarah continued to shriek, howl, and squirm with frenzied panic while Amanda struggled with one hand to readjust the child's underpants and stockings. And during this nearly impossible task, Sarah's bare bottom tempted her mother's restraint almost beyond bearing. Breathless, her chest heaving from exertion, Amanda found the latch and pushed the door open with her shoulder when she was finally finished. "Here," she snapped, thrusting her daughter at Jason. "Take her back."

The strained expression matched the heated tone. Jason quickly conquered a smile while he comforted the little girl sobbing on his shoulder. "Just out of curiosity . . . What is a patter-rab?"

"How the devil am I—" She took a deep breath for control, not at all appreciative of being the source for the jolly amusement lurking within his eyes. "Some imaginary creature who has a penchant for haunting outhouses, I would venture to guess."

"Logical," he mused. "Ready?" Jason started to reach for the lantern inside the door.

"Leave that, please," she requested, forgetting inhibitions in the face of annoyance and necessity. "I would like a few moments of privacy and solitude."

"Of course." The velvet texture of his voice barely subdued an outright guffaw. "Watch out for those patter-rabs."

Finally alone with only the chirping of crickets to

disturb the glorious silence, Amanda's eyes roamed the interior of the outdoor toilet. If Sarah could, in the dim light, create imaginary terrors, Amanda could hardly wait for morning when the very real creatures in the form of wasps, spiders, and the occasional yard snake, seeking cool shelter, began to inhabit this structure.

Straightening her skirt, she found herself indulging in an involuntary shudder at the discovery of spiderwebs clinging to her hem. Brushing them off, she vowed to see this disagreeable necessity thoroughly cleaned and swept free of spiderwebs. "Spiderweb?" She said aloud as she looked back at the thick profusion of webbing clinging to the wood beneath the shelf of the toilet seat. "Patter-rab?" Had Sarah, in her hysteria, jumbled the word? A snort of laughter burst from her throat, followed quickly by another until she was bent double in mirth. Tears ran down her cheeks until, with a gasp, Amanda slumped against the door and fought to check the rampant rise of emotions, recognizing that she was skirting the edge of hysterical shrieking herself.

"I'm tired," she admitted. "And scared."

The ridiculous scene with Sarah had managed to restore Amanda's lost sense of humor. It did not, however, remove the tickling sense that fate had played a very perverse little trick by throwing herself and Jason together again.

"Ridiculous," she scolded firmly. After all, if they were meeting for the first time, would she even be giving him a second thought? "Patter-rabs," she repeated on a chuckle, leaving the unpleasant sanctuary of the outhouse. Jason was the very least of her worries. She would not give him more importance than was his due. They were both adults now. Surely they could deal with each other on that level.

Amanda entered the kitchen and rewashed her hands. "I'm sorry to keep you waiting," she apologized before taking the vacant chair next to Sarah.

"No problem, sugar," Julie said, beaming at her from across the table. Jason held the typical male place of honor at the head of the table, adjacent to Sarah. Amanda folded her hands and bowed her head in preparation for the saying of grace. When silence was immediately followed by a bowl of mashed potatoes being thrust at her, she swallowed her surprise. After scooping out a small helping for herself, she then served Sarah before passing the potatoes on to Jason.

The platter of chicken and the vegetables followed. Amanda puzzled this radical change in custom while Jason and Aunt Julie discussed tomorrow's chores. How clearly she remembered Uncle Todd's voice booming out the blessing before every meal. Had Julie become lax in observing this ritual since his death? Surely Jason, reared in the household of a bombastic minister, would consider a few words of prayer part of daily routine.

Then Amanda remembered what he'd once confided regarding his strict, almost fanatical upbringing:

"I've been prayed over, preached at, and held up as an example, a warning to those who are tempted to sin. My foster-father has made me his personal crusade, but is beginning to despair the salvage of my savage soul. Daily the good Reverand and his wife wring their hands and ask God why He should burden them with so great a trial. They don't realize that God—if he really exists—hasn't any more use for me than he had for my mother."

"Amanda, honey," Julie's voice yanked Amanda's attention back to the present. "Is there something wrong?"

"No. Of course not." She forked a small bite from the chicken breast on her plate. "This is wonderful, Aunt Julie." A glance toward Sarah discovered the little girl was refusing to have any part of the food upon her plate.

"Is something wrong, sugarplum?" Amanda asked while Sarah toyed with her meal. "Does your tummy hurt?"

Sarah didn't respond, continuing to play with her food, using a crisply fried leg to push potatoes and green beans toward the center of her plate until they blended into an unappetizing mixture.

"Sarah, please don't play with your food."

Amanda's initial concern escalated to impatience. "Sarah, if you don't feel like eating, then please keep your hands in your lap. It's not polite to put your elbows on the table."

An obstinate lower lip was thrust forward, but Sarah relented. Within moments though, she was at it again, stubbornly testing the waters of her mother's temper by nudging potatoes and beans off her plate and onto the tablecloth. "That is quite enough of that, young lady," Amanda stated, whisking the plate away to place it on the sideboard directly behind her chair.

Always the peacemaker, Julie Danfield pushed

her own supper away. "Don't know about the rest of you, but my appetite's off kilter tonight. Must be the excitement." Her brown eyes fixed on her niece's tight face with a clear message.

Amanda smiled tightly. Putting her fork down, she said, "It's been a long day."

Jason shook his head while wearing a rueful expression. With a resigned sigh, he wiped his mouth on a napkin and pushed away from the table. Then he offered his hand to Sarah. "Come on, kiddo. Let's you and me clear out of here before your mama and Aunt Julie decide it's our turn to do dishes."

Sarah blinked in surprise. She was too young to realize her instinctive, rather than conscious, ploy to divide and conquer had been effectively thwarted. But she knew she felt very much like she always did when her friends outvoted playing with dolls in favor of hide-and-seek—outnumbered. Without a whimper she allowed Jason to lead her from the room.

Amanda let her face sink slowly into her hands. "Your beautiful supper," she moaned. "Ruined by a cross six-year-old. I'm so sorry, Aunt Julie."

"Oh, I think we'll survive a skirmish or two. She'll come round. All this has got to be hard on the poor little thing."

Amanda looked up, tears sparkling in her eyes. "Sometimes I think she'd be happier if I'd died instead of her father. He petted and pampered, and granted her every wish. I guess we both spoiled her. But she was such a happy little thing. Now it's as if she's punishing me for living."

"Nonsense!" Julie scoffed. "She's just feeling

confused and lost, and too young to understand why. I remember another girl who acted very much the same way when she lost her mother. You were just sixteen, an age when you needed your own mama most, when Elizabeth passed on. Madder than hades, you were. My brother was at his wit's end with worrying over you. See these gray hairs—" Julie lifted a thick strand. "You put most of them there singlehanded that last summer you spent with us."

If only you knew the half of it, Amanda thought ruefully before changing the subject. "Let's get these dishes done."

"You leave that chore to me and get that poor child settled in for the night." Julie refused to hear a protest. "There ain't nothing difficult about a few piddlin' dishes. I've been doing them by myself for many a year." She was already up and clearing the table. "I've put you in the same room you had before. Sarey's in that old sewing room of mine directly across the hall."

Reluctantly Amanda rose, giving in to her fatigue and her aunt's firm insistence. "I feel awful about all this. It's not a very auspicious beginning, is it?"

"*Asspicious?*" Julie chortled. "Is that a fancy way of saying supper was a calamity? You tell Jason I've got fresh peach cobbler for dessert."

Amanda found Jason and Sarah on the threadbare sofa in the parlor. The little girl was curled on his lap, sound asleep.

"I was telling her a story about a princess who starved her subjects when she conked out. It was one of those moral-of-the-story tales."

Amanda smiled warmly. He certainly had a way with Sarah. Her heart twisted when she realized the hurt he must still feel over the loss of his own little girl. Her thoughts must have been reflected in her eyes because Jason swallowed heavily before he said, "It feels good to hold a child again. I hope you won't mind if I borrow her now and then."

Tears clogged her throat, making her voice thick. "Of course not. Sarah needs friends, and it seems you're her first choice."

In a single motion he stood, careful not to disturb the sleeping child. "And her mother? Does her mother have need of a friend?"

Again those forest-green eyes probed, asking more than Amanda wanted to answer. Friendship meant a certain intimacy, a sharing of one's self she wasn't certain could be possible between them. She couldn't give Jason what he wanted, so she compromised. "Her mother is content not to have enemies."

It wasn't much, but at least it said she bore him no lasting malice for the hurt he'd caused in his wild youth. In a way it was better than he might have expected. "I understand. Now shall we get this little pickle tucked in for the night?"

She directed him to the small bedroom Julie had designated, going straight to the single bed to draw back the quilt. Everywhere she looked there was evidence of her aunt's thoughtful preparation. The bedspread she was folding back was of cheery, quilted yellow gingham, appliquéd with lambs and kittens. Scattered about the room were Sarah's personal treasures, which they had shipped ahead of their arrival. Unpacked, they awaited a little girl's discovery.

Jason gently placed Sarah on the mattress, his dark fingers caressing the pale hair resting on the small brow. "She's a beautiful child, Mandy. Sorry . . . Amanda," he corrected, stepping back.

She wanted to tell him she truly didn't mind the nickname, but something held the words that might have bridged the distance she'd put between them.

"Good night, Jason."

Amanda woke with a start, going from deep slumber to total awareness in seconds. It took less time to identify the source of the disturbance. Pressed tightly against her back, teeth grinding at irregular, yet strangely predictable intervals, Sarah had taken total possession of the bed and covers. After a few cautious attempts to retrieve the quilt, Amanda resigned herself to the morning chill, preferring not to chance disturbing the child completely swathed in blankets.

When her nightgown had been adjusted, and her cold feet were tucked beneath the thin cotton, Amanda reached for her daughter. Drawing the tiny form close, she savored both the warm body and this rare moment of tenderness.

The sweet fragrance of cornsilk hair filled her nostrils. She pressed her lips to the baby-soft velvet of Sarah's cheek. The knowledge that she'd been sought out to provide security in the darkness of night brought a measure of optimism in the dim light of a new day. Perfectly content and prepared to snuggle with Sarah until full daylight, Amanda was caught unprepared for the elbow driving deep into her ribs. Sarah's restless thrashings eventually drove her mother out, and then barred any hope of return when the little girl immediately took advantage of the vacancy and sprawled crosswise on the bed.

Despite being chased from slumber at the crack of dawn, Amanda felt completely rested. It had been a very long time since she'd slept so soundly. Stretching up on her tiptoes, she felt a strange restlessness building within, an excitement she couldn't explain, in the joy of being free, if only temporarily, from the oppressive melancholy of recent months.

Reacting strictly on impulse, she pulled her nightgown over her head and reached for her discarded clothing draped over a nearby chair. Her spirit sang with the need to be free of walls and restrictions. She crept about the room, wincing at any little noise, for fear of waking Sarah. Leaving her hair in the braids she'd hurriedly fashioned the night before, Amanda picked up her shoes and stole through the house, hardly daring to breathe until she stood outside beneath the gray sky of predawn.

"Oh, the stillness," she sighed, and then clamped a hand over her own wayward mouth, finding the total absence of sound more glorious than she ever imagined. Stars were still visible in the sky. And beneath those tiny dots of brilliant light were the hills, rising just beyond the rail fence and surrounding the ranch buildings.

With an agility she had thought lost in childhood, Amanda easily negotiated the uneven logs of the fence, gasping when the damp, spiky grass tickled the bottom of her bare feet.

Like a child, she skipped across the mist-laden meadow, her shoes dangling from her fingers while her arms swung in exaggerated motion. Laughter bubbled from carefree lips. When the first slender rim of the sun appeared, the sky lost its leaden cast, and the milky fog swirling around her knees seemed to rise higher with the dawn, enveloping her in a pink haze until she was completely lost within a rosy cocoon. She began to twirl, letting her shoes fly helter-skelter from her fingertips. There was no Amanda, only this creature of magic, dancing in a mystical world where anything was possible, and dreams were real.

Amanda's arms lifted with the mist, her hands extending to grasp the moment, helplessly letting go when the huge orange sphere of the sun burned it away. It dissipated into just another memory, something too fleeting to mourn.

It took longer than she might have thought to find her shoes. During the search, she found wildflowers, watched birds and jackrabbits, and generally procrastinated returning to the house for as long as she dared.

The climb back over the fence proved difficult without the child to aid the woman. Her skirt snagged on the rough-hewn logs, catching the hem on a long and sharded splinter. She was still attempting to free herself without ripping cloth and stitches when the sound of running water, splashing against a man-made surface, drew her attention.

In front of the long, stone structure of the bunkhouse, Jason, his torso bare, was pumping water from the underground well. Unaware of an audience, he bent beneath the pump, dousing his head and shoulders with the water gushing from the spout. The icy water brought a bellowing shout; a visible shudder jolted his body. His beltless trousers slipped precariously low on his slender hips while his hands repeatedly cupped beneath the pump to spread liquid over his arms and chest. Fluid muscles knotted and quivered, rippling from back to shoulder to those sinewy arms, so beautifully formed, so solidly and majestically male, that Amanda's femininity responded in a manner predictable to nature as nerve-shattering needles of physical desire scored every inch of her flesh.

Dear God, this was madness. She commanded her brain to cease and desist the untoward signals it was directing. But her eyes seemed determined to ignore orders as they swept over the firm, defined muscles of his chest. His flesh was smooth and hairless. The blood of his ancestors and a hot sun had baked his naturally dark skin until, with the moisture running rivulets down his body, it took on the hue and luster of burnished copper.

Harry had been firmly fleshed for his age and city-bred lifestyle. But rarely had Amanda viewed him without his shirt, and never, never had he affected her with such a bold, shameful lust. She wanted to die for it. Her fingers were desperate as she renewed her efforts to free herself of the fence.

He musn't see . . . she couldn't let him discover . . .

Rending cloth and a soft cry sounded in the quiet like the brass section of Mr. Sousa's marching band. Jason whirled, every muscle tensing, while the towel made a quick swipe across his face. His vision cleared just in time to see Amanda sprinting across the yard, her braids swinging behind her as she dashed madly for the house, her bare feet crushing the grass. It was a telling flight, and one that brought a wide grin.

Chapter Three

A GIANT ACHE HAD LODGED ITSELF AT THE BASE OF Amanda's spine, but it was not the cause of the harassed expression she wore. "I'm sorry about the laundry, Auntie," she apologized again while feeding the sodden bedsheet through the wooden rollers of the ringer, cranking furiously until the sheet was free of excess moisture.

Julie stepped back from the washtub to flex her red and shriveled fingers. "Well, accidents will happen."

"*Accident?*" Amanda's eyes were wide with disbelief as the sheet dropped into the basket. "You can

40

watch an entire morning's wash pulled off the line and ground into the dirt and call it an accident?"

"Sarey was just having some fun. Matter of fact, I rather enjoyed watching her put the fear of God into that cantankerous old rooster. That was quite a sight."

Amanda stifled a reply that would have turned the air blue. After one month of being so frightened of the chickens that she would scream herself hoarse if one escaped the coop or clucked at her from behind the wire-encased chicken yard, Sarah had determined, this particular morning, to make a pet of the rooster. The chase had ended when the child and chicken ran afoul of the clothesline where Amanda and Julie had just finished hanging the week's wash.

"You look exhausted, Auntie. Why don't you lie down for a while. I'll finish up out here and then start supper."

Although she'd never admit it verbally, Julie Danfield's body forced her to concede she was worn down to a frazzle. "Guess I could put my feet up for a while. Maybe I'll just fix me something quick to eat now and forget supper. Will you see that Jase gets fed?"

"Of course."

Julie didn't miss the slight tensing of Amanda's shoulders at the request. She was beginning to suspect that her niece's strained nerves were only partly caused by the pranks of a rambunctious little girl. One sight of Jason, or the mention of him, could coil Amanda tighter than a Kansas twister.

"At least it don't look like rain," Julie said brightly.

A short burst of frustrated laughter escaped Amanda's throat. "Is that the bright side of our day?"

Julie returned the younger woman's grin with a good-natured chuckle. "You know what I always say about looking for rainbows—"

Amanda moaned a little as she lifted the heavy laundry basket. "I know, I know. And it's also darkest before the dawn." She looked up at the sky. "If there were clouds up there, would they be lined with silver?"

"You bet they would. We could use some rain."

"You're impossibly optimistic," Amanda groaned. "Go on now and take that nap."

While she smoothed the muslin sheet she'd folded over the line until it was as wrinkle-free as possible, Amanda was already thinking ahead to the ironing that would have to wait until the heat of the day tomorrow, since it was doubtful the laundry would be dry early in the morning. She looked up at the sky and wagged a threatening finger at seemingly endless blue. "No rain, you hear? If I have to haul water and do wash again tomorrow . . ." Her voice trailed off as she marched over to the washtubs.

With a ragged sigh—she did a lot of sighing lately—she grappled with the metal rim until the ancient, heavy copper tub spilled its contents, soaking her shoes and the hem of her dress in the process. Soon, Amanda thought, before my back is permanently stooped, I'm going to speak to Auntie about getting tubs with drains and stoppers. The second tub was managed with a loud grunt and a snarl.

That chore finished, Amanda wiped a hand across

her wet brow and made a futile attempt to push back the hair that was falling into her eyes. Lord, what she would give for a full bath. Her eyes strayed longingly toward the bunkhouse where she'd been informed the only bathtub resided. Somehow the thought of stripping down to her altogether inside Jason's domain had encouraged a temporary contentment with the inadequate basin baths. But Amanda was weakening, and her inhibitions were looking more ridiculous by the day.

She'd had a great many foolish thoughts and strange feelings since arriving at the TJ, many of which she had not yet dared examine too closely. Some she'd determined would never be viewed or acknowledged in the light of day.

Lifting the hem of her skirt, she squeezed out the moisture as her eyes made a quick sweep of her new home, looking objectively without that first morning's magic . . . without the distraction of Jason.

Only four weeks . . . sometimes it felt like forever. The morning when she'd played in the mist seemed a dream, a fantasy. Now she was fully awake and finding the reality of ranching life more difficult by the day. The outbuildings around her had once glistened white in the glare of the sun. Now their surfaces were blistered, the old paint cracked and peeling from too many years of neglect. Except for the barn and the smokehouse, all the buildings were abandoned, the skeletal remains of a ranch that had once hummed with flesh-and-blood vitality. Had the heart of the TJ stilled with Uncle Todd's death? Sometimes Amanda feared the security she had sought was sitting on quicksand, and slowly, but irrevocably sinking.

She'd told Jason she wasn't afraid of hard work. True, she wasn't. The problem was, Amanda hadn't known the true meaning of the word until just recently. The city girl had found that the rich, creamy butter she loved to spread thick on her bread lost some of its sweetness after hours and hours of churning. A plump stewing hen, simmering in a pot, surrounded by light, airy dumplings, could now turn her stomach after she had personally been the executioner. However, there was one chicken in particular she'd very much like to have by the neck—

Another heavy sigh exploded from her chest. "Stop that, Amanda," she scolded herself. "Things will get easier once you accustom yourself to the routine and know what you're doing."

Pushing away her gloomy thoughts, Amanda started for the house. Her damp, slightly sticky clothing brought a grimace of distaste. She would have to change and wash before fixing supper . . . before Jason came in from the pastures.

It was dark by the time Amanda finished the first round of dishes and took Sarah her bedtime snack of cookies and milk. She found the little girl in her nightgown, seated in a straight-backed chair she had pulled up to the open window. Her sad little face was cradled in her hands. Amanda placed the saucer and the glass down on a bedside table and joined her daughter. "What is so fascinating out there?"

"Jason," Sarah responded, looking up at her mother briefly before her gaze returned to the man working in the blacksmith's alcove just inside the old stable. "He's still fixing Whiskey's shoes. I've been watching him."

Sarah's disappointment at not being able to share dinner with her hero was thick in her voice. Everyone had kept their own schedule with supper tonight. Julie had retired hours ago, and Amanda was keeping Jason's food warm while he repaired a loose shoe on the bay he favored above the other three horses servicing the ranch.

"He's putting nails in poor Whiskey's foot, Mama. Does it hurt?"

Sarah's question seemed to come from a great distance, but it was effective in distracting Amanda's attention away from the flexing muscles in Jason's naked arms and shoulders. "I really don't know, sweetheart. But I don't think so." She touched the little girl's neck. "Come away from the window now and eat your cookies. It's bedtime."

While Sarah munched on the oatmeal and molasses confections, Amanda drew a hairbrush through her child's baby-fine hair. "Sarah, do you understand why Mama was upset with you today?"

The blonde head shook from side to side. Amanda put the brush down and began to braid the golden silk. "Pulling the clothesline down caused hours of extra, unnecessary work. That was very careless and inconsiderate—not so much for myself, but because of Auntie. She's not young anymore and hasn't been very well. We need to take good care of her so she doesn't get sick again."

The little lip quivered. "I didn't mean to, honest. When Cluckey tried to run away under the covers I . . . I thought I could catch him. It wasn't 'tentional, Mama. Really. I didn't know everything would fall down." She looked back over her shoulder, her blue eyes swimming with tears and sincerity. "Auntie won't die like Papa did, will she?"

Amanda's arms went around Sarah and she pulled the little girl against her in a fierce hug. "Oh, sweetheart, of course not. At least not for a very long time, I hope. She's not sick that way." She kissed Sarah's temple. "Don't you start worrying about Auntie dying. We just need to see that she gets more rest. Older people need more rest than we do."

"Is Jason mad at me, too? Is that why he didn't eat with us?"

Amanda felt like the wicked witch again. "Heavens, no, Sarah. You are Jason's best girl. He doesn't even know about the laundry, so how could he be angry? And now that Mama understands it really was an accident, I'm not angry, either. Now, give me a hug. It's past your bedtime."

Kisses and hugs were exchanged, along with a lot of playful tickling and giggles, before Amanda finally tucked Sarah beneath the thin sheet. With her rag doll snuggled in the crook of her arm, Sarah yawned. "Cluckey is a bad chicken for getting me in trouble. I don't think I'll play with him anymore."

Amanda felt a tight knot form in her throat. Sarah must be very lonely. She vowed to spend more time with the little girl. "Good night, sweetheart. I love you."

"I love you, too," Sarah whispered back.

There were tears in Amanda's eyes when she went to turn down the lamp, but they didn't prevent her from seeing Jason slip into his shirt and lead his newly shod horse from the stable.

She hurried toward the kitchen, but stopped just short of the door, her hand automatically smoothing the sides of her hair, and checking the fit of her fresh blouse. There was something revitalizing about changing out of plain calico. She always felt so much better in the evenings after she was washed and neatly clothed. Amanda never equated her vanity with the man now entering the kitchen, at least not consciously. She moved into the room.

"Amanda," he said by way of greeting, slipping into his chair.

"I've kept your supper from getting cold in the bun warmer," she stated. She took one of the quilted pot holders that were hanging on a nail next to the stove, grasped the porcelain handle, and opened the door of the warming oven. "Careful," she warned as she placed his food before him, "the plate is hot. Would you like some coffee?"

"Yes, please." Jason was folding back the dust cloth covering the jam and the butter crock. When she placed a steaming mug of coffee near his right hand, he glanced up, letting his eyes linger on the new crop of freckles beginning to spread across her nose and cheeks. "Sit down and keep me company, Amanda."

The request sounded urgent to his own ears. He quickly covered the rawness with a chuckle. "After spending daylight to dark in conversation with four-legged creatures, my ears ache for the sound of a human voice." As expected, she hesitated, turning her face away just long enough for his hungry gaze to rake over the soft, white lawn blouse. The high, ruffled collar and lace cuffs heightened her femininity, making him sharply aware of the woman. She always smelled of fragrant soap, even on the hottest days, and the light, flowery scent of her cologne brought a thickness to his throat and a heaviness to his groin. "Please," he added.

To refuse would have been unnecessarily churlish. Amanda poured herself a cup of the coffee before joining Jason at the table. "Sarah missed you tonight."

"I missed her, too." Taking a bite of the chicken-fried steak, Jason followed her lead and kept to safe topics. "This is unusually tasty tonight. Julie usually turns steak into shoe leather. Where is she, by the way? Is she not feeling well?"

Amanda flushed with pleasure over his unknowing compliment, but didn't correct his assumption that Julie had done the cooking. "Aunt Julie was worn out from having to do the week's laundry twice in the same day."

"Why was that?"

Amanda began to recount the tale of Sarah and the rooster, noting how the weariness seemed to drop away from his face as he listened. When her narrative brought that enchanting smile to his face, she warmed to the telling, even embellishing on the story to bask in the warmth of his laughter, surprising herself by sharing his enjoyment.

"It really wasn't at all amusing at the time," she finished with an attempt at sobriety, failing when his husky laugh vibrated within the room.

Jason wiped his eyes on a last guffaw, rearing back in his chair to study her smiling face. "It's good to hear you laugh again, Mandy." He wasn't aware that the nickname had slipped out, or that his voice had almost caressed the name—and the woman. But he was very much aware of the changed atmosphere within the room, and was puzzled by it. "Can I expect baked or fried rooster in the near future?"

She popped out of her chair to carry her empty cup to the counter, fighting the unreasonable reaction caused by his innocent slip of the tongue. She very methodically washed and dried her cup until she felt sufficiently controlled to return to the table. "Are you finished?"

"Yeah," Jason said dully, accepting her coolness because he had no choice. To relieve his inner turmoil, he stretched his arms over his head and reached up toward the ceiling. "God, I'm beat tonight!"

When he linked his fingers and turned them inside out, the ropelike muscles in his forearms jumped, and the veins in his dark skin stood out in sharp relief. His dark blue shirt strained at the seams, stretching taut across his chest and belly. Amanda suddenly couldn't get his tableware away fast enough.

"You work too hard," she said in a rush, gathering the silver and his plate, nearly running with them to the counter.

"Well, I don't know a cure for it. Right now I'm mostly babysitting while the herd—what's left of it—grazes. I've been repairing the fences and keeping track of the water supply." He frowned. "The calves need branding and the young bulls need . . . fixing." Her crimson face told him she understood what kind of fixing. "There just aren't enough hours in the day, and most definitely not enough of me. However, hiring a man, or several men, is out of the question right now."

"Could I help?" she asked impulsively, knowing the offer was ridiculous. Amanda couldn't see herself as a rope-throwing, hard-riding cowhand.

Jason couldn't see it, either, but before she could move away, he captured her wrist and pried the coffee mug from her fingers. Turning her hand, his thumbs explored the smooth, delicate surface of her palms. "Too soft. Not at all cowhand material . . . not yet, anyway. But then it's not your hands that need toughening up for that chore, is it?" he teased, smiling up at her, the grin fading at the frozen expression on her face.

Amanda jerked her hand away, and rubbed the tingling flesh against the side of her skirt to erase the feel of those dark, square fingers. Averting her head, she didn't see Jason's face grow stormy over the way she had repulsed the physical contact. "Oh, you'll be working cattle before this summer is through, Amanda. Don't doubt it," he said gruffly, letting his chair slam down. "But for now, I've got another job in mind . . . if you're serious about wanting to help."

His tone clearly indicated a lack of faith in her sincerity. The fact that he'd seen through her empty gesture didn't stop Amanda from bristling defensively. "I don't make a habit of saying what I don't mean, Jason." Well, that much, at least, was partly true. She didn't make stupid statements as a general rule—

"Good." He slapped the edge of the table and

rose from his chair. "Do you think you could meet me in the barn before dawn in the morning?"

"How far before dawn?" Good heavens, getting up with the sun was difficult enough.

"About a half hour." Jason had moved to the door and was waiting for her answer, searching her face to see if their meeting in the barn held the same significance for her that it did for him. What he found was only that damned detachment he was growing to despise. "Amanda?"

"I'll be there."

"I'll expect you."

With his departure, she finished cleaning the kitchen. It wouldn't occur to her for nearly another hour that she'd not asked, nor had he volunteered, exactly what job it was he had in mind.

Amanda was too busy engaging in a fierce inner battle, fighting feelings, old and new, that came unbidden as if in whispers of an unwelcome secret that couldn't be shared or passed on for fear of the consequences.

To her horror, Amanda overslept. The rooster was crowing loudly when she finally burst through the open barn door, her fingers busy securing the top three buttons at the neck of her second-oldest work dress of yellow gingham. "Jason?" she called, not seeing him, thinking he'd grown tired of waiting and had left.

"Over here," he called out, directing her with his voice to the stall where he presently had his hands beneath a very fat dairy cow.

"I'm sorry. I overslept." She eyed the cow with

trepidation, backing away from the animal's wildly swishing tail. "Am I too late?"

"Let's say I started without you," he grinned, and vacated the stool, indicating with a sweep of his hand that he expected her to take his place. "Sit down, Amanda. Bess here"—he slapped the animal's hide —"gets cranky if she's made to wait too long."

As if to prove the veracity of his statement, the cow bellowed, and then smacked Jason's backside with that vicious tail. Amanda was already shaking her head with a fearful denial. "I . . . I don't think I—" She looked at Jason pleadingly. "Is this what you wanted me to do for you?" Amanda had never felt particularly comfortable around creatures possessing more than two legs with a height exceeding her kneecaps.

"Don't let this old grump scare you." Jason had a firm grip on her elbow and was pulling her into the stall, forcing her down on the stool. "She'll settle down the minute you start milking. Go on . . . grab hold."

Amanda was too frightened to hear the underlying amusement in his voice. She flinched every time Bess whacked him with her tail. Jason prompted her again. Her hands reached out and then jerked back several times before she found the courage to allow her fingers to close around the cow's teats. A visible shudder quaked through her body, part fear and partly surprise to discover that what she'd always imagined to be soft, like human flesh, was actually rough and thick in texture. Closing her eyes, Amanda squeezed. Nothing happened. She opened her eyes and squeezed again. This time the cow twisted her huge head to look at Amanda with an expression closely akin to human disapproval.

Jason squatted down beside her, shaking with silent laughter. "Like this, Amanda." His hands closed over hers, manipulating first the right and then the left. Streams of warm milk began to squirt into the bucket with his steady alternating rhythm, only to cease immediately when he pulled back to let her continue on her own.

Amanda made a small whimpering sound of defeat. "I can't do this."

"Sure you can," he said reassuringly. "Squeeze harder. You won't hurt the cow." When she still couldn't seem to manage to get more than a dribble, he again encouraged the flow of milk by adding his experience to her inept bungling.

"It feels so funny," she breathed, looking directly into his face, her heart skipping several long beats to find his nose only inches from her cheek. Both sets of hands stilled. The distance between them was so slight Amanda could see the rarely visible dark brown flecks in his green eyes, which were fixed upon her mouth.

The cow, only aware of its half-done discomfort, caught Jason on the back of the head with a blow that sent him tumbling into Amanda's lap. "Damn you, Bess," he snarled, trying to right himself using Amanda's soft thigh for leverage.

His fingers sinking into, and between, an intimate part of her anatomy brought Amanda off the stool. "Watch where you're putting your hands, Jason Thorne," she spat, not realizing his gropings were unintentional until her upward movement caused his precarious balance to falter, sending him backward to sprawl on his backside. She wanted to crawl into the empty stall behind her to escape the angry probe of his glare.

"Let's get one thing straight here and now, Amanda. If I touch you, it won't necessarily mean I've got lustful intentions toward you. When and *if* I do make a move in that direction, you can be damned certain there won't be any sneak attack involved, and little chance to misread my intent. Now sit back down and start milking this cow before she knocks my head off!"

He jumped to his feet. She immediately plopped down on the stool wondering why people didn't die from mortification. "I'm sorry," she apologized in a small voice, taking a firm grip on the cow's teats again. Her high emotional level lent strength to her hands. The cow trembled with relief when milk began to fill the bucket.

"That's better." He looked down at the part in her hair between the two pigtails draped over softly rounded shoulders. With her hair braided, her face flushed with embarrassment, she was too much like the Mandy of his memories, of his dreams; the penny-bright girl who had lived in a secret part of his heart all these long years.

That she looked the same made it all the more difficult to accept the woman who blew hot and cold toward him. Mandy had been enchanting with her open directness, her inability to camouflage her thoughts and feelings. Amanda kept him perpetually off balance, pivoting constantly with the rapid changes in her mood. One moment she could be laughing with him, sharing herself and her child, showing an awareness of herself as a woman by taking pains with her appearance beyond the necessary, instinctively enticing the male. And he was most assuredly male.

But a touch, an inflection of voice, allowing his eyes to linger on her face for a single moment longer than she thought necessary, could turn her into a block of ice, distant and so far removed he feared he'd never be able to break through her reserve. Jason was beginning to wonder how she might react if she knew the depth of his feelings or his determination to see those emotions and desires carried through to their inevitable outcome.

"I think it's finished," Amanda said, folding her hands in her lap. Jason squatted down again and gave the cow's teats a hard, testing pull. "She's finished." He couldn't quite keep the hard edge of exasperation out of his voice. "Are you ready for Daisy now?"

"Is she mean-tempered as well?"

"All creatures have limits to their patience, Amanda." He was sick and tired of dancing around her, behaving like a polite stranger. He'd hurt her once, yes. But dammit, surely she must realize how much more hurt could have been done . . . .

Jason snatched up the bucket and dumped the contents into a large container. Her hatred would have been preferable to this indifference and those few moments when she allowed that cold mask to slip and ignite hope within him. Patience had never been a strong suit with him, which Amanda should very well remember. He passed her the bucket. "Do you think you can handle Daisy on your own?" he rasped.

Amanda couldn't understand his anger. True, she had overreacted, but he was certainly making too much of this as well. Any woman would have behaved in a like manner. It had merely been a reflex action. *Was it, Amanda?* whispered a little voice that would not be stilled. *Surprise, alarm, indignation—those would have been natural responses to an unexpected intimate touch. However, you didn't jump up and protest for any of those reasons, though, did you?*

"I'll do my best," she answered stiffly, moving to take her place beside the cow while Jason went to attend the three horses stabled in the huge barn.

Seemingly within no time, spurred by an anxious desire to finish this chore and remove herself from Jason's company, Amanda was pouring out the bucket of milk and asking, "Do you want to check if she's empty?"

Her choice of words brought a chuckle. Jason quickly checked the animal. "She's empty," he said, turning back to her with a smile. Framed in the doorway with the morning sun catching wisps of her hair and turning them to flame, Amanda represented twelve years of impossible dreams come true. He wanted her—here and now, tomorrow and always. Since learning Amanda was free, his every action, every plan, had Amanda at its center. He knew she needed time to adjust to his presence, to learn to trust him and to face those feelings she built defenses to protect. In fact, it was her steadfast determination to hide behind that fortress which told him the past was no more dead for her than it was for him. In time, with the hills surrounding them, Jason knew he could conquer her fears. But it was time that might prove his greatest enemy. The future of the TJ was uncertain, and his control over that future tentative. Here, he could afford the luxury of patience. Outside this protected environment—

"Where should I put the bucket and stool?" Amanda felt increasingly uncomfortable beneath his silent scrutiny.

As Amanda began to massage her neck, Jason closed the distance between them. "Can I count on you to be the morning milkmaid? Julie will probably want to continue the afternoons."

"I'll have to train myself to awaken earlier, but, yes, I'm quite sure I'll manage."

God, how he wanted to blast through that aloof shell.

When his hands fell onto her shoulders, Amanda consciously commanded her muscles to relax, his earlier admonishment still ringing in her ears. She had no intention of making a fool of herself twice in the same day. "I'm sorry about my behavior earlier."

Jason's expression was impassive while his fingers gently worked over the area between her shoulders and neck, easing the strain caused by the unfamiliar exercise. "Next time, put your head against the cow's flank. It will relieve some of the pressure back here." His fingers met at the back of her head and locked together.

Amanda's eyes opened wide as her head was immobilized. There was no misinterpreting his hungry gaze now. "Jason . . . don't . . ." she began, taking a step back.

He took a step forward, keeping her at arm's

length, but refusing to allow another inch of separation. "Don't ever get too complacent, Amanda. You have control only up to a point—" He unclenched his fingers and jammed his hands into his pockets. "But God help you, Mandy, should you indicate, directly or indirectly, that you remember, as I do, just how it once was between us."

His warning shattered any possibility that they might continue coexisting within the safe bounds of a lukewarm truce. Not waiting for the dust to settle, Jason fetched his horse and swung himself up into the saddle. "Tell Julie I fixed my own breakfast." Then he rode out of the barn without a backward glance. He'd accomplished his purpose. Her protective shell had crumbled before his eyes.

Chapter Four

AMANDA STOOD PERFECTLY STILL UNTIL THE BAY STAL-
lion's departure could no longer be heard. Then she
walked outside and slumped against the side of the
weathered old barn, shielding her eyes from the
glare of full sunrise. Between the hills and sky, the
lone horse and rider were cast in silhouette as they
raced across the rolling pasture. The sight was so
typically devil-may-care, so like the recklessness
evident in the young man she'd once known, Amanda was helpless to prevent a sudden, vivid flash of an
unwanted memory. . . .

* * *

In all her sixteen years, Amanda knew she'd never been more miserable, bored, and lonely. She wandered aimlessly within the smelly old barn, wishing she were home with her papa, worrying about him, wondering if he was missing Mama as much as she was.

She stifled the sob that rose in her throat. Aunt Julie was right. This awful moping over her mother's sudden death had to stop soon. It wouldn't bring Mama back, and it certainly wasn't helping Papa. If only she had something to do, someone to talk with other than older people who just didn't seem to understand.

With a heavy sigh and a frustrated flip of her skirt, Amanda left the dark confines of the barn. Leaning back against the wall she began to jab at the ground with her toe, digging a fair-sized hole, only to fill it up again by sweeping the dirt she'd loosened back into the depression with the side of her foot. Switching feet, Amanda repeated the apathetic activity.

Suddenly, she was distracted by the sound of a horse's whinny. Looking toward the fence, she watched the reckless approach of a hard-riding ranch hand. Amanda's boredom quickly vanished. With a muted gasp she pushed away from the barn wall, her body tensing as her hands came up to prevent her eyes from witnessing the collision of horse and fence, and certain injury to the man. She shuddered when she heard his wild yell, fully anticipating subsequent groans of pain, or worse—no sounds at all.

Her heart was pounding violently within her chest when Amanda finally found the courage to peek through her fingers. The young man slid from his saddle, took three running steps, and vaulted cleanly over the high rails.

His sure hands slapped hard against the wood. The muscles in his arms bunched, taking his full weight as his feet left the ground. His legs swung up and out and over, his slender hips swiveling, shifting, clearing the fence easily by several inches. Then he landed with only the slight flex of his knees, immediately breaking into a run as he headed toward the house.

Again he yelled. This time, however, Amanda recognized the self-congratulatory note. She bristled over his cockiness after he'd nearly scared her half to death with that careless, harebrained display. Or had it been an exhibition of superior control? She felt a spark of admiration for the fluid agility in his graceful movements, even for the tooting of his own horn when he'd assumed there was no one else around to applaud his accomplishment. But as he dashed past, Amanda's eyes flew open in shock just before a gurgle of laughter erupted over the sight of the very revealing tear in the seat of his somewhat baggy trousers.

He whirled, his hands flying to the exposed part of his anatomy, and Amanda's laughter died in her throat. Stormy eyes were fixed on her face in such a threatening glare that she recoiled back into her safe shadow with a gasp. She watched as his gaze moved over her from head to toe. She flushed hotly, averting her eyes. The low, velvety sound of his chuckle brought her eyes snapping back just in time to see him whip the dusty flat-crowned hat from his head and sweep it before him in a bow. Hair black as a raven's wing tumbled over his tanned brow, and when he lifted his head she could see his deep green eyes. The lazy smile remained, and it was doing funny things to her stomach. He was, without doubt, the best-looking young man she'd ever seen, and obviously far too aware of himself.

His cool arrogance and cocksure manner were annoying, especially when he released the torn flap of his trousers and thrust his thumbs deep into the front pockets of those overlarge pants. The earlier tension was gone. He really was much, much too handsome, and younger than she'd originally thought, no more than eighteen or so. But there was nothing about him even vaguely like the gangly, awkward boys she knew back home. Good heavens, he was bold, too much so in her opinion. After nearly five minutes of meeting him stare for stare, Amanda lifted her chin and snubbed him soundly.

She didn't see the cocky smile fade, nor witness the momentary flicker of pained disappointment before the young man turned with a resigned shrug and proceeded toward the house, letting his nearly bare backside catch the warm breeze.

When the screened door slammed shut, Amanda quickly looked back over her shoulder and knew a moment's disappointment to find he'd been discouraged so easily. The temptation to follow him into the kitchen was great, but her inexperience with boys made her hesitate. There was also those strange, fluttering feelings she couldn't explain to encourage not risking another confrontation. She felt different all of a sudden, and it was this strange emotion, not any natural timidity, which drove her to seek the concealment of the barn. Near the door she had a clear, unobstructed view of the entire yard, where she could wait and watch without being obvious.

Fifteen minutes later she was watching his progress back across the yard, choking on her laughter at the sight of a bright red patch on the seat of his baggy pants. Not once did he look her way, and as he neared the fence it became necessary to poke her head out the door to keep him in view, her body following inch by inch until she was completely out of the barn.

He was already springing back over the fence when she impulsively lifted her hand and shouted, "Wait!"

She could have sworn there was a sudden tensing, a slight, infinitesimal break in his agile stride before he swung himself back up into the saddle. She ran toward the fence, but he was already riding away with an ear-splitting "Yahoo!"

Dejected, she watched him race away, her spirits dropping to zero once again. With a hard kick to the bottom rail of the fence, Amanda was just about to turn on her heel when he suddenly reined his horse to a skidding stop, whirling his mount around until they were once again facing each other across the spread of the meadow. Amanda raised her arm and gave him a tentative wave. She thought she saw the flash of white teeth before his hat left his head to return the gesture of farewell. Then he was galloping away, and the air was carrying the sound of a lusty shout. . . .

With a furious mental shake, Amanda pushed away the memory and returned to her unfinished chores. She slung the milk pail and stool into a likely corner, letting her temper give her the strength and courage to open the pasture doors and shoo the cows outside to graze. The cantankerous Bess received a sharp slap on her rump when it looked as if she might balk short of the door. Amanda had completely forgotten to be afraid of the cranky cow in the heat of her anger.

"God help you," he'd said with that conceit and arrogance which had been so typical, only more obvious, in the younger Mr. Thorne.

There was one area, however, where Jason had been all too correct. She *had* allowed herself a measure of complacency with him. Not so much where her feelings were concerned, but with his, assuming he had no greater desire to stir up the dead embers of a youthful passion than herself.

Why should she think otherwise? Until last night he'd not touched her except for an accidental brushing of shoulders, the innocent grazing of their fingers in the exchange and passing of food at the table. If his gaze had often been too intense, too searching, Amanda had managed to rationalize it away in ways too numerous to catalog. It had been more comfortable to treat Jason as the platonic foreman, necessary to the ranch, friend of her aunt and daughter, while never assigning him any particular role in her own life.

"God help you, Mandy, should you indicate, directly or indirectly, that you remember, as I do, just how it once was between us."

Had he meant it as a warning? A challenge? Or were Jason's surprising words inspired by a need to let her know that his feelings were still strong?

Stop it! Good heavens, Amanda, act your age! she

chided herself fiercely. You're a grown woman, a mother, not some silly schoolgirl weaving romantic fantasies of a never-ending love.

You acted the histrionic old prude over nothing when Jason's manner toward you has been exemplary in every way. He undoubtedly decided if you were going to cry wolf, then you might as well have something to really holler about.

Can you blame him?

Amanda pulled the barn door shut behind her with a determined yank. Behind this old rough-hewn portal were the shadows of the past. They lingered in every corner and echoed throughout the rafters, and would be waiting again tomorrow, and the next day—every day—to remind her vividly of a young man and the girl who had loved him too well.

The next few days passed with such routine and normalcy Amanda was convinced that the incident in the barn had resolved itself, and she put the episode entirely out of her mind.

She was far too content as she browsed through the merchandise displayed in Hardy's General Store to allow anything to spoil her pleasure. It felt wonderful to leave the isolation of the ranch and enter civilization for a few short hours.

She fingered pretty bolts of cloth and gave longing consideration to the scented lotions and colognes displayed atop a glass-enclosed counter. She had just tested a bottle of fragrant skin cream, rubbing a small amount on the back of her hand, when Sarah burst through the door like a whirlwind.

"Mama!" she cried as she dashed across the room, nearly upsetting a wicker basket filled with lacy parasols in her excitement. "Jason says we are going to have a soda or an ice cream before we go home."

Amanda looked toward the door as the bell jingled, hailing Jason's arrival. "That's very nice, Sarah," she said somewhat absently, watching his approach. Wearing faded denim pants, and a stark white shirt beneath his customary leather vest, Jason looked impossibly handsome. By contrast, Amanda felt frumpy in her poplin skirt, topped by the yellow shirtwaist she'd never particularly liked. The color had been tolerable when her skin had been porcelain pale. But now, after several weeks of sun, she was certain this particular shade turned her complexion sallow.

Jason would not have agreed with Amanda's assessment of herself. In his opinion she'd been born to wear bright colors. She looked like sunshine. "Have you picked out your purchases?" he asked.

She replaced the lid on the floral-scented cream and gave him a polite smile. "There isn't much, only some tooth powder and soap. I gave Aunt Julie's list to the shopkeeper to fill." She looked over toward the main counter. "I don't see her now, but I'm certain she has everything ready."

Sarah's attention was rivited on the pretty jar her mother had just returned to the counter. Before Amanda knew what she was about, Sarah had it in her hands and had taken the lid off. "Oooh, this smells pretty," she trilled, shoving the cream at Jason, forcing him to take a whiff before her own nose dipped again; this time coming back up tipped in creamy white.

"Sarah," Amanda scolded. "Put that back."

At that moment, Maude Hardy, the shopkeeper,

reappeared. "Should make you add that cream to the purchase now the child's stuck her nose in the pot," she said in the cool tone Amanda had noticed since walking into the store. "It don't seem quite sanitary for folks to be sticking fingers and such in my merchandise, spreading only God knows what to some unsuspecting person who takes that home."

Amanda bristled, but not because the woman didn't have a valid and well-justified complaint. She did. It was more her general attitude of discourtesy —or was *hostility* the more appropriate term?— which had been evident the entire past half hour. She squared her shoulders and gave Maude Hardy a quelling glance, "I never had any intention of not purchasing the cream," she lied. The item was entirely too expensive and frivolously unnecessary.

It was Jason who took the jar in contention from Sarah. "Good," he said with an amused quirk of his lips. "I like the fragrance. It suits you." He moved to the woman and handed her the jar. "How much do I owe you, Mrs. Hardy?"

She refigured the items and snapped out the total. "I hope you've got enough cash to cover this, 'cause Clyde would have my head if I put anything on account for the TJ."

Amanda saw Jason's spine stiffen, but he said nothing as he reached into his pocket and counted out, to the exact nickel, the money she had requested. When it had been deposited in the register, the woman handed him the filled basket. Then she looked at Amanda, pointedly directing her next words around Jason. "You tell your aunt it ain't nothin' personal, but there won't be no more credit for her here."

Not really understanding, Amanda looked at Jason questioningly. His expression was stormy, but he didn't reply to her silent query. "Let's go," he snapped.

They had almost reached the door when Maude Hardy spoke again. "You can also tell Julie that havin' Thorne around ain't helping things one little bit. And you might also ask her if she's wondered why he decided to show back up after all these years? A lot of folks would like to know the answer to that one."

Amanda was already bristling over the woman's blunt demand to be paid in cash. She had had too many of her own run-ins with shopkeepers who valued the almighty dollar above the right to human dignity as they demanded payment and denied credit without regard to feelings or pride. But when she started talking about Jason as if he weren't present, invisible, beneath her regard, Amanda rounded on her.

"Madam, I'd suggest you ask Mr. Thorne personally if you're so curious. And *if* it's any of your business. Furthermore—"

Jason nudged Amanda out the door just as she was getting warmed up to the tongue-lashing she was about to deliver. Taking a firm hold on her arm, he began to guide her toward the drugstore. Still wearing her mutinous expression she looked at him, baffled by his unperturbed demeanor. "You should have let me tell that old witch off," she snapped.

"Cool down, Pepper," he said, his voice fairly vibrating with humor. "Old Maudie has always been irascible. Don't pay her any attention. Besides, you'll soon discover she's not alone in her opinion that this county would be better off if I'd stayed away. This prodigal son hasn't found a warm welcome upon homecoming. But then, I didn't expect one."

Amanda thought about what he'd said until they reached their destination. Sarah darted inside the drugstore when Jason opened the door. Amanda held back, and the question that had been burning inside her for several weeks just seemed to burst from her lips. "Why *did* you come back, Jason?"

He appeared to ponder his response at length while his eyes searched her face, as if he might find the answer within the warm depths of her honey-gold gaze. "This is home, Amanda. For better or worse . . ." He lightly caressed the arm beneath his hand. "Don't attempt to do battle with these people in my behalf. It's a waste of time . . . and effort." When her eyes ignited as if she would argue with his softly spoken command, Jason silenced her by placing his fingers against her lips. "We've just set a little girl loose inside a drugstore. Shouldn't we go in and keep her out of trouble?"

They found Sarah sitting on one of the four stools in front of a long, marble-topped soda fountain. She was twisting back and forth, her little legs swinging as she jabbered to the smiling man behind the fountain. He chuckled, and Amanda heard Sarah saying something about Clucky the Rooster. But the man's genuinely pleasant expression faded the minute he spotted Jason. He slammed the tall soda glass he'd been drying down on the counter, and only a miracle kept it from shattering. Amanda cried out

69

softly when she thought of the damage that might have been done should that glass have shattered, sending fragments dangerously close to Sarah's eyes and face.

Jason, too, must have realized the danger because his face darkened, losing the almost benign expression he reserved for the citizens of Stockton. He looked positively murderous when he plucked Sarah off the stool. "You'd better exercise more caution, Mr. Stein. If that glass had broken and caused any injury to this child, you'd have regretted it, I'm certain."

There was an unspoken threat which didn't go unnoticed, except for the little girl who was oblivious to it all as she squirmed in Jason's arms. "I want a great big cherry phosphate," she ordered over Jason's shoulder, giving the pharmacist her biggest smile before Jason put her down on a chair at a table in front of the window. "The very biggest!" she repeated.

Mr. Stein had the good grace to look ashamed of his actions, flushing beneath Amanda's cool, accusing stare. "W-what will the rest of you folks have?"

The tension was thick within the little drugstore as they placed their orders for beverages. Sarah was the only bright spot. Her big blue eyes were drinking up the room, darting here and there. "Mama, this is just like Carney's back home, isn't it? They even have 'lectric lights and a telephone. Why doesn't Auntie have a telephone? Everybody had one where we used to live." She cocked her head. "Are we still poor, Mama?"

Amanda was struck dumb by the question, wondering where it had come from. But before she could think of a response, Jason tweaked the little girl's nose. "Pickle, how could we be poor when we're so rich with love? Do you feel poor?"

She shrugged. "I was just asking. We never had any money when we lived in Kansas City. Well, I guess Papa did, 'cause he was always buying me presents and stuff. Mama never had any, though, and Mr. Carney used to get awful angry every time we went in there, 'cause he said Papa owed him lots of money, and Mama would yell at him 'cause she said he ought to know better than—"

"That's enough, Sarah!" Amanda was dying inside. Her child had just waved some very dirty linen in Jason's face. Obviously Mrs. Hardy's refusal of credit had triggered this memory. Although it was hardly a secret that they'd had financial difficulties after Harry's death, Amanda had never told her aunt, or anyone else, of the troubles that had plagued nearly every day of their married life. She couldn't meet Jason's gaze and was saved from further mortification when another customer entered the store, immediately calling Jason's name.

"Thorne," the man said brightly, coming directly to their table. "You've saved me a long drive out to the TJ. I spotted your automobile and decided to track you down before you started back."

"How fortunate," Jason drawled sardonically. "This must be my lucky day, Winston."

Because this was the only genuinely friendly face they'd met the entire morning, Amanda was confused and shocked by Jason's unwelcoming manner. Hoping to take some of the bite out of his rudeness, she smiled at this very attractive blond-haired man, marvelously dressed in an elegant pin-striped suit.

Bright blue eyes twinkled, and he flashed Amanda a pair of boyishly charming dimples as he returned her smile. They made him appear younger, but the intelligence and maturity he wore like a second set of clothes confirmed him to be in his middle thirties.

"You must be Mrs. Danfield's niece," he said smoothly. "Grant Winston at your service, Mrs. Ames. Your aunt has spoken of you and your lovely daughter often. I'm extremely pleased to finally make your acquaintance."

When he extended his hand, Amanda didn't hesitate to give him her own. She had to crane her neck up at him. He was really quite tall, a big man for all his sophisticated elegance. She suddenly felt like a brown mouse, sandwiched between two such handsome men, darkness and light. "Would you care to join us, Mr. Winston? We were just about to enjoy some cool beverages."

"I'd be delighted!" he exclaimed happily, not giving Jason a glance as he pulled out the extra chair and sat down.

Amanda, however, made the mistake of glancing toward those dark, stormy green eyes. She squirmed and gave him a look of apology, her eyes so mutely appealing that the glower left his face, replaced by indifference.

"How are you making the adjustment to our quieter country living, Mrs. Ames?" Grant Winston questioned affably.

"Fairly well, Mr. Winston. Are you a native of these lovely hills?"

"Heavens, no. Like yourself, I'm city born and bred. However, several months ago I decided to move my law practice from Kansas City to Stockton."

Mr. Stein chose that moment to deliver one cherry phosphate and two root beers, taking Grant Winston's order at the same time.

"How does your wife feel about such a move?"

Jason's head snapped up at Amanda's bald curiosity into Winston's marital status, and an indefinable glint appeared in those disturbing eyes.

"I'm not married, Mrs. Ames," Grant responded pointedly, grinning broadly so his dimples were being used with effect.

Amanda realized her question might have been construed as flirtatious, though it had not really been her intent. She had felt comfortable in his company immediately, and sensed his interest in her as a woman. Why not? He was good looking, easy to talk with, they shared similar backgrounds. Why then did the terms dull and predictable also come to mind? Thrusting those thoughts aside, Amanda smiled warmly.

She didn't hear Jason's muttered curse before he leaned over and whispered in Sarah's ear. The little girl gurgled delightedly at his jest, but clamped her hand over her mouth too late to prevent a spurt of cherry liquid, which spewed from her mouth.

"Oops," Jason said, his lips twitching as he covered a laugh with a loud cough behind his fist.

Grant Winston was mopping his face with a monogrammed handkerchief he'd pulled from his breastpocket.

"Oh, dear," Amanda wailed. "I'm so very sorry, Mr. Winston. Sarah, apologize to this gentleman for your bad manners."

"Sorry," the little girl mumbled between deep pulls on her paper straw.

Amanda would also have liked to hear an apology from Jason for his part in this, but knew better than to ask it of a man struggling so hard to control his laughter that his eyes were moist. "Children will be children, Mr. Winston. We have to occasionally make allowances for their behavior." She was looking directly at Jason.

Although Thorne had chosen a rather unusual method, Grant had little difficulty interpreting the clear message. The lovely widow was not available for a casual flirtation—or anything else, he suspected. Grant liked a challenge much as any other man, but this was not the time or the place. He'd allowed himself to be distracted from his purpose too long already.

Before the beverage he'd ordered could arrive, Grant was reaching into his coat to pull out an envelope. "Thorne, you'll be pleased to hear Mr. Brinkman has decided to be more reasonable. I'm certain Mrs. Danfield can't help but be pleased."

Jason took the letter, then refolded it so that the envelope would fit in his back pocket. "The confidence you and Brinkman have is overwhelming, Winston." He stood in one single motion. "It's getting late, Amanda. We had better be starting back."

She would have complained about his rather high-handed manner, but the argument stalled on her lips when Sarah hopped down off her chair and followed

Jason to the door. "It was pleasant to make your acquaintance, Mr. Winston," she said uneasily as she rose from her own chair.

"We'll meet again soon, I'm sure," he promised.

Jason and Sarah were already halfway down the street when she caught up with them. "You might have let me finish my root beer," she grumbled.

"Couldn't," he shot back, an unmistakable edge in his voice. "It was getting so deep in there, I was afraid I'd have to shovel our way out."

Chapter Five

"ARE YOU CERTAIN AMANDA DIDN'T PICK UP ON ANYthing during your conversation with Winston this afternoon?" Julie put her dishrag down and turned away from the sink to face Jason, who was still sitting at the table. Amanda and Sarah were outside, watching the sunset.

"I'm almost certain," he replied, looking up from the figures he'd been studying for the past half hour.

Julie shook her head as if baffled. "Not even after that mouthy Maude Hardy said right out there wouldn't be any more credit for the TJ?"

Jason closed the ledger book and leaned back in

his chair. He didn't need to continue looking at those numbers to realize they weren't adding up. "How much has Amanda told you about her marriage, Julie? Were they happy together? Has she hinted there might have been financial problems before Harry's death?"

"She doesn't talk much about Harry Ames at all. I know he sure left them in a pickle when he died, but far as I can tell from what Sarah has said, he was generous with gifts." Julie paused for a moment before continuing. "Now that you mention it, though, Amanda certainly doesn't seem to have anything particularly fancy in the way of clothing or fripperies. Although they shipped out more toys and playthings than any ten children could want or need. I remember my brother crowing about what a fine catch his little girl had made. Of course, just seeing her married eased poor Frank's mind. He knew he had that cancer growing in his stomach. I really just don't know much about Amanda's marriage, when I think on it. I've always thought it wrong to saddle a young girl with a man near old enough to be her father. However, she seemed happy enough."

Twice today, once in Hardy's store, and then later when Sarah had started babbling about money and being poor, Jason had seen Amanda go white. Her eyes had clouded with an almost panicked distress, and the tension in her usually supple body had been visible. She seemed more than content to keep herself uninvolved in the business of the TJ. In many ways she behaved more like a guest than a permanent member of the household.

Jason told Julie about the reactions he'd witnessed

in Amanda while in town. "Doesn't it seem odd that a man with his own dry goods store, one well established for almost two full generations, would die destitute? Surely Amanda could have sold his business and garnered some kind of profit. Since they lived in a home purchased by Harry's parents, why would she be forced to sell at a loss unless the house was mortgaged? Does that speak of affluence?"

Julie didn't respond as she joined him at the table, resting her arms atop the checked cloth. He didn't fool her for a minute with all this talk about Amanda's problems. Jason was doing his damnedest to distract her from those two documents he'd brought home from town today. Finally she spoke. "Well, by coming here she sure has jumped from the frying pan into the fire, hasn't she? Could be the women in my family have a special talent for tossing prosperity out the window in the blink of an eye. Look at me. It took me less than a year to bring this ranch to its knees."

"With a little help from your friends . . . and enemies," Jason reminded her quickly. He hated it when she started beating herself, taking blame where there was none. "Don't start up on this again, Julie. How could you possibly have foreseen that Stoney Markum, a man who had been your trusted foreman for more than ten years, would have sold you out?"

"He contracted for the entire herd, Jase," she said, her voice still disbelieving, even after all these months of living with the reality of Stoney's betrayal. "Or tried to, anyway. All I had left after his deal with Brinkman were those fifty cows, and some mighty big unpaid debts. Guess I should be grateful Stoney miscounted. At least we'll be able to keep beef on our own table for a while longer." She took a deep breath. "What makes a man turn on a friend?"

Jason knew Julie wasn't just referring to her former foreman, who was doubtless living high and free somewhere on the traitor's fee he'd collected from Brinkman. He reached across the table to capture her tightly clenched hands. "Julie, it will be a cold day in hell before we're forced to start butchering those cows for our survival. As long as I draw breath—"

"That argument isn't going to work with me this time, Jason Thorne. Not after what you brought home to me today." She pulled away from his grasp to snatch up two folded sheets of paper, waving them in his face. "You know well as I do that this final offer of Brinkman's is more an ultimatum than anything else. He's starting to get nervous, impatient because we're not going belly up fast enough to suit him. And he's probably starting to wonder why. He didn't plant Grant Winston in this town just to spread his propaganda. Or do you suppose it's just the wind which keeps opening up those pasture gates and scattering cows all over yonder two or three times a week? It sure wasn't any act of nature that twisted the windmill shaft all to hell just about the time Amanda and Sarah arrived. Shoot, the way Brinkman sees things, he probably thinks we're starting to bring in reinforcements. How else can he explain our taking on two additional mouths to feed when, according to his figures and all reason, we shouldn't have two spare nickels to rub together by now. Stoney might not have been able to count, but Winston can add up two and two quick enough. There was fifty head left on that range last fall after Brinkman's men drove off my herd. There's fifty-six now, counting calves. We're not eating our own beef, Jase. Yet by all appearances we are hale and hearty. And just how long do you figure it will take before word gets back to Brinkman that you pulled cash out of your pocket for those supplies today?"

Her voice wavered, and tears filled her eyes as she slapped that second offending sheet of paper down onto the table. "But this . . . this, I think, is the final straw. A petition, signed by people I've known and called my friends for the better part of my life, requesting I get my bustle right out of the county. Politely phrased, of course. It seems Winston has them convinced that unless Brinkman gets hold of the TJ, he'll take that meat processing plant he's promised elsewhere. You know, I'm half of a mind to give these thankless, so-called friends what they want and quit torturing myself with the worry of it all."

"You don't mean that, old girl," Jason soothed, trying not to show his alarm over what he hoped was merely an empty threat.

"Why shouldn't I mean it?" she countered while brushing away the moisture that had fallen to her cheeks.

"Because your conscience would give you no peace if you did," he said with quiet assurance, his gaze gentle as he pulled his handkerchief from his pocket and passed it to her. "We both know Brinkman has no intention of turning elsewhere. He's too sure of his victory here. The TJ will be only his first conquest. Once he has this ranch, he'll simply start gobbling up everything in sight. They won't have a chance against that kind of power."

"And we do, I suppose?" she said sarcastically.

He grinned slightly. "You know we do. Julie, you're hurt. Justifiably, I'll admit. But you'll be playing right into Brinkman's hands if you let this petition sway you. It's what he's counting on."

"Maybe," Julie conceded. "However, letting this deadline run out won't necessarily stop Brinkman's plans. He'll just find some other poor fool to ruin, and then what will we do? We'll really be cut off then. He'll control the cattle market around here. Even if we manage to find a buyer for our beef, how are we going to get them to the rail lines with Brinkman owning all the land around us? Cows can't fly, you know."

Again he chuckled, not at all fazed by her snippy tongue. He was relieved by it. If she could still give him sass, her spirit wasn't entirely broken. "I hope he does start looking elsewhere to get his foothold. The sooner the better. People might not think so highly of their saintly Mr. Brinkman and his smooth-talking attorney when they're standing in our shoes."

"Well, they've surely been begging for the opportunity," Julie said bitterly, the pain of old friends turning against her nearly more than she could bear.

Jason muttered a vehement curse beneath his breath, wishing he'd had the good sense to burn that damned petition. "Listen here, old girl. Not everyone in this community put their names to that list of deluded idiots. I believe you still have friends."

"Yeah? Where are they, then? They sure haven't been rushing my door to offer help."

Jason frowned, but didn't sidestep the issue. "Has it occurred to you that by having the half-breed around you have been denying yourself the very support needed?"

Julie's dark brown eyes ignited. "Half-breed my . . . mother's nightshirt. You don't have enough Cherokee in you to work up a decent war whoop. Your mama might have claimed some piddlin' bit of Indian heritage, but that's not what folks hold against you. We both know—"

"The reason doesn't matter," Jason told her abruptly. He pushed away from the table and went to stand before the screened door. "I'm here. That's excuse enough for this town to give you a wide berth."

"Yes, you are here," Julie said gently, going to him. She gave that rigid back a comforting pat. "Which is something I thank God for every morning, every night, and a half-dozen times or more in between." She stood beside him, following the direction of his gaze. She could see her niece near the corral fence, and hear Sarah's shrill laughter. "I don't even much care that it wasn't entirely for my sake you showed up last January. You saved my life, Jase. And you've stood by me since, even though that's also not entirely for my sake."

He gave her a quick, puzzled look. "Don't tell me you've joined ranks with those in town who are convinced my sole purpose is to ruin their plans and turn your silly old head?"

"I might be silly at times, and I certainly can't deny being old. One thing I'm not, though, is blind. You, Jason Thorne, are as transparent as this here screen. I'll confess I was surprised when you started writing me not long after Lucy and Susan died—not that I wasn't glad to hear from you. You needed somebody to talk out your grief with, and I was proud you thought of me. But sometime after that first year, you started asking after Amanda. At first, I thought you were just being polite. Then I realized good manners had nothing to do with your interest. You were just plain starving for information about my niece. Tell me, Jase," she asked with a probing stare, "just how well *did* you and Amanda get to know each other that last summer?"

"By *know,* do you mean in the biblical sense?"

"I most certainly did not," she protested, flushing to the roots of her hair. "And you'd best not be telling me that you messed with that child—"

"I loved her, Julie," he responded simply, earnestly. "Too much to have hurt her that way. I swear." Not entirely, he amended silently.

Although he'd stated his feelings in the past tense, Julie had known for a very long time they were very much part of Jason's present. "How does she feel about this?"

"God, I wish I knew," he breathed, his eyes drifting shut for a brief moment. "She doesn't seem to bear me any real hatred. On the other hand, if I get too close she jumps and runs like a frightened doe."

Julie knew that emotions strong enough to burn hot within a man for twelve years couldn't have survived unless they'd once been returned full measure. "I suspect she wouldn't jump at all if she were indifferent. I think you threaten that safe little world she's trying to hide herself in. She's avoiding you, just as she has done her best to avoid involving herself in the TJ's troubles. But by the look in your eyes every time she walks into a room, and the way things are going with Brinkman, I don't imagine Amanda's going to be able to hold off reality much longer." When Jason made no response to this, continuing to watch a woman and her child, Julie took a deep breath and forged on.

"What are we going to do, Jase? About Amanda? About Brinkman's deadline for buying this place?"

Jason rolled back against the wall, his thumbs seeking the pockets of his trousers. She looked to him for answers, solutions, and he felt the weight of her trust resting heavy upon his uncertain shoulders. "With Amanda, the right thing would be to sit her down and force her to listen, insist she hear the facts whether she wants them or not. That's what we *should* do. However, I'll admit to some purely selfish reasons for wanting to keep her in the dark for a while longer. We need time; time without further complications. There's enough of the past to reconcile between us. Too much of the present could make that difficult, if not impossible. As for Brinkman: Do I really need to restate my position?"

"I guess not. Though I'd think this would be the last place on earth you'd want to put down roots. Still, I'm not easy in my mind. It is getting harder and harder to believe Brinkman will make a mistake, or the Good Lord is going to work us a miracle. It's not that I want to give up. I don't. But lately I can't help wonder and worry about what might happen should Brinkman and Winston decide a little harmless harassment isn't working. We're vulnerable out here. What if they start getting mean? What if—"

"Whoa there," Jason cautioned, pulling her close against him. "Don't let your imagination run wild on you. Think logically. Would Brinkman chance arousing suspicions toward his real purposes with an obvious act of violence? Right now he's seen to it we're pegged as the villains in this game. I don't imagine he'd risk switching roles at this late date. People around here have their faults, maybe more than their fair share. But they wouldn't stand still if any real harm should come to you. We're safe enough. At least until the end of July."

Julie was easy to convince because she desperately wanted to believe Jason's reassurances. "All right, Jase. We'll let that toad sweat a while longer. You, on the other hand, had best not wait for any golden opportunities." For the first time this evening, mischief began to dance in her eyes. "My advice is that you kiss that girl silly the first chance you get. Because when she starts asking questions—which she will soon enough—I'm for telling her the truth. Do you agree?"

A single dark brow arched while a slow smile spread across his handsome face. "Agree about what? The kissing or the telling?"

"Oh, you devil!" Julie chortled, giving him a hard push toward the door. "Get on out of here! You've got some serious romancing to get started on!"

* * *

Amanda laughed softly at Sarah's efforts to capture fireflies, leaping and twirling, running in circles, reaching for those twinkling imitations of God's stars brought down to earth.

Muffling a sleepy yawn, she glanced toward the house, wishing Aunt Julie and Jason would conclude their business so she could find her bed. Once in a while these private conferences caused a little ruffling of her feathers. But then she'd acknowledge her total ignorance regarding the operations of a ranch, and knew her presence would be ridiculous. If there was anything of importance she needed to know, Amanda trusted them to keep her advised.

Closing her eyes, Amanda inhaled the wonderful fragrance of the summer evening. It was absolutely heaven to be free of worry. And if she were dreaming this glorious contentment, she hoped she never awakened. Twice today she'd felt the twinges of that old, familiar stirring of smothering panic. Countless times she had faced men and women like Mrs. Hardy, watched their eyes grow glassy, their mouths narrow, their expressions turn ugly just before they would launch into a vociferous demand for payment on some account. Attempts to be discreet or polite were rare. She was harrangued on her front porch, accosted in the street, confronted in public buildings, shamed in front of friends and neighbors until there weren't any friends. For ten years she lived with the march of creditors until she cringed inside, her spirit shriveling more with every year as she lived with her forty-year-old child.

She tried so hard to forgive Harry now in death as she'd not been able to in life. Much of the blame was her own, she admitted. When they married she had been little more than a child herself, and equally irresponsible. But how could she have known that Harry's nature, lighthearted and wonderfully fun loving, was also a symptom of weakness and lack of character. She could blame his mother, who kept the leash too rigid. Unfortunately, the son had needed the unyielding control. She might excuse him for the heart condition—something he never bothered to reveal—which made him grasp for every minute of life with greedy hands. Or she could continue to flog herself for not being stronger, wiser, effectual in making him see reason. In the end there was only Harry, who cared more for his play and pleasures than for his wife and his child.

Of course, Sarah believed her papa had been perfect. Amanda had worked very hard to maintain that illusion. Harry brought home lavish gifts to his wife and little girl. Amanda would return hers immediately, and often she would beg the owners of the store not to extend Harry credit. To pay for his generosity, Harry would take money from his own store until there was never any profit. Disgruntled employees quit faster than they could be hired when their salaries were delayed, cut, and often ignored entirely. Their employer's careless business practices often encouraged outright theft. Amanda had attempted managing the store for a time. A miscarriage, caused by stress and overwork, had put her flat on her back long enough for Harry to ruin any gains she might have made. By the time she was well enough to return, he'd bankrupted the business, selling out entirely, retiring on the second mortgage he'd taken on the house.

Harry had not survived six months of his retirement. Amanda had tried very hard to grieve for this man she had once genuinely adored. But love and passion had not endured the butcher, the baker, and the candlestick maker when their accounts went unpaid.

It had been hell, she admitted. Ten very long years of constant worry and despair. Only Sarah had kept her sane.

Thank God, it was over. They were both safe now.

Jason had been standing only a few feet away from Amanda for quite some time. He watched her intently as she struggled with some painful internal conflict. In the moonlight her lovely face reflected emotions he couldn't begin to fathom. She clutched herself tightly, and he could see the rapid rise and fall of her chest, knowing if he touched the pulse at her throat it would be racing wildly.

He began to pray to a God he wasn't even certain existed that no memory they shared was the cause of such awful distress. It was all he could do to maintain his distance and not pull her into his arms, and tell her he would never, never let anything hurt her again.

When she finally appeared to conquer her private demons, he cleared his throat softly.

Amanda started almost violently at the sound. "Jason," she breathed, feeling foolish to have jumped so high. "I didn't see you there. Is the meeting over?"

He moved closer, propping his foot on the rail near where she stood. "For tonight. Do our private meetings bother you?"

Surprised by the question, Amanda was uncertain

how to respond. Part of her realized she was quite happy to delegate the worry and responsibility of the TJ to her knowledgeable aunt and this man. But there was also a tiny shred of guilt over dumping the full burden onto others.

"Not really," she finally told him. "I'm better off doing only what I'm told. What do I know of ranching?"

Her answer was too nonchalant, but before Jason could persue the subject, Sarah ran up and pushed her way between both adults.

"Mama! Jason! Look'ee what I made," she said, breathless with her excitement. When her hand was extended for their admiration, Jason winced slightly at the glowing circlet which surrounded her little ring finger. Several fireflies had made their luminescent sacrifices to adorn a child's hand. "Isn't it pretty?" she sighed.

Amanda and Jason exchanged looks of consternation before Amanda patted the little girl's head. "Yes, that's very pretty, sweetheart. But you really shouldn't hurt the little bugs. If you take their lights, they might die. Also, they won't be able to twinkle for us anymore. Do you understand what I'm trying to tell you?"

"Yes, Mama," Sarah returned dully, clearly disgruntled. "They're just bugs," she added with a sidelong glance that said she thought grown-ups were awfully strange.

When she stomped away from the two tenderhearted adults, Jason turned to Amanda. "Bloodthirsty little thing, isn't she?"

Amanda chuckled. "No more so than any child her age. Now, don't try to tell me you never massacred a firefly or two in your youth? I'm certainly no saint."

Jason gave her a tender smile, not bothering to deny the charge even though he couldn't honestly remember a single time when he'd had the freedom to chase fireflies. Right after supper, every night of the week, there had always been those lengthy, knee-breaking hours of prayer until bedtime. Play had not been a word in his vocabulary, let alone a reality in his life. At least not until one summer, when a girl had taught him to laugh and tease and run with no purpose but the joy of it. "How do you feel about starting your refresher course in riding tomorrow?"

She frowned. "Do you want an honest answer?"

"Let me rephrase that. We *are going* to start your riding lessons tomorrow."

"Well, then, I suppose I'm as ready as I'll ever be." A thought struck her. "Jason, I don't have anything to wear. My wardrobe has never felt the necessity for such a costume."

"Damn," he muttered. "I should have thought of that while we were in town today. I doubt Julie has anything that wouldn't go around you three times. And, before you tell me alterations could be made in a day or two, let me remind you that my free time is limited. Plus, I'm not letting you get out of this so easily. I've got an idea that might work." He pushed away from the fence and took off in a running lope toward the bunkhouse, leaving Amanda still mentally sputtering over the conversation he'd just had with himself. When he returned seconds later with a pair of his own trousers and a shirt, she found her tongue.

90

"Don't be ludicrous, Jason. I can't wear men's clothing!"

He was holding the trousers out in front of him, eyeballing her for size. "They'll be a bit long, and maybe too big, but I think they will do nicely." He tossed them at her, following with the same routine for the shirt. "Actually, trousers will be safer for the kind of work we'll be doing. Those split skirts are fine for just riding, but there's too much danger in getting them snagged or tangled up."

"Jason," Amanda repeated, drawing out his name with exaggerated patience, "I cannot—will not—wear your trousers at any time, or anywhere. . . ."

Twice Amanda nearly fell flat on her face in the unaccustomed boots. It had taken two pairs of heavy woolen socks, and still her aunt's contribution to this ridiculous costume felt a full size too large. When she caught her heel on the bottom step outside the kitchen door, Amanda muttered an uncharacteristic curse before she righted herself again. Jason's pants were much too large around her waist, and she tightly gripped the excess material. But she was more embarrassed by the tight fit of the pants elsewhere. They clung to her hips and thighs scandalously, almost as if they'd been painted on her body. Without the tentlike proportions of the shirt, Amanda would never have stepped outside the house. Fortunately, the shirttails dangled nearly to her knees, and that was just where she intended they would stay.

Her chin was thrust out aggressively as she made her way to Jason leading a chestnut mare out of the barn. When Jason didn't even bother to mask his amusement, tossing back his head to roar with laughter, she was grateful it was necessary to hold on to the trousers. Otherwise, she might have smacked that grin right off his face. "The boots are still too big," she informed him coldly. Her tone only brought more humor to glint in those dark eyes.

"I think we can find another pair of socks," he offered helpfully.

"My feet are melting as it is," she shot back. Deep down she knew she was covering her apprehension with false anger. Standing this close to the mare, the horse looked impossibly tall, strong, and subsequently threatening.

Jason suspected that the source of her snippiness was rooted in a purely false bravado, so he purposely continued to aggravate her temper. "Do you need a belt to hold up those trousers? Or are you clutching your stomach in abject terror?"

Her fear-glazed eyes cleared and heated with irritation, but before she could think of some cutting remark Sarah was there and cooing with unfeigned envy. "Oooh, Mama, can I get some trousers, too? Is it fun to dress like a boy?"

Having taken advantage of Sarah's appearance to fetch a length of rope for a makeshift belt, Jason returned just in time to hear Sarah begin pleading to take her mother's place on Fancy's back.

"Later, Pickle. When your mama and I are finished, I'll set you up there for just a short walk. But for now your aunt needs help in the garden."

The little girl scampered off with only a wrinkling of her nose in protest. Amanda's feelings were much stronger. Once again he'd snatched the prerogative of parental authority as if it were his God-given right. "I wish you'd stop interfering with my daughter's discipline," she told him waspishly.

Jason quickly looped the rope around her waist, giving a little tug, which she, of course, resisted as he measured and cut to proper length. "You know, I didn't intend to interfere between you and Sarah." His halfhearted apology was immediately spoiled when he rudely jerked the tails of the shirt up so his hands could feed the makeshift belt through the loops on her trousers. She froze with surprise. "Actually, Amanda," he said casually, pulling the ends of the rope tight, knotting them securely around that beautifully narrow waist, "I was more concerned with preventing another one of your excuses to keep you off this horse," Jason continued, his voice becoming gruff. He hoped his reaction to the discovery of her shapely hips and long slender thighs couldn't be read on his face . . . or anywhere else, for that matter.

"Come on, Amanda," he said more gently, extending his hand. "Fancy is well trained and gentle as a lamb."

There would be no more putting this off. Ignoring his hand, mustering every ounce of her courage, Amanda stepped up to the animal. She wiped her sweaty palms against the sides of her trousers and took a firm grip on the saddle horn. Her mind was racing, and her heart pounded when she placed her left foot in the stirrup and pushed off the ground.

The animal, sensing her fear, shied away just a little, causing Amanda to shriek in terror. The result was panic in both horse and rider. Fancy's hindquarters swung away in a wide arc. Amanda had one foot in the stirrup and her right leg was flying wildly.

Terrified she would lose her grip on the saddle, she closed her eyes and screamed, "Jaaa—son!"

On the next pass of Fancy's backside, Jason caught Amanda's hips. Her high-pitched cry of fright soon became a outraged cry of protest as she was boosted up and rudely put in the saddle. Her legs felt as if they were being wrenched from their sockets, and her bottom was tingling from the slap of leather and the strong hands that had been intimately curved there.

Amanda heard Jason's chuckles over the furious rushing of her blood as it returned to her body. She was attempting to catch her breath, along with her wits, to tell him off soundly when she noticed he'd been distracted. She followed his narrowed dark gaze to the man who was standing at the edge of the garden, flanked by her aunt and Sarah. "Oh, no . . ." she moaned, recognizing Grant Winston. Amanda wanted to die because it was patently obvious, by the look on his face, that he'd witnessed this entire fiasco.

"Jason," she rasped. "Help me down . . . please." Out of the corner of her eye she could see Winston walking toward them. She simply couldn't greet the man with any dignity while sitting on the back of this damned horse. "Jason! Help me down!"

He glanced back at her. "Down is just reverse of up, Amanda."

Her jaw tightened at his glib response. She took a careful measure of the distance to the ground. Gingerly she shifted her weight and began to lift her right leg, silently praying Fancy wouldn't move a single inch. She heard Jason's grumbling, "Oh, Christ," and then Amanda was lifted free of the saddle. She was acutely aware of every inch of his lean, sinewy form as he slowly lowered her, letting her slide down his entire length. In his eyes was a heart-stopping mixture of roguish amusement and a sensual awareness.

Standing a few feet away, Grant Winston didn't miss much of the exchange between Thorne and the pretty, if somewhat unconventionally dressed, widow. He coughed lightly when it appeared neither was taking much notice of his presence.

The sound broke the sensual spell. Amanda whirled, her face flaming, to meet those charming dimples and a perfect set of teeth. "H–Hello," she said with attempted brightness.

"Good afternoon, Mrs. Ames." He looked at Jason. "Thorne," he added somewhat less warmly.

"What brings you out here, Winston?" Jason demanded in a tone that sounded more an accusation than a question.

Julie, who had just come up to join them, took charge at this point. "Mr. Winston and I have some piddly business to discuss. You two just keep right on with what you're doing." She linked her arm through the attorney's. "Besides, Grant, you told me the mayor was expecting you for Sunday dinner. And if I know anything about Miles Davis, it's that he expects folks to be punctual. If we stay out here jawing, you're liable to be late."

As she spoke, Julie was drawing Grant Winston toward the house, giving him little choice but to follow. Short of the door, he turned back. "It was a pleasure seeing you again, Mrs. Ames," he called out.

"Come again soon, Mr. Winston," she returned.

Jason made an objectionable sound deep in his throat. Then he began to mutter. "Oh, yes, please do come back, Mr. Winston. Wear out the god-damned road."

Amanda turned back to him, totally mystified. "What on earth is the matter with you? If there's some reason why I shouldn't be pleasant to that gentleman, I do wish you'd tell me."

"Pleasant?" he groaned. "Good God, Amanda, you practically ooze all over that overdressed, ego-tistical city slicker!"

"That is not so," she denied, her voice rising with her temper. "But even if it were—what business is it of yours whom I choose to be friendly with? And, in case you haven't noticed, I just happen to be a city slicker myself!"

"Listen here, lady . . ."

They were practically standing nose to nose when Sarah hopped off the fence where she'd been sitting since Grant Winston's arrival. Tugging hard on her mother's shirttail, she looked up into those two angry faces. "Why are you fighting?" Her big blue eyes were bewildered and bright with tears.

Jason reacted immediately, squatting down to ruffle her hair. "We weren't fighting, Pickle. We were just having a loud discussion."

Sarah sniffed. "That's what Mama always used to say when she and Papa would yell at each other. But it wasn't true." She shook her head slowly from side to side. "It always scared me. Kiss and make up like Mama and Papa used to do."

Jason rolled his eyes up at Amanda. "Well . . . ah . . ."

"Sarah," Amanda said patiently, putting her hand on her daughter's shoulder. "Sometimes adults have disagreements. It has nothing to do with you. There's no reason to be upset, or scared." When the tears continued to fall, Amanda tried again. "Honey, people just don't get along all the time."

"It's not working, Amanda," Jason said as he rose to his feet.

"Well, you convince her, then. I don't know what more—"

Jason's arm hooked around Amanda's waist, and he captured her mouth for a hard brief kiss before she could manage more than a strangled gurgle of complaint. "How's that, Pickle-face? All better now?"

Sarah was positively beaming. Jason's eyes were dancing with mischief, and he looked quite pleased with himself. Amanda wasn't certain what she was feeling. Not certain at all. "Wouldn't . . . wouldn't it have been simpler merely to reassure her we weren't really fighting?"

"Well, I thought so, but you get all prickly when I interfere. And who was it who had to go into all that rigmarole about disagreements and people not getting along?"

"I was only trying to be reasonable—"

Sarah jerked again on her mother's shirttails. "You're fighting again!"

Jason's brows shot up. "Sarah, I do believe we are," he drawled.

This time Amanda was prepared as she danced back. "Oh, no you don't, Jason Thorne." She darted around the mare, placing the animal squarely between herself and Jason's grinning threat. "You stay right there!" she warned, pointing her finger at him over the saddle. They made two full trips around the horse before Jason caught her, only to let her off lightly with a tweak on the nose. She heard uninhibited laughter, and was surprised to discover it was her own.

Chapter Six

JASON DIDN'T LIKE THE LOOKS OF THE SKY. AMANDA, riding at his side, was unaware of the approaching storm. She was concentrating too hard on maintaining control over her horse. He silently cursed the fact that he'd allowed her to talk him into this little jaunt. After only a week of instruction—an hour here and there—she wasn't ready to handle the mare and nature both.

Where in the hell had those clouds come from? he wondered. When they'd started out right after Sunday dinner, only a few dark smudges marred the perfection of a crystal blue horizon. Now the winds were beginning to gust, and dark rain clouds were collecting, racing over their heads, while inter-mittent sunshine chased shadows upon the ground. At this slow pace they'd never make it back to the barn before all hell broke loose.

He urged Whiskey close to the mare and captured the chestnut's bridle, pulling her up. "Amanda, we have a storm which is going to cut loose any time now," he told her calmly, hoping she wouldn't panic.

She did. Her face drained of color. "What should I do?" She wasn't ready to handle this situation. They should have stayed within the ranch enclosure, but the day had been so beautiful, and the hills had seemed to beckon.

Jason knew there was only one option now. A terrified rider, plus a skittish horse, was asking for trouble in spades. He dismounted and gave the bay stallion a hard slap on the rump. "Head for the barn boy!" Whiskey took off like a shot, and the mare would have bounded after him, if not for Jason's tight grip on the bridle.

"Scoot up, Amanda. We'll ride double from here."

She did as he instructed without hesitation, kick-ing her foot free of the stirrup so he could mount behind her. When she felt his weight on the saddle, her body tensed slightly in reaction to the man who was settling himself close to her back. Too close. Her backside fit tightly between his legs; his thighs pressed against her own. And when his arms came around her, taking the reins, she felt as if she'd been enveloped.

"Just relax. Lean back against me." His voice was

low in her ear. Her back was flush against his chest. "We'll be moving pretty fast, but trust me not to dump us both."

Jason's command was almost imperceptible, but the mare responded immediately, lurching forward to gallop for home. It seemed they had barely been traveling when the first flash of lightning and the resulting rolling of thunder shook the ground. Amanda jumped, and would have lost her seat if not for Jason's strong arm around her waist holding her securely. It was as if the electricity crackling and flashing above also electrified their bodies, charging through their heated flesh, as they moved together with the rolling gait of the mare.

Just as the current flowing between them began to reach dangerous levels, Fancy raced through the gate, and a swift, sharp turn brought them into the barn.

Jason's face was taut as he tried to control the desire coursing through him, making his pulse hammer. He swung down from the saddle, then lifted his arms up for Amanda, wanting more than anything in his life for her to fall into them and answer his need with her own. But he knew, as his hands encircled her waist, it was not to be; not this time. He lifted her free of the saddle, but his trembling, and her eagerness to flee dangerous, threatening emotions, conspired against them both. She fell hard against him and she felt his arousal.

He didn't quite understand the silent plea within her golden eyes until he realized how tightly he was holding her, molding her to every square inch of his heated flesh. "Amanda," he whispered, his hands moving up her back, his gaze burning over her face with an eloquent plea of his own.

"No . . . Please . . ." she begged on a shuddering breath.

Jason's arms fell away, and he stepped back. Amanda gave him no time to reconsider, stumbling away to flee toward the house. He slowly followed her as far as the door, seeing that she made her way inside safely just before the first large drops of rain began to splat against the dry ground.

Suddenly he was assailed by the memory of another stormy evening that had ended much in the same way. . . .

Jason was listening rather absently to Amanda's nonstop chatter about some silly incident that had happened at her school. He had little interest in the story, but delighted in watching her animated face as she recounted the tale. She was stretched out on her stomach in the meadow's thick, summer grass, kicking her legs up behind her, unconcerned about the show of stockinged legs. She really could be quite trying at times, he thought even as he grinned, pretending to be interested. But this girl had become precious to him, important in ways he couldn't understand.

She was too slender, almost flat-chested, and not his type at all. Secondly, they argued more often than not whenever they were together. She had quite a temper, which he guessed went along with her hair, that looked as if it had captured the brilliance of a sunset. She was good at verbal fighting, giving tit for tat, not at all afraid to go nose to nose. It was the first time Jason had ever fought with someone without that awful knotted dread of knowing pain would soon follow and blood would flow.

Not only could she make him madder than hades, she could also make him laugh, which was rare. Everything about this girl was a surprise, a new experience for him. She had become his friend. Jason had never known the closeness, or the acceptance, of a friend before.

In the early days his emotions had scared him to death. He'd put up barriers which she ignored. He said things intentionally to hurt and wound. She'd stood her ground and told him off proper. Then, in desperation, Jason had used his final weapon to cut the binding threads that were slowly ensnaring his heart. He'd coldly, with calculated purpose, thought to scare her off with his tainted blood and bastardy. Amanda had listened quietly. When he'd run out of ugly words to describe his inferior placement in the world, she'd looked at him with those warm honey eyes, shrugged slightly, and said, "So?" There had been a sense of peace, a gentle stillness settling deeply inside of him, and Jason had realized, for the first time, that he'd been shaking almost his entire life.

"Jason Thorne, you aren't listening. I'll bet you can't repeat a single thing I've said."

"Who'd want to? You weren't saying anything— just talking. There is a difference, you know."

He barely managed to avoid the clump of dirt she sent sailing at his head, falling backward, only to arch upright. "Hell's bells! Where did those clouds come from?" A storm squall was rolling in fast. Jason jumped to his feet and hauled Amanda up off the ground. Holding her hand, he dragged her along as he ran across the meadow. He quickly discovered she possessed another fault. She couldn't run worth a damn.

Slowing his pace to match hers, the storm broke before they could reach the fence. Sheets of water were drenching them as he vaulted over the high rails, and then reached for her. "Come on!" he snapped impatiently while she struggled to climb over, hampered by soggy skirts. "Oh, hell," he grumbled, and fitting his hands beneath her armpits he pulled her over. He'd already turned her toward the house when a lemon-sized hailstone glanced off his head. Amanda cried out as the sky began to hurl balls of ice with hurtful force.

The barn was closer than the house and Jason shoved her in that direction, pushing her inside. Once they were safely out of the storm, he fell into a cushion of hay, breathing heavily. "Whew! I sure didn't see that coming. Are you all right?"

"I—I think so," she said through chattering teeth. "I'm c-cold." Amanda crossed her arms over her breasts, and her hands were furiously rubbing up and down her shaking arms.

Jason rolled off the hay and went in search of something warm and dry, but found nothing, not even a smelly old blanket. "Maybe we ought to try for the house." Outside the hail continued to fall and gather upon the ground, making a double hazard.

"Amanda!" Todd Danfield's booming voice cut through the noise. Jason went to the door and called out to his employer. "With me, sir!" he yelled at the top of his lungs. "In the barn!"

"Thorne? Amanda's with you?"

"Yes, sir!"

"Good! Stay put until this passes over!"

Amanda had come to stand beside him while the messages were hollered back and forth. She stood close and her voice was still unsteady as she said, "I guess we're trapped for the duration, huh?" Jason looked at her. Water was running off her braids, further soaking her thin cotton blouse, which was already plastered to the chest he'd always thought too flat to be of any interest. Jason saw now that he had been hasty in his judgment. Although her breasts were small, they were disturbingly perfect in shape with nipples that seemed to be jutting out at him as if eager to be touched. He swallowed hard and jerked his eyes away.

"How long do you think this will last?" she asked, moving closer to him for warmth. Jason recoiled when her breast grazed his arm. "How the hell am I supposed to know?" He burst out, using anger to shield himself against the sudden rush of feelings he couldn't seem to control.

She glanced at him strangely, but chose not to comment on his inexplicable irascibility. "Golly, have you ever seen hailstones so big before?" She poked her head slightly out the barn door.

"Jesus!" he yelled, pulling her back. "Are you stupid!? Do you want to damage what few brains you've got!? Don't you have any sense at all?"

"Obviously not!" she shot right back. "If I did, I certainly wouldn't put up with your nasty nature and ugly disposition. Good heavens! Sometimes you are so moody my head spins just trying to keep up with you."

"If it's such a trial, why bother? I sure as hell don't need the hassle of trying to entertain the boss's precious little niece."

They'd had equally ridiculous shouting matches before, swapping insults, neither of them even knowing how it started. This time was different. Jason had intentionally set out to hurt her, and it cut him as deeply as it was lancing through Amanda. She whirled away from him, putting distance between them before she covered her face with her hands and burst into sobs.

Not since Jack Granger and his brother Billy had caught Jason on the way home from school and broken his nose for the first time could he remember anything hurting so badly as did the knowledge he'd made Amanda cry.

"Oh, God," he groaned, unable to bear the sound of her hurt. Neither could he keep away. "Oh, God, Mandy," he groaned, putting his arms around her, pressing his cheek against her wet hair. "I'm sorry. Don't cry. God, please stop. Dammit, Mandy, you'll have me bawling in a minute if you keep that up any longer."

The thought of Jason Thorne wimpering like a baby must have struck her funny, because she choked out a laugh and lifted her head from his shoulder. "I'd like to see that," she said cheekily with a loud sniff. "We sure act stupid sometimes, don't we?"

"Mmmm," was all he could manage. His throat seemed to be clogged. He didn't think he'd hated anything more in his life than the sight of those tears which still lingered on her lightly freckled cheeks and gathered at the corners of her trembling mouth.

Impulsively he kissed them away. Amanda must have thought he was teasing her again. Instead of pushing him away, she raised up a little on her toes and smacked a childish kiss square on his mouth.

Jason felt her touch, inept though it was, all the way to his toes. It worried him, and he made light of it. "You kiss just like a baby," he teased, thinking she would flare up at the insult.

"I do not," she challenged, as he'd expected, thumping his chest.

"Do, too." He gave her a light push.

"Don't!"

And so it went, back and forth, push and shove, until suddenly Amanda grabbed his neck and slammed her mouth against his.

She was surprisingly strong and resisted his startled attempts to loosen her fierce grip. It was obvious she'd never been kissed, didn't know the first thing about what she was doing. But as he struggled to free himself her mouth softened, and he forgot everything except the feel of her lips. His hands curved around her chin, and his thumbs used gentle pressure to tilt her head just so. He caressed her mouth with his own until she learned too well the lessons he was attempting to teach. No longer did she need his hands to guide the soft, gliding motions, so he let them travel elsewhere, across her shoulders, down her back to pull her against him.

Her small breasts seared his chest. Never again would those plump pillows he'd thought so necessary to inflame a man's passions give him the same satisfaction.

Amanda *was* the flame, igniting the barren dryness of his soul, giving life where none had truly before existed. He became desperate to fill himself up with her warmth. His mouth became wild; searching, finding, taking all she could give, wanting more with every conquest.

Suddenly she pulled away, and her lips were bruised and swollen, wet and glistening from the strokes of his tongue. Her eyes were flooded with questions and confusion, though he found no fear there. Still, when he reached for her, she backed away, holding up a small, trembling hand to ward him off. Then she turned and dashed toward the door, but paused for a brief moment to look back at him. She smiled at him, and Jason thought his chest would explode as the sunshine of that smile burst upon him.

"Mandy," he said, taking a step toward her. She ducked out of the door before he could reach her. With his shoulder resting against the splintered frame, Jason watched as she ran through the rain, slipping and sliding, sloshing through the puddles, and kicking hailstones on her way. . . .

Amanda was jolted from a restless sleep by a loud clap of thunder, followed by Sarah's piercing shriek of terror. Instantly alert, the disturbing dream wiped away by a mother's concern, Amanda was already out of bed when Sarah came flying into the room. "Mama!" the little girl wailed as the lightning flashed and the house trembled. Obviously the brief thunderstorm earlier in the day had been but a forerunner of this more violent onslaught of nature.

There wasn't a breath of space between the constant barrages of thunder and lightning. Windows rattled, and the wind howled at gale force. Amanda held Sarah tightly, her own anxiety mounting, for she knew this was no ordinary storm. Soon Aunt Julie joined them, the lantern in her hand clearly reflecting the old woman's distress.

Outside, Jason was fighting the gusting wind as he ran toward the house. Loosened shingles swirled about the yard, flying through the air, and skittering across the ground. When he opened the screened kitchen door, it was nearly jerked out of his hands, the rusty hinges straining against the force nature was about to unleash.

Once inside, Jason moved swiftly toward the bedrooms, shouting, "Julie! Amanda! Grab blankets. We've got to get into the storm cellar!"

Amanda didn't hesitate, scooping both Sarah and her quilt up in a single motion, and met Jason in the hall. Julie hung back. "Aw, Jase. It isn't all that bad. This old house has survived dozens of blows worse than this."

Jason didn't take the time to argue. Taking Sarah and the quilt from Amanda, he said, "Drag your stubborn aunt along." He didn't look back to see if Julie was giving her niece any trouble.

Amanda was terrified by the time they reached the storm cellar. They were forced to cling to one another just to remain upright against hurricane-strength winds. Bracing herself against the side of the house, she took Sarah from Jason so that he could unlatch and throw back the heavy flat doors of the underground shelter. Her hair whipped free of the braids, stinging her skin, lashing at her eyes. She pressed Sarah's face tightly against her shoulder to shield the little girl's eyes from the flying debris.

When he finally had the doors opened, Jason

reached out his hand, yelling above the noise until he felt Amanda's fingers curl around his own. She descended the narrow stairs first, waiting for Sarah at the bottom. Then Jason pulled Julie away from the wall, giving her a little push before she would go down into that darkened pit. He joined them, pulling the doors shut behind him, plunging the small, musty-smelling room into pitch blackness. They closed with a thud. Sarah cried, and Julie Danfield whimpered.

"Easy," Jason soothed. His deep voice was solid and reassuring. "There's a lantern just behind the stairs." He searched blindly until he found the ancient storm lantern and the matches always kept near its base. Within seconds he had dispelled the dark.

While Sarah's greatest fears were being alleviated with the light, Julie's were being alarmingly confirmed. Roaches ran across the dirt floor, spiders vibrated in their webs, and beneath the shelves laden with airtight jars of preserved fruits and vegetables, small red eyes winked.

Julie shuddered violently, her skin already crawling, certain that a rat or a roach would run across her bare feet any second. She froze in place.

Jason spread the quilt against the bare rock wall, and then he dragged Julie across the small room, firmly shoving her down until her back was pressed against the wall. When she gave him a mute look of appeal, he patted her shoulder gently. Amanda, with Sarah clinging to her, joined Julie on the floor.

It was then the howling wind stilled.

"See . . . I told you—"

"Hush," Jason barked as he sat down between the

women and placed an arm around each of them. They all huddled together, listening intently to that awful, unnatural calm.

They all knew when it began to happen.

Amanda stifled a cry when the silence was broken by a sound that, once heard, could never be forgotten—the deafening roar of a tornado. Suddenly it seemed as though all the air was being sucked out of the small cellar. The doors shuddered.

"Dear God," Julie muttered.

Amanda instinctively leaned closer to the man next to her. She felt the stubbled scrape of his chin and the softness of his lips as they pressed against her cheek. "We're safe here," he whispered against her skin. "Safe," he repeated, drawing all of them closer together.

Almost as quickly as it had begun, it was over. The air surrounding them returned to normal, cool and sweet, scented with gentle rain.

They had been inside the cellar for five minutes; another fifteen would pass before Jason felt confident that the danger, and the storm, were over. Still he was cautious, leaving the women behind while he went out to judge the sky and search for damage.

Julie scooted over next to Amanda while they awaited his report. "As much as I hated coming down here," she confided, "I'm more afraid of what we'll find when we leave."

Sarah yawned and began to squirm. It seemed to take forever, but finally Jason called down. "We've got bright stars and only minor damage."

Julie's heavy sigh of relief as she quickly scrambled off the quilt and dashed for the stairs brought a chuckle from Amanda. She followed immediately, looking up into Jason's smiling face as he lifted Sarah free of the stairs.

His smile faded on a harsh indrawn breath as Amanda left the cellar. The heat of Sarah's body, where she'd been cradled against her mother, had dampened the front of the thin cotton nightgown, making it nearly transparent as it clung enticingly to her breasts and belly. The night air, which had become significantly cooler, brought about an involuntary reaction. Amanda's nipples tightened, becoming unintentionally provocative, stirring again the passions that were becoming increasingly difficult for Jason to control.

That she was aware of the revealing gown was abundantly clear when she crossed her arms over her bosom. Neither did she waste any time in hustling herself and Sarah into the house.

Jason stared after her as if in a daze until a sharp elbow jabbed him in the ribs. Julie was eyeing him with both censure and amusement.

"Why don't you walk me around," she said. "The exercise would do you good."

Chapter Seven

IT HAD TAKEN SARAH A LITTLE WHILE TO SETTLE BACK down and drop off to sleep. She'd been full of questions and unresolved apprehensions, but Amanda felt certain there would be no lingering terrors beyond a child's natural fright of thunder and lightning.

But now, as she searched the bureau for a dry nightgown, Amanda was purposely feeding her own fears, occupying her mind with all the horrible things that might have happened. It was the only way she could banish a storm of another sort, one more personally threatening than any nature could unleash, one that created a maelstrom within herself.

She nearly tore her gown getting it off, still able to feel the heat of Jason's stare. The violent storm couldn't hold a candle to the turbulent reawakening of her own long dormant passions. They had come upon her swiftly this afternoon, bringing with them the images of other times, made too vivid by the smell of hay, the rain, and the hard arousal of Jason's body.

"God help you, Mandy," he'd warned.

What a fool she'd been to rationalize his words the morning in the barn as a lashing out of anger. That would have been a child's response. Jason Thorne was not now, nor had he really ever been, a boy. He was a man, strong and virile, and he'd been telling her for weeks by look, touch, and word that he wanted her as a woman.

But was that entirely true? Wasn't it more likely that Jason wanted his Mandy, the passionate, reckless girl he'd once known?

Impulsively Amanda turned to view her naked body in the mirror, seeing for herself the woman Jason thought he wanted, finding nothing of the girl she'd once been in her own reflection. Her body had matured, blossomed with the birth of a child. She'd known fully a husband's passions, and had been helpless with the loss of that one truly fine and beautiful part of her marriage. It had not survived Harry's excesses. Neither had Jason's impetuous, spirited, thoughtlessly trusting Mandy. The girl was no more . . . gone . . . dead and buried.

Or was she?

"Yes," Amanda whispered vehemently, denying the spark of desire that was trying very hard to sputter into flame.

Why did it frighten her so?

The sound of her aunt entering the house saved Amanda from tormenting herself further. She pulled the clean nightgown over her head, muttering a soft little curse when the single button at the neck, popped off and rolled across the floor. She went after it, chasing it under her bed. On her hands and knees she crawled beneath the metal rails, grumbling all the while. The sound of her own voice masked the heavy footfalls in the hall. With her head and shoulders thrust under the sheet, she was also oblivious to the man standing in the open doorway, a quilt slung over his shoulder.

Jason's first impulse was to laugh at that wiggling backside. His second would have gotten him arrested. Unaware she was being observed, Amanda backed out, sat back on her heels, and began to brush away the dust that had collected on the front of her nightgown. The garment had fallen off one shoulder, and as she swept her hands across the bodice, the material strained. Not bothering to readjust the gown as she got to her feet, Amanda continued the downward stroking of her hands all the way to the hem.

The gaping fabric revealed to Jason the mature fullness of her breasts, generous now as they'd not been twelve years ago. He had thought her beautiful then. Now she was perfect beyond all the wild and empty dreams that had haunted him through the years. He filled his hungry eyes, all the while knowing the piper awaited payment. But the time for a polite cough had long since past, and if the price must be paid . . .

When Amanda began to rise she caught a glimpse

of a taut male thigh above a slightly flexed knee. She straightened so rapidly that her head began to spin. Their eyes locked and it was long moments before she found her voice.

"What do you want?" she finally managed.

Jason chose to ignore the obvious response as she adjusted her gown, covering the creamy whiteness of her shoulder. "I remembered your quilt was still on the floor of the cellar. It will get cool before morning so I brought a replacement."

The excuse sounded frail to his own ears. Both of them knew there was a hall linen closet filled with quilts. Truthfully he'd forgotten. However, the momentary lapse had been damned convenient. He'd wanted to see her again as she'd been outside. What he'd found, as she was right now, made him want far more than a look.

His gaze burned, and his features were sharp with unveiled desire. Although he'd not moved a muscle from where he leaned indolently against the doorframe, she felt the tension rolling within him, as it was within herself. She began to tremble, quivering inside and out. Amanda was afraid to move, wondering what he might think if she asked him to toss the quilt, fearing what might happen should the distance between them be closed.

"You're shivering, Amanda," Jason observed in a husky voice, pushing away from the door. In three long strides he was standing before her, unfurling the folded quilt to drape it around her shoulders. He held the edges together just above her breasts, noting the agitation in her quickened breathing. "Why are you trembling?"

Amanda shook her head, unable to respond verbally. Her senses were being assailed by the sleep-warmed scent of Jason, which had been absorbed into the quilt from his bed.

"Tell me, Amanda," he prompted even as he privately acknowledged it wasn't important she say the words. When her eyes lifted shyly, and he heard, "I—I don't know," Jason smiled at her tenderly.

"Don't you?" he whispered.

His lips lightly brushed her brow, traveling slowly over her eyes and cheeks, inching toward her mouth. He gave her all the time she needed to stop him. But in the end, when he heard his name on her lips in a faltering appeal, any good intentions he might have possessed went straight out the window.

"Too late," he growled, taking her mouth in a sweet possession.

Her conscience, which had always lagged behind good sense when this man touched her, failed her once again. There wasn't even a halfhearted struggle as he kissed her in that way which had always robbed her of thought, of will. It was not a boy who was rediscovering the shape and texture of her mouth with lips and tongue, but a man who was remolding her mouth, making it his own.

Amanda felt herself melting against him and a shuddering sigh acknowledged her full surrender to his kiss as she answered the tender strokes of his tongue.

The quilt fell unnoticed to the floor to be replaced by Jason's strong arms around Amanda's giving softness. God had made them so perfectly for each other that they fit together like two halves of one whole.

Jason could feel her flowing against him, her hips a

cradle to hold and welcome him home. "Mandy," he moaned against her mouth, his hands moving down over her shoulders to cup her bottom and pull her closer as his need grew to wildfire proportions.

It was that name, spoken as an endearment, and meant for a young girl lost many years ago, which broke the spell. She tore her mouth away and pushed hard against the unyielding wall of his chest.

"Stop it," she breathed. "Stop this right now."

Through the haze of dreams being fulfilled, Jason heard the desperation in her ragged tone. With effort, he moved his hands up from her hips, but only so far as the curve of her waist. He was reluctant to release her entirely.

"It's still strong between us, Mandy. You can't deny that," he said softly.

"I can . . . I do," she said vehemently. "Because I'm *not* your Mandy. We're neither of us irresponsible children anymore. Good heavens, we are actually little more than strangers." She pulled away from him, crossing her arms over her breasts in a protective gesture. "Think about this reasonably. We've known each other the sum total of less than six months, and that includes that summer twelve years ago. We were too young then to know our own minds. Besides, didn't someone once say time lost cannot be found again?"

Amanda looked at him then, and her eyes were earnest. "Don't make this situation impossible, Jason. We can be friends, but nothing more."

He met her gaze. "There's also an old saying that covers ladies who protest too much." When she would have disputed this, Jason hushed her by placing a single finger over her still trembling, well-kissed lips. "You've had your turn. Now it's mine. No, we're not children, thank God. Frankly, I've no desire to relive that hell again. Secondly, *Mandy* does still exist. I've seen her countless times; in ways you probably wouldn't recognize. And thirdly, we were *always* friends, Amanda. Our friendship was a major part of what we had together that summer. But it wasn't enough for us then, and it won't be enough now." He bent to retrieve the quilt, quickly tossing it at her to stall further discussion. "Now, if you want me to leave this room tonight, let me suggest you not challenge me to put my theories to the test."

The way she pressed her lips firmly together was confirmation, she knew, as he did, what the outcome of such a challenge would be. Their eyes locked for a long moment before Jason gave her a rueful smile and headed toward the door, stopping just short of the hall to turn back.

"I'm not certain what you're afraid of, Amanda," he said softly. "But everything will be all right. I promise."

Even as he made the pledge, Jason knew she could not possibly comprehend all the things his vow encompassed, but he felt compelled to reassure her anyway. Then he quickly departed, pulling the door softly shut behind him.

Amanda stared at the closed door for a very long time before she moved woodenly to extinguish the lamp. Still wrapped in Jason's quilt, she fell across her bed, not holding back the sudden flow of tears—tears that had been damned up inside for too long.

* * *

The perfect, cloudless blue sky made the previous night's storm seem unreal. It also ceased to be a thing of beauty after five hours of the most back-breaking labor Amanda had ever known.

Amanda dropped the empty bucket she carried and leaned back against the bed of the wagon. Tearing off the floppy old hat Jason had jammed down on her head at the beginning of this endless day, she wiped her brow, grimacing when her sleeve was soiled with the damp and dirt. The hat, meant to protect her from the broiling sun, had become an instrument of heated torture. Never could she remember being this tired, hot, or truly achingly miserable.

Although the tornado had spared the house and the main structures of the ranch, it had dipped in and out of the clouds as it traveled across TJ land. They were working along the border of the northeast pasture, where nearly a half mile of barbed-wire fence had been destroyed. Wooden posts, for the most part, had been ripped right up out of the ground, the wire mangled beyond repair. And they were lucky, very lucky, it hadn't been worse. The damage was minor: an uprooted tree, boards driven through rail fences, the ground chewed up here and there. Not one cow had been hurt, which was a primary relief, though Jason had found one calf wandering aimlessly several miles from the herd. The young steer had seemed dazed and somewhat battered, but otherwise unharmed. Jason believed the animal had been picked up off the ground by the capricious twister, carried aloft, and then gently set back down. Such an unbelievable miracle wasn't surprising to Amanda, who'd grown up in the middle of this country. She'd heard tales even more improbable which had proved true.

"Amanda, could you bring me more water?"

Jason's voice intruded upon her rest. Although she readily admitted he could not repair this fence alone, Amanda knew she was swiftly becoming a very useless ranch hand. Dear God, she didn't think there was an inch of her body that didn't ache unmercifully.

With an anguished groan, she crawled up onto the back of the wagon to fill her bucket from the large barrel they'd carried out here with them. Getting back down was easier, but she nearly screamed aloud when she attempted to lift the heavy bucket.

The first chore this morning when they arrived at this site was to clear the twisted wire from approximately a quarter-mile area. Because Jason didn't want Amanda anywhere near the spiked and thorny barbs, her task had been to salvage the posts he intended to reuse. Now they were in the process of resetting those fence posts.

With pick and shovel, Jason dug the two-foot holes. She carried water to the spot to soften the hard, dry ground where he was digging.

Jason turned at her approach, and seeing the pain in her face, he knew that Amanda was near the end of her rope. She moved jerkily, unable to hold the heavy bucket steady to keep the water from sloshing out. He tossed the pick aside and met her more than halfway. When he'd taken the bucket from her, Jason resigned himself to finishing up for the day, even though they still had several good hours of sunlight left.

"Go sit down in the shade of the wagon," he

ordered gently. "You've done enough for one day. When this post is set, we'll head back for the house."

She wanted to bawl with relief. Instead she said, "I—I'm all right . . . really."

"Like hell," he growled, turning her around and marching her back to the wagon. Once there, she needed little urging before flopping down on the ground with a telling moan, her sunburned face contorting with pain. "Stay put, I'm the foreman here, and I call the shots."

She nodded weakly as her head fell back against the wheel. The spirit was willing, but the body couldn't walk another step. Through half-closed eyes Amanda watched Jason as he worked, amazed by his seemingly tireless energy. This man had been up, and working, before the dawn. Before she had lifted her head from the pillow, Jason was riding the entire perimeter of the TJ, checking for damage. Since then he'd barely paused to eat, going without water longer than she considered possible. Amanda could have drunk the entire barrel dry several times this day if he would have allowed it.

Through it all, not once, by word or gesture, had Jason mentioned last night. Today he was the foreman; she the ranch hand. Nothing in his manner indicated he thought about the passionate kisses, or the words they'd exchanged.

Perhaps he had given the matter more thought, deciding she could possibly be right. And why, in the name of all that was sane and reasonable, did that possibility rest like a leaden weight upon her heart?

Amanda shifted her position, but there was no comfort to be found. She carefully raised her knees, and clasped her arms around them, letting her head fall forward. Within seconds her eyes closed.

Almost an hour later Jason tossed the shovel into the back of the wagon. It clattered noisily when it landed. Amanda didn't flinch. She was exhausted, and he found no pleasure in seeing her this way. But there was no help for it.

Right now the cattle were content to hold close to the smaller ponds on the western range. Unfortunately, without a significant, steady rainfall, those shallow watering holes would soon be dry. Yesterday afternoon's brief squall, and the subsequent blow which had followed, barely touched the surface of what was needed in the way of moisture. Soon he'd be forced to move the herd in search of water. The windmill, which should have been pumping water into its tank reservoir, was useless to them with it's battered shaft. Man and nature seemed to be joining forces, conspiring against them. Or was it a test? Many times in his life, Jason had flaunted himself before God, challenging proof of His existence. Perhaps it was his turn to be challenged, and prove himself worthy before any prayers would be answered.

Gently, with a tender smile, Jason lifted Amanda and placed her upon the makeshift bed in the back of the wagon. She cried out softly when she was placed on the tarp, but didn't awaken. He then climbed aboard the hard seat and turned the horses for home.

Amanda woke with a vehement groan of protest that immediately became a cry of real pain when Sarah continued to bounce upon her bed.

"Mama, get up!" the little girl scolded impatiently, prodding her mother's shoulder with a sharp little finger. "Auntie says supper's on the table and to 'come and get it now.'"

Disoriented, Amanda lifted her head slightly off the pillow. "Is it morning?" she asked weakly.

"No, silly. It's still today."

Amanda's brow furrowed. The last thing she could remember with any clarity was resting against the wagon wheel. But there was also a vague image of Jason lifting her out of the wagon and carrying her into the house. Heavens, what a scene that must have made.

Inching her legs off the bed, she slowly rose to her feet. Someone—Aunt Julie, no doubt—had stripped her of her soiled working clothes, leaving her only in her camisole and drawers. The thought of dressing was simply too much. It would kill her.

"Sarah, apologize to Auntie for me," she said, turning back to the bed and crawling onto that downy cushion. "Tell her I'm not hungry. I just want to rest." What she really thought was that she preferred to die in peace.

"Are you sick?" Sarah sounded worried, making Amanda feel guilty for causing alarm.

"No, sweetheart," she quickly reassured her child. "Mama's just very tired and a little sore. I'll be fine with a little rest." She hoped her voice sounded convincing. "Crawl up here and give me a kiss, and then go eat your supper like a good girl."

When Sarah left, Amanda sighed heavily and gave her body up to fate. But her eyes had barely closed before she was being rudely awakened again. "Don't shake the bed . . . please," she begged. "Let me sleep."

"You'll not thank me in the morning if I do, Amanda Jean," Julie Danfield said sternly. "Fact is, you won't be able to leave that bed for a week if I let you lie there. Come on and pull yourself up. Jase is filling the tub in the bunkhouse for you to have a good, hot soak. And I've got the liniment ready for a rubdown. Do you want to condemn yourself to that bed for days?"

Amanda thought the sentence sounded heavenly, and said so. Julie was having none of it, browbeating her to her feet while she forced Amanda's aching arms into the sleeves of a robe. When it was finally belted securely around her waist, Amanda was pushed toward the door.

"Auntie," she pleaded. "I don't think I can walk that far. I hurt all over."

"We'll give you some help, then." She called for Jason. He must have finished filling the tub and been waiting just outside the door, because he came in immediately.

Although he gave her a look of tender pity, there was little mercy as he hoisted her left arm across the width of his broad shoulders. Julie moved to Amanda's right side and did the same with that arm. Amanda felt as though her arms were being wrenched from their sockets as they stretched across the two bodies practically dragging her out of the room.

Somehow she survived the trip, and when she was up to her neck in steaming, soothing hot water, Amanda was grateful for their care.

"Don't you fall asleep and drown in there," Julie cautioned while she draped Amanda's clean underthings over the arm of a nearby chair. "I know you're miserable. But I swear I don't know a soul who has died of sore muscles yet. Sure hope you won't be the first."

"Mmmm," was all Amanda could manage, her eyes drifting shut.

"Keep alert, girl! I don't have the time to waste standing over you so you don't slip down. You've got exactly thirty minutes to soak. By then you should be able to get yourself out of the tub. I can't help you there because my old back won't support your weight. The alternative would be sending Jason in here after you. I doubt you'd want that—though it wouldn't be the end of the world. There's a clock right above your head on the mantel."

Amanda glanced up, but missed the clock entirely. Instead her eyes fixed upon a photograph of a lovely blond woman and a dark-haired little girl.

"Did you hear me, Amanda?"

"Thirty minutes," was the absent response. She couldn't seem to tear her gaze away from the portrait.

Noticing what had captured her niece's attention, Julie moved closer to the huge stone fireplace. She fingered the brass frame. "It's a real heartbreaker about Jason's family, isn't it? Especially that little girl. Looks the spittin' image of him, and I know he worshiped the very ground she walked on. Oh, he grieves for Lucy, too, but more because I don't think he feels he loved her like she deserved."

Amanda's eyes snapped to her aunt's face at that. "Why would you think that?"

"Just a hunch based on some things he's told me. I got the impression there was somebody else; someone real special. Knowing Jason, though, I doubt Lucy ever felt slighted." Her wistful tone changed as she grinned from ear to ear. "Shoot, a woman would have to be plumb crazy, or dead, if she had Jason Thorne between the sheets at night and didn't think herself one lucky female. Oh, he's not perfect. But a whole lot of faults can be forgotten between dusk and dawn with a man like that one." She clacked her tongue and gave Amanda a wink. "You can agree with that, can't you?"

Wide awake now, Amanda knew she was staring open-mouthed with shock. "I can't believe we're having this conversation."

Julie laughed heartily. "Well, either that water's too hot, or there's some other reason your face just went blood red, Amanda. Lordy, girl. I'd almost think you were some silly little virgin. Women have those needs, too." She frowned a little then, her face going serious. "Or is it that Harry never—"

"Of course he did!" Amanda scoffed, wanting to end this subject quickly.

"I'm glad to hear it. Always did worry me that you married somebody old enough to be your father. A body just naturally slows down as a person heads into his middle years. Now, with me and Todd that was never a problem because we both sort of slid into old age together. We sure did have some wild young years to look back on when the fires started losing heat though. The memories, and a little extra effort, sure did warm many a cold night." She chuckled again. "Enough of this nonsense. You remember to keep alert. If I have to send Jase in

127

here after you, you're liable to find out firsthand just what we've been talking about."

Her aunt left the bunkhouse still chortling, and Amanda was left with some very disturbing thoughts. Needing to distract herself, she let her eyes roam the bunkhouse. Her attention had not been on her surroundings when she'd first entered this male sanctum. It was really very pleasant, and not at all what she'd anticipated.

The old bunks had been removed, and the scratched wood floors she remembered were mostly covered with large braided rugs. There was clutter, but for the most part Jason's home was spotlessly clean. Did Julie sneak in here on occasion? No, Amanda knew the older woman hated housecleaning of any sort. She did only what was absolutely necessary and had gladly turned the keeping of the house over to Amanda.

To her immediate right was a large, attractively upholstered sofa, flanked by a matching chair. The gramaphone she occasionally heard playing Sousa marches rested on a table nearby.

He'd sectioned off the oblong room into separate living quarters with strategic placement of furnishings. She was bathing in the parlor.

At the opposite end of the room was a huge brass bed. In between was the dining area, complete with a small cookstove, a pantry, and a round table surrounded by two chairs.

The implications of what her eyes perceived were slow to reach her mind, but soon they were shouting at her with strong statements that spoke of home and permanence. She didn't want to hear, was afraid to trust what her eyes beheld. If she did, then someday there might come a morning when she'd awaken to find him gone . . . like before.

Suddenly too many thoughts were crowding her mind. Things of the past and of the present. Bits and snatches of conversations, very recent and from long ago.

Almost of their own volition her eyes were drawn toward the mantel. The blond woman smiled down on her. What had she been like, this pretty woman who had been time-frozen in a photograph?

Lucy Blane. Wasn't it strange how the mind could capture a name and hold it fast through the years. Until tonight Lucy had been only a name, faceless, and yet not forgotten. . . .

Chapter Eight

"WOULD YOU CUT THAT OUT," JASON COMPLAINED, HIS eyes darting up and down the empty street.

"What's the matter with you today, anyway?" Amanda shot back at him, refusing to let him see her hurt. "I thought we came here to be alone. Or have you decided you don't like kissing me anymore?"

Jason's eyes rolled skyward as he fell back against the knotted trunck of a huge tree. "Holy sh—cow, Mandy. If I kissed you every time you wanted, my lips would fall off." He grinned in spite of himself, reaching out to tweak her on the nose. "Besides, this is hardly the place. If someone should see us together . . ." he said, as he glanced toward the church uncomfortably near.

Amanda was regretting the hours she'd spent pleading and begging just to get him into town for the Founder's Day celebration. He wouldn't participate in anything, kept shy of the crowds, and acted as if he'd rather be anyplace else on earth than here with her. "Are you ashamed to be seen with me, Jason?" She knew she wasn't pretty like other girls. She had no shape, and too many freckles. Her hair wasn't bad, as far as color was concerned, but it was naturally unruly and difficult to restrain. Jason probably only felt sorry for her.

"Christ!" he exclaimed. "Don't start that nonsense again. Where you got that silly idea you were plain-featured, I can't imagine. But when you frown like that, it's almost true."

As if to take the sting out of his words, he pulled her close, hugging her fiercely. "Oh, Mandy, it's this town that makes me crazy. Not you. Never you. If they saw you with me, you'd get smeared by the same mud they sling my way. I couldn't stand that. I would hate it if you started seeing me through their eyes."

She pinched him hard in the fleshy area of his ribs even as she settled herself comfortably in his arms.

"Talk about nonsense," she said pressing her cheek to his. He felt so good, even though she sometimes wished he were taller, or she shorter, so she could be the cuddly girl she knew boys preferred. But it wouldn't be nearly so easy to kiss him. With a giggle she took that kiss, stealing it, and his breath, by proving what an apt pupil she'd been over the past three weeks.

"Damn," Jason said in a breathy tone. "You've got to stop doing this to me, girl. I'm going crazy. Pulling back is getting harder and harder every time. . . ." He held her away and looked at her intently. "You don't know the first thing about what I'm trying to tell you. Do you?"

"No," she admitted honestly, frustrated by another repeat of this confusing lecture. "But I wish you'd tell me so I'll stop whatever it is that bothers you so much."

Jason took a deep breath. "Well, it's like this. . . ." he began, searching for the right words. "Kissing you makes me want other things. I—I don't want to stop there. Can you understand that?"

"Oh, that's just clear as mud, Jason. Thanks so much for taking the time to explain. . . ."

Her snippy sarcasm was lost on him. Jason was staring over her shoulder. She started to look behind her, only to have her arm nearly yanked from the socket when he pulled her behind the tree. "Crap," he mumbled. "I hope he didn't spot me."

"Who?" She tried to peer around the tree trunk.

"Don't look!"

"I didn't see anybody, Jason."

He looked again, and then let out a heavy breath of relief.

"Well, he's gone now. Let's get out of here." Taking her wrist, he made a mad dash toward the church, ducking around the corner of the building. When they'd drawn abreast of the back door, Jason dug through a weedy flowerpot until he found the key hidden there.

"I knew this would still be here. The Reverend is

terrified he'll find himself locked out of the church when the need comes upon him. Of course, it doesn't bother him much that he locks out everybody else when he's not present. I really believe he thinks God takes a break unless he's here to supervise."

Amanda watched apprehensively while he unlocked the door with a casual familiarity. She hung back when he motioned her inside. "I don't think we should, Jason."

"Oh, for heaven's sake. I practically grew up here. It's like a second—" He broke off. "Forget that. It's not a second, or any other kind of home. I spent most of my life here. I'd say that gives me some rights to take shelter from the sun if I want. Besides, it's a church, Mandy. It belongs to all people, doesn't it?"

"I guess," she agreed with a shrug, stepping inside. Jason shut and bolted the door behind her. "This must be your foster father's office."

"The *Reverend's* office," he corrected. "He's no father of any sort to me."

Sometimes it was nearly impossible for Amanda to believe the bitterness Jason felt toward the people who had raised him and the town where he'd grown up. Was all he told her true? Doubting him hurt her. But it all sounded so exaggerated and unreal. "Would he be angry if he found us here?"

"Sweet Mandy, he'd pitch a fit the likes of which you don't care to see." Jason flopped down in the leather chair behind the Reverend's desk.

"Maybe we should leave, then?"

"And maybe we shouldn't. We're in the house

133

where sinners are supposed to be saved. Since I'm standing an inch away from hell, it might do me some good."

She flew at him. "Would you stop that! You're always saying stupid things like that about yourself. They aren't true, Jason Thorne. Do you hear me?" She was nearly shouting. "They aren't true!"

He pulled her onto his lap, pressed his cheek hard against her small breasts. "I hear you," he said hoarsely. "Oh, how I hear you." Eventually he looked up, and he was smiling again. "Let's make a deal, you and me. I'll stop being stupid about my questionable salvation if you'll start believing me when I tell you that you're the most beautiful girl I've ever known."

"I'll try," she whispered with a deep blush.

"Not good enough," he chided. "God, if you could only see yourself through my eyes." Jason cradled her face and his eyes were eloquently sincere. "The only thing in the world wrong with you, Mandy, is that you're too damned young. If you were just a year older, I'd tuck you away in my back pocket and run away with you to the very ends of the earth."

"I'm not so young. Only two years younger than you." she insisted.

"Maybe not," he mused, drawing her to his mouth. "Maybe not . . ."

"What is going on here!"

The bellowing roar behind them brought Amanda off Jason's lap with a shriek. With her hands clasped over her thundering heart she found herself facing the most accusing pair of coal-black eyes she'd ever seen. Her skin crawled as they raked over her before sliding to Jason and then back to her again.

"Jezebel!" he shouted, waving his finger, pointing it at her head. "You bring shame to your aunt and uncle. Unenlightened though they might be, they don't deserve to shelter a daughter of Satan!"

She was already backing away when Jason jumped to his feet. "Damn you!" he shouted at the wild-eyed minister. "I'll kill you if you say another word against her!"

Terrified he meant it, Amanda grabbed his arm. "Jason . . . don't. . . ." He was forcing her to the door, opening it to shove her outside. "Get out of here, Mandy," he ordered. "Go find Todd and Julie and stick by them." Jason must have seen the terror coiling deep inside her because his harsh expression softened a little. "Do as I tell you . . . please."

The door closed in her face. Had she been inclined to follow his bidding, her trembling legs would have refused to cooperate. She leaned back against the brick wall of the church, trying to catch the breath that was coming in rapid gasps, as if she'd been running for a long distance. Her blood pounded loud in her ears, but not loud enough to block out that bombastic voice that drifted through the doors and walls.

"Fornicator! Spawn of Satan! Have you lead another young innocent to wickedness? How many others have been used to satisfy your carnal appetites? Have you fathered more bastards like you to blight God's earth?"

She couldn't hear Jason's reply clearly. Then Reverend Thorne was bellowing again. "Because of you, I'll be driven from this town . . . my church. Henry Blane will not rest until the name Thorne is eradicated. I pray to the Almighty that the cursed seed you have planted in Lucy Blane will wither and die in the womb!"

The door slammed back against the wall, nearly striking Amanda where she stood. Jason ran past her, unseeing, as if the devil were truly at his heels. She would have gone after him, but found her arms captured in a steel grip.

"Repent, child!" the minister canted with a savage vehemence. "Denounce your unholy alliance with that creature from hell!"

Truly terrified now, Amanda didn't think; she only reacted, freeing herself from this maniac by drawing her foot back and giving him a hard kick to his bony shins. Before he could recover, she was racing back toward the town square, rushing into her uncle Todd's arms to babble incoherently against his strong, protective chest. . . .

A loud cough brought Amanda back to the present and sent her diving for the depths of the bathtub. The guffaw that followed—distinctively feminine— brought her back up with a sputtering complaint. "Auntie, you scared me half to death!"

"I was afraid you'd get too comfortable in there," Julie replied, still grinning until she got closer to her niece. "Honey, is something wrong? You're looking really peaked now." She placed her hand on Amanda's brow. "Well, you do feel a little warm, but that could be the heat and the bath. Don't you go getting sick on us. Jase has been flogging himself all evening for working you too hard today as it is."

Amanda carefully managed to emerge from the tub on her own. "I'm not getting sick, I assure you. Tell Jason he needn't lose any sleep on my account."

"My words exactly," Julie chimed in, seeming not to notice Amanda's thorny tone. "Even so, he's insisting you have a day of rest tomorrow while he goes into town to order the wire. In my opinion, you'd be better off getting right back out there so those muscles don't have a chance to tighten back up on you. But I guess Jase knows that as well as I do, since he's suffered it often enough himself."

Amanda listened without comment. Julie talked nonstop while her niece dressed, then they made the slow trek to the house. Once back in her own bedroom, Amanda shrugged out of the robe and stretched out—per Julie's instructions—on her belly, crosswise on the bed. Sarah wandered in, and crawled onto the bed.

"This rubdown is bound to be a tad uncomfortable for you, Amanda. Keep in mind we're only doing what's best."

She left the room, and Amanda assumed she was going after the liniment. The soothing effects of the bath were wearing off and the painful aching was returning. Sarah leaned over and patted her mother's shoulder.

"Poor Mama. You'll be better soon," she commiserated. Amanda made some halfhearted response of agreement, letting her eyes drift shut. The only genuinely positive feelings she could bring forth were for the pleasant breeze flowing in through the open window, cooling the exposed flesh of her arms and legs. Also the resurgence of physical discomfort allowed her to firmly close and relock that private

Pandora's box of memories, which had served no purpose except to dig up incidents that were better left alone.

The pungent smell of liniment alerted Amanda to her aunt's return. She closed her eyes even tighter, clenching her teeth in preparation for what was certain to be an unpleasant experience. At first the liquid which touched her skin felt cool, then quickly it began to burn like fire as it was rubbed into the sunburned area at the base of her neck. The mattress dipped at the very same instant her head reared up on a gasping cry. The strong fingers digging into her neck and shoulders were punishing. She thought she would die of the agony until she turned her head slightly to beg for a reprieve. Then she felt certain she would die of mortification instead.

On the bed, straddling her hips, Jason loomed over her half-naked body. "A-Auntie!" she cried out.

He pushed her face back down, his sinewy legs tightening when she would have attempted to scramble away. "Don't be unnecessarily prudish, Amanda. I'm here with Julie's full blessing. She doesn't have the strength to see this done properly. Besides, we're being well chaperoned by your own daughter. So keep quiet and relax. If you stay board stiff, you'll only feel that much worse for it in the morning."

"I—I—Oooh!" His thumbs discovered a particularly tender spot above her shoulder blades, and he worked the area over with concentrated effort, rubbing and kneading, ignoring her loud moans until they became soft sighs of relief. Arms, neck, and upper back were soon responding to the alternately painful, and soothing ministrations of his massage.

Amanda soon lost all will to protest the impropriety of this unconventional situation. The pleasure was too great. When she began to cooperate completely, Jason crooned his approval, moving his hands down her back above the thin chemise. "Oh, that's wonderful," she sighed when he finished with the small of her back, easing the ache with those magical hands.

By the time he reached her legs, she was nearly floating with sleepy malleability. The flesh beneath Jason's hands was supple, satiny, and yielding. Gradually his strokes gentled, becoming more the lover's caress when his fingers brushed along the edges of her lace-trimmed drawers. Only Sarah's presence kept him from sliding his hands beneath the cloth where he would discover the essence of her womanhood.

Gradually, through the fog, Amanda began to perceive the change in his touch. There was also an alarming altering within her body, a slow, building heat which was banishing her former lethargy, making her restive so that she squirmed slightly upon the mattress.

So closely in tune with the body he was now purposely arousing, Jason knew the second she began to respond as a woman. He groaned inwardly, silently cursing Julie's insistence on their small watchdog, who was currently yawning and watching him intently through sleep-clouded eyes. He wished her that way, but Sarah was committed to her assignment. What would happen, he wondered, if he just casually said, "Pickle, why don't you go to your own room so I can love your mother the way she needs loving."

All hell would break loose, without a doubt, although Sarah wouldn't be the one having the fits. Maybe he could direct his comments to Amanda: "Send the little girl away, and I'll ease that tormenting ache I've caused."

Nope. She'd accuse him of playing unfairly, of catching her in a vulnerable state. Which, of course, he had. Giving himself a hard mental kick, Jason moved off the mattress and recapped the bottle of liniment. The smell was hardly an erotic inducement. His eyes slid to the vanity where Amanda kept the fragrant, flowery-scented cream he'd bought her. Next time . . .

Amanda was doing battle with her traitorous flesh and didn't know whether to sob with relief or frustration when Jason's roaming fingers stilled and moved away from her tortured body. Her bottom lip was swollen from the pressure of her teeth. She'd bitten it in a futile attempt to distract herself from the throbbing sensations that had blossomed deep within the very core of her being. They pulsed there still.

"I'll find Julie and see Sarah gets tucked into bed," Jason said, his voice natural and deep. She, on the other hand, didn't dare speak for fear her state would be betrayed. She managed a slight nod.

"I'll find Auntie," Sarah offered, scooting off the bed before Amanda could call her back, darting to the door with a "Sleep tight, Mama" tossed over her shoulder.

It would appear all of Jason's wishes would be fulfilled. All he had to do was take those few short steps to the door and throw the bolt. The temptation was great. Unfortunately the reality didn't quite conform to his idea of a romantic moment, or the collected fantasies of twelve years.

Amanda could hear him breathing. Her own respirations were rapid and shallow. She waited in turmoil, having no idea what he might do, or how she might react. Her entire body went rigid when she felt a sharp, stinging sensation on the inner part of her thigh. "Ouch!"

"Still hurting, are you?" Jason asked as he washed the liniment from his hands in her basin. "Well, rest is the best medicine. Sleep as late as you wish tomorrow. I'll take care of the milking in the morning." She had turned slightly on her side and was eyeing him warily while he dried his hands. He flashed that Pan-like grin. "Sleep well, Amanda."

"I intend to," she assured him more steadily than she'd expected. After he left, she carefully moved to right herself on the bed. Unconsciously she rubbed that small spot on her thigh which still tingled. She shifted her legs until she could examine the area. "What in heaven's . . ."

Her head snapped up, jolting the muscles of her neck and shoulders, making her wince. Imprinted on the fleshy whiteness of her thigh were the distinct, unmistakable impressions of human teeth.

"I don't know why you are being so stubborn about this, Amanda," Julie said, clearly exasperated. "Didn't you tell me, not more than fifteen minutes ago, you felt *just fine* this morning with hardly an ache or a pain?" She handed Amanda the last of the breakfast dishes for drying. "Well?"

"What I said was that I'm feeling better than I'd anticipated. I am not, however, up to being bounced and jostled around Jason's automobile. Surely he has enough intelligence to match up two spools of thread without my supervision. Auntie, if you can't trust the man on a simple errand, how on earth can you give him full authority over the TJ?"

Julie grumbled beneath her breath. Marching to the back door with the dishpan, she kicked the screen open and tossed out the murky water. "Amanda," she said slowly as she turned back around, "have you ever known a man—any man— who could be trusted with a woman's errand? Even if he did remember, there's no tellin' what he'd come back here with. Maude Hardy wouldn't help him match up those colors. Shoot, that woman wouldn't give him the time of day." The dishpan clanged as it was dropped back onto the counter. "Well, I guess if you're not feeling up to the trip, then that's the end of it. Sarah will just have to understand those dresses I promised her for her dolls will have to be post- poned until the next trip into town—whenever that might be. I'd hoped to cheer her up some since it's a good bet she's coming down with a case of the sniffles." With a very expressive shrug, Julie re- moved her apron.

Amanda carefully shook out and folded the dish- towel. Julie had started out trying to bully her into accompanying Jason to Stockton. Now her tactics had changed to manipulating with guilt, using Sarah as her weapon. She didn't believe for a minute the thread was so urgently needed. Sarah would neither notice, nor care, if three different shades of thread were used in the making of her dolls' wardrobes. The last thing Amanda wanted was to spend another day alone with Jason. She needed time to sort out her feelings and get herself under control. And it appeared as if her aunt was attempting a little matchmaking scheme.

"Auntie, what is this *really* about? You must have a better reason than any I've yet to hear for being so adamant about this."

Julie Danfield glanced down at the floor and then back up again, meeting her niece's level gaze.

"Should have known you'd see right through me. Honey, you saw for yourself that folks give Jase a pretty hard time. Oh, he claims it don't bother him. But I can't quite swallow that. I think having you around might encourage them to hold their nasty tongues some. Of course, that's no guarantee."

"Why don't *you* go into town with Jason?" Amanda asked quite reasonably. Not once, since Amanda's arrival, had Julie left the ranch. "I would imagine getting away might be good for you. Surely your influence would be greater than mine. Besides, if Sarah isn't feeling well, then I should be the one staying home to look after her, wouldn't you say?"

The girl sure had neatly turned the tables back on her, Julie thought ruefully. She could hardly tell her niece that if she went into town, there was likely to be a riot. Somebody would say something hateful, and she'd like as not slap the daylights out of them. While she searched for a reasonable answer, Julie fiddled with the straggling strands of her iron-gray hair and found her solution.

"Lordy, child, you can't expect me to be seen in public lookin' like this? If I'd have thought you wouldn't be going, I'd have taken a bath and washed this mop of hair. But when you decided to use the tub again this morning to wash off the liniment and soak out the night's stiffness . . ." She shrugged again. "I might be old, Amanda Jean, but I've still some pride over my appearance left. I wouldn't be caught dead on the streets of Stockton looking like this."

Amanda felt like screaming, but knew further argument was futile. "All right," she said tightly. "I'll go, if it means so much to you."

"That's my girl," Julie said, positively beaming. "You'll enjoy yourself once you get on the road. I'll go tell Jase to wait up until you can change out of that old dress. Wear something pretty. It's good for the morale, and you've been looking a little frayed around the edges lately."

When Amanda was alone in the kitchen, she let go with a muted scream of helpless defeat. She'd just been outmaneuvered by a cagey lady bent on doing a little matchmaking. Somehow Julie had sensed the growing tension between her niece and foreman, and had decided to give nature a little helping hand.

"Oh, God," Amanda groaned, moving off down the hall, pausing to check on Sarah. The little girl was playing happily with the elaborate dollhouse Harry had given her shortly before his death, so Amanda decided not to disturb her. She needed some time to collect herself—an eternity or two just might be long enough.

Once in the privacy of her room, Amanda pressed her fingers to her throbbing temples. Since the night of the storm, she'd not had a single peaceful moment. Now, added to her own turmoil, was the problem of discouraging Julie from continuing these transparent efforts to encourage a romance.

"You could simply confront her, tell her you see

right through her schemes, and ask her to stop," Amanda muttered.

What then do you tell her when she digs her heels into persuing this subject and demands to know *why*.

Start out with the old convenient "once burned, twice shy" excuse, but refuse to explain any further. Or you might mention Jason's obvious lack of financial security; something most women could understand, being the helpless, subjugated creatures we are. And, of course, there's the fact Jason Thorne might indeed be the devil incarnate, because he takes your breath, steals your soul, and your very reason with the merest touch of his hands and lips.

Insofar as those less-than-rational reasons were concerned, Amanda knew each one to be wretchedly close to the truth. Yet not one of them—singly or collectively—was having the least effect in preventing her from falling hopelessly in love with Jason all over again.

Chapter Nine

By the time Jason parked the automobile in front of Hardy's General Store, he felt as if the entire right side of his body was incased in ice from Amanda's cold shoulder. Any attempts at casual conversation had been met with cool one-word responses. It had been a mistake to have her along this trip, and he wished Julie hadn't meddled. Their situation with the TJ—Brinkman's deadline only a couple of weeks away—was reaching the critical stage. As was the relationship with Amanda, which was rapidly approaching the point of no return for him. Obviously, for her, it was all coming too fast. He wished again for a slower, easier pace between them, but knew himself too well for that. His need for her was too strong, and his patience was nearly gone. Jason Thorne freely admitted he was a man with a short fuse. There was also the added worry that things could easily blow up in all their faces.

After hopping out of the vehicle, he opened Amanda's door and offered his hand, which she pretended not to see. Her pained expression told him the bouncy ride had aggravated her aches and stiffness. He once again tried to lighten things between them by asking, "Are you going to be all right?"

"I'm fine," she snapped, smoothing her printed muslin skirt and stepping around him.

"You don't look fine," he insisted, quickly moving beside her to help her out of the automobile. "In fact, you look like a lady ready to *bite* somebody."

Amanda went stone rigid at the word bite, her face flooding with a telling shade of crimson at his deep chuckle.

Jason was still grinning when they stepped inside the store, but the smile faded immediately when three men, leaning negligently against the main counter, turned to face him. He swore softly beneath his breath and gave Amanda a brief, apologetic glance before speaking.

"Bert," he said with a nod toward the stationmaster. "Jack . . . Billy," he added tonelessly, greeting the Granger brothers much in the same way a man would acknowledge two rattlers—with extreme caution. When the brothers smiled broadly, Jason knew it was time to face the music. Unfortunately, all the notes were sour here.

"Well, well," Jack Granger said with his lazy,

eager grin. "Would you look what dragged through the door, Billy."

"Speak of the very devil," chimed his younger brother.

Bert Taylor moved away from his companions. "I've got to be getting back to the station." Halfway across the room Bert paused in midstride. He looked first toward Amanda, then his gaze moved to Jason and his dark eyes communicated a surprising regret. "Jason, I—"

"It's all right, Bert," Jason told him, trying hard not to show his shock at this unexpected show of concern in a man he'd never called friend, who had always been only slightly less antagonistic than the others.

Looking a little shamed, Bert grumbled something unintelligible and continued out of the store.

Intuitively Amanda moved closer to Jason. There was a palpable, distressing current of excitement flowing from the two men leaning indolently against the counter. It sent tremors of alarm throughout her body despite the fact that on the surface everything appeared normal. By appearance, the men Jason had called Jack and Billy were ordinary farmers. Dressed in faded bib overalls, their clothing bore the stains and smells of the barnyard. Both men were quite tall, but they were already starting to wear the pauchy bulk of gluttony.

Jason felt Amanda come up behind him, but didn't take his eyes from the Granger brothers. "Why don't you wait outside while I order the wire, Amanda," he requested in a casual tone.

"Auntie's thread," she reminded him, not fooled by his attempt to cover up the anxiety which was growing by the moment. She could feel it in the taut muscles of his arm when she stepped up beside him, their shoulders brushing.

"Amanda . . . ," he started, but Clyde Hardy's entrance from a back room stalled Jason's intended command.

"Jack," the storekeeper was saying, "it seems I'm fresh out of . . . ?" He faltered at the sight of his newest customers, his narrow face going quite pale as his eyes began to dart between the Granger brothers and Jason. "Thorne," he finally spat with contempt. "Get out'a my store. I don't want any trouble."

Jason heard Amanda's soft gasp just before he felt her hand creep between his side and elbow, pushing through the narrow space to cling to him tightly. "Neither do I, Mr. Hardy," he stated with steady calm. "Our business shouldn't take that long. The storm took out about a mile of fence, so we'll be needing two spools of the Glidden double-strand. If you'll have Jerry bring it out, I'll pay extra for the freight." He glanced quickly at Amanda. "There *wasn't* anything else we needed, *was* there?"

Amanda caught his message and quickly responded in the negative. Never had she wanted anything as badly as she wanted to get out of this store and safely home. She knew now her sense of danger was real, not a product of her imagination. But why? Jason's background again?

"Are you deaf, Thorne? Or just stupid?" Clyde Hardy grated. "I thought we'd made it clear the TJ's business, or residents, wasn't welcome here anymore. And you can tell that bird-brained woman you're working for folks aren't going to put up with her stupid stubbornness much longer. If she ain't got enough sense to know—"

"I get the message, Clyde!" Jason ground out, his dark eyes going hard and cold. "Come on, Amanda. Let's get out of here. There's still enough time to drive over to Peabody and purchase our supplies there."

"Yes," she agreed quickly. Amanda was so eager to get away that she didn't think when she released Jason's arm and rushed for the door. It was a mistake she immediately realized when she heard a bellowing roar of triumph. She turned just as the youngest Granger brother came charging straight for Jason.

He wasn't a coward to hide behind a woman's skirts, but Jason had known from the beginning what would happen should Amanda leave his side for a minute. Therefore, the second she moved away he'd prepared himself for the initial attack. For all his size Billy Granger had speed. Jason barely had time to drop down and lower his shoulder before two hundred pounds of bulky fury went rolling over his back. Jason flipped Billy over, pushing the younger man's legs high so that he landed hard, all the air being driven from his lungs when he made contact with the unyielding floor. China vibrated upon shelves, and Clyde Hardy groaned loudly when some of the dishes tottered and fell, shattering into a million pieces.

Breaking glass drowned out Jack Granger's muffled cry when Jason blocked the larger man's intended blow, countering the move with a left hook which sent Jack flying back against a bin filled with coffee beans. A delicious scent wafted through the room as the bin overturned, spilling the dark beans all over the floor.

Jason had won round one, but these two brothers were veterans of many battles. They also were strongly motivated by the years in which they'd been denied their favorite victim. They also had the advantage of size, and the belief that a fair fight was only for fools. One to one, Jason Thorne could easily whip them, and they weren't about to give him that chance.

The minute Billy regained his feet, he was back into the fray with a roof lifting "Yahoo!" His beefy arms were around Jason's middle before the slighter man could swivel to face his new foe. "I got him, Jack!" Billy shouted gleefully, lifting Jason clear off the floor, jostling him up and down, slowly squeezing off his air with rib crushing strength.

"Hold the son of a bitch!" Jack said unevenly, his head still whirling from the punch he'd taken. "I'm going to kill him now!"

For Amanda the next few minutes would forever remain a vague blur in her mind. One second she was hugging the door, frozen with terror; the next she was bashing Jack Granger over the head with a parasol lifted from a nearby stand. Surprised by the suddeness of this attack from an unexpected source, the older Granger's well-aimed kick went far wide of its goal, and it was his younger brother who shrieked in agony, his arms going slack.

Drawing a deep breath to fill his burning lungs, Jason caught Billy in the stomach with a powerful drive of his elbow. The man doubled over, putting his chin within range. Billy's head was snapped back by Jason's fist, and he blinked rapidly from the pain radiating through his face. "Damn," he muttered just before backhanding Jason halfway across the room.

Jason's back slammed against a table loaded with bolts of cloth. The legs of the table scraped against the floor as it was pushed back by the propulsion of Jason's body. Without its tentative support, Jason lost his footing and he went down, striking the back of his head on the sharp edge before he landed dazed on his backside. With his senses reeling, he tried to gain his feet but the room began to spin wildly, going a little dark.

He shook his head sharply, trying to regain his focus, mystified by the strange vision of flowers on a field of swaying green. He'd had lights explode in his head from a hard blow before, but never daisies. Slowly the haze cleared away, and Jason realized the flowery field was the cotton print of Amanda's skirt. She had stationed herself over him and was swinging a parasol with the deadly cunning of a warrior brandishing a broadsword.

"Move her out'a my way, Billy!" Jack Granger roared, still rubbing his aching head, which had been repeatedly abused.

"*You* get her out of the way," Billy countered, not wanting to tangle with this red-haired virago who took a wild swipe at his midsection and then gave him a painful gouge with the pointed tip of that frilly umbrella.

"Well, *goddamn*," Jack barked on a lunge, grabbing the weapon and jerking it free to break it in two pieces over his knee. "Now, get out of my way, bitch!"

"What is going on here!" bellowed a new voice.

All heads turned to see Grant Winston striding across the room. When he snatched the parasol out of Jack Granger's hands, Amanda's knees gave way with relief and she slumped down beside Jason.

"Get out of here," he snapped at the Granger brothers, "or I'll see the both of you brought up on charges for assault on this woman."

"We didn't do nothin' to her, Grant. It was Thorne we was after. She just got in the way, that's all."

"Out!" Winston repeated, his blue eyes glittering with anger and disgust.

The two brothers looked decidedly unhappy, but they obeyed the sharp, commanding tone. "Good to see you again, Thorne," Jack said on his way out the door. "I'll be lookin' forward to the next time. Leave the lady at home, though, will ya?"

Amanda fought the urge to giggle hysterically at the almost friendly, benign tone from a man who had, only moments ago, been determined to commit murder. She cried out softly when she saw the blood streaking down Jason's chin from the cut on his lower lip. Her hands shook violently as she fumbled inside her reticule for a hankie. When a folded white cloth was dropped into her lap, she looked up at Grant Winston with gratitude flooding out of her eyes. She immediately pressed the handkerchief to Jason's mouth.

"Easy," he cautioned on an indrawn breath, taking charge of his own injury. His gaze was still a little bleary when it worriedly went over the disheveled woman at his side. "Are you—"

"Mrs. Ames. Are you injured, dear lady?" Grant Winston's booming voice of concern drowned out

Jason's own query. He watched the man assist her to her feet while he was still struggling to get his legs beneath him. Jason felt a surge of jealousy, and another prick to his already wounded pride.

Amanda was glad for the strong arm to lean on, but she felt stupidly embarrassed that once again Grant had caught her in less than flattering circumstances. She looked around the floor for the hairpins that had scattered, causing her hair to tumble helterskelter over her face and straggle down her back. "I'm fine," she managed shakily. "I think."

Jason had finally managed to rise with the help of the table. He discarded the handkerchief to examine the huge lump on the back of his head, wincing when his fingers found the tender spot. Thankfully his scattered wits were starting to return. Just in time, it would seem. Clyde Hardy, huffing and puffing with fury, his eyes snapping with the need to issue blame for the disaster done in his store, was coming straight at him. In the older man's hand he was waving the limp, broken remains of a parasol.

"This is all your fault, Thorne!" he raged. "Look at my place! I knew the two of you meant trouble the minute you walked in!"

"How dare you, sir!" Amanda said between clenched teeth as she rounded on the man who would accuse them unjustly. Ten years of holding impotent rage inside boiled up and over. "We entered this establishment as honest-paying customers, only to be rudely informed our business wasn't welcome. If anything, your high-handed attitude only encouraged the attack which followed. Nor, might I add, did you lift a single finger to protest, or make an attempt to stop that unprovoked assault once it had begun; not even when they turned their violence toward myself. If my uncle Todd were living today, he'd see an apology on your lips, or you, sir, would be spitting teeth!"

When Clyde Hardy's lips curled in a sneer and a snort of derision bubbled from his mouth, Jason's eyes closed. Here it comes, he thought, unable to stop the inevitable.

"Is that so? Well, little lady, for your information the name Danfield don't mean shit around here anymore!" He ignored Grant Winston's request to mind his language, advancing on Amanda, his narrow chest heaving. "I thought we made that point clear enough in the petition we signed a few weeks ago. But she obviously don't give a damn about the rest of us, so why should we extend her, or anybody connected with the TJ, any particular courtesy? Isn't it plain enough she ain't wanted around here anymore?"

Something in Amanda's stricken, confused expression, or even possibly his own guilty conscience, took some of the fire out of Clyde Hardy's eyes. "She's busted, dammit! Is it fair we should all suffer 'cause a stubborn old woman don't know when to call it quits? Hell, Brinkman's made her a fair offer for the TJ. Why ain't she got enough sense to know she'd be better off someplace else, livin' easy in her old age?"

"W-what is he talking about, Jason?" Amanda turned frightened eyes on the man who had come up to stand at her side.

Jason slipped an arm around her waist. "You've said enough, Clyde." Although his tone was soft, the underlying threat was clearly heard, and ignored.

"I'll say any goddamned thing I please in my own place, Thorne!" The old man shot right back. "I especially don't want to hear nothin' from you! We all know it's your doin' that's keeping Julie from doing the right thing and selling out. Why'd you bring your unwanted carcass back here in the first place? Tell me that, will you? She was talkin' reasonable to Winston here until you showed up and turned her head with God only knows what kind of stupid notions! Well, it ain't gonna make any difference! We'll have that meat packing plant, and Brinkman will get hold of the TJ. Do you want to know why? Well, I'll tell you! It's 'cause you'll be buying *all* your supplies over in Peabody from now on. This town is cutting you off. And you'd better keep your eyes wide open while you're driving that motorized buggy of yours from here to there. Some folks around here just might be waitin' to encourage you to keep right on going—clear out of the state."

"Is that a threat, Clyde?" Jason asked dryly.

"Threat—warning," the older man said with a shrug. "Take it any way you like, but take it seriously." On that he spun on his heel and stomped off in search of his broom and dustpan.

Jason felt a brief surge of respect for the old storekeeper. If he could be convinced Brinkman, not Julie Danfield, was this town's enemy, he'd make a valuable ally.

For Amanda, this entire morning had taken on the quality of a terrible nightmare. She didn't understand all that she'd heard, but enough to make fear coil inside of her. Julie was busted. Someone wanted the TJ. These people wanted that someone—she couldn't remember the name—to get the TJ. Julie

Danfield wasn't wanted here anymore. Anyone connected with Julie Danfield wasn't wanted. Jason had been threatened and attacked.

She looked at Jason with pleading eyes, wanting so badly for him to tell her it all had been a horrible dream. When she heard him say, "I'm sorry, Amanda," her hope was shattered. With it went her protective numbness and she felt each of his words as if they were sharp blows. She wrenched away from the arm encircling her waist.

The sight of her pale face, and the gold eyes glazing with uncertainty and fear, made Jason want to shout with rage. Or yank her into his arms and swear everything was going to be all right. In his gut he knew it to be true, but personal convictions, intuitive feelings, held little weight in the harsh world of facts and figures. Amanda was of that world. It was going to take a powerful lot of convincing to make her part of his own.

Amanda looked to Grant Winston and saw his eyes shift away guiltily. Did everyone know? Was she the only duped fool in this town? "Jason . . ." she started.

"Not now, Amanda," he said more sharply than he'd intended. "Find someplace to sit down before you fall down."

She made no response, but only stared at him for what seemed an eternity, her thoughts unreadable. Then she spun on her heel and walked briskly toward the door. Jason let her go. There wasn't any point in stopping her. The Grangers would be half-way home by now. And he knew he'd find her just outside when he was ready. Amanda didn't have anywhere else to go.

He turned his hard green gaze on Grant Winston, causing the attorney to take several steps backward before he shifted his regard to the storekeeper. "I'll tell Julie Danfield you send your warmest regards, Clyde. She's always pleased to hear from old friends."

The old man flushed a deep shade of crimson, which could have its source in either anger or shame. Jason strongly suspected Clyde Hardy suffered from the latter.

"Good day, gentlemen."

Chapter Ten

JASON BROUGHT THE AUTOMOBILE TO AN ABRUPT STOP beneath the grove of trees in front of the house. Amanda was already groping for the door handle, forcing him to lunge at her in order to prevent that hasty escape.

"Don't do this, Amanda," he said with a desperate urgency, holding firmly to her arm. "Let us explain before you judge and condemn . . ."

"Let go of me," she returned coldly, keeping her face averted.

He would have maintained his grip and argued this out if Julie and Sarah hadn't appeared at the corner of the house. "All right," he rasped. "But this isn't finished between us. Also, be warned. If you start dumping bushels of guilt and recriminations on your aunt's head, you'll have cause to regret it later, I promise." He released her. As he'd known she would, Amanda fled the vehicle and ran straight for the house. She didn't even pause to acknowledge the little girl running toward her, the little face wreathed in smiles.

The sight of her niece's disheveled appearance stopped Julie dead in her tracks. She started to reach for Sarah to pull the child back, but wasn't quick enough. Sarah shot past and was following her mother into the house before Julie could collect her suddenly alarmed wits.

For a moment she debated whether to follow the pair, but that was settled quickly enough when Jason walked around his vehicle. Even from this distance, her eyes were sharp enough to see the puffy swelling of his lower lip, the pained expression in his dark green eyes. When he jammed his thumbs into the front pockets of his trousers, she knew for certain they had trouble. Even when he was a little boy, made to stand at the front of the church where all could see him, the example and the evidence of sin, he always took this stance. Most saw this careless, relaxed positioning of his body as a defiant arrogance, a flaunting scorn toward those who would save him from himself. Julie had always believed the casual way he held himself was a defense against letting anyone see how very vulnerable and lonely he felt; often frightened, and sometimes very near tears.

"What happened," she asked softly as she approached.

"What didn't happen?" he countered with a humorless snort of laughter. "Let's see, first there was the Granger brothers." He heard Julie's indrawn breath and gave her a sad smile. "Yeah, they're always good for openers."

"You don't look much like a man who's gone a round or two with Jack and Billy. For one thing—you're still on your feet."

Jason had to agree with her, giving Julie the highlights of the fight and his rescue from an unexpected source. "God, she was something to see, Julie. With just that flimsy parasol and more courage than most men could claim, she took them on all by herself." The tender smile that had lifted the uninjured corner of his mouth faded. "Then Clyde Hardy had to get up on his high horse . . ."

"No need to tell me the details of that," Julie said with a shake of her head. "I can just imagine all that Clyde had to say about one crazy old woman and her stubborn, bullheaded hold on a broken-down ranch." She patted Jason's arm, needing no more confirmation than the grim set of his mouth. "Well, I'd better get myself in there and try to smooth things over."

"Julie, she's not exactly in a receptive mood," he warned. "She's scared, and she is hurt and confused. After Jack and Billy, Amanda probably expects a vigilante committee to run us out of town. Convincing her those two would have come after me simply for the hell of it won't be easy."

"But it's the truth. Somehow we'll just have to convince her things aren't the black picture painted back there."

Julie crossed paths with Sarah as she entered the

house, and the little girl came moping out the door. When she spotted Jason, her somber expression brightened somewhat and she came skipping across the lawn to him. He swooped her up, hugging her tightly, but reared away when her curious little finger would have prodded the tender flesh of his mouth.

"Oooh, that's nasty, Jason. Does it hurt?"

"Only when I laugh," Jason told her. But when she kissed his cheek only inches from his mouth, announcing, "There—I made it all better now," he felt more like crying. This loving child did indeed make things all better, easing the pain of an unending empty hurt. Although his arms would always ache to hold another child, one lost to him forever, Sarah helped fill the void created by Susan's death. And he'd learned to love this little pickle just for herself.

Carrying her toward the bunkhouse, Jason told her the story of how he'd been clumsy enough to walk right into a door.

Outside Amanda's closed bedroom door, Julie steeled herself to face her niece's justifiable outrage. However, when she stepped inside the room she encountered a scene she hadn't expected.

Amanda was moving methodically from the tall wardrobe to the bed. Draped over her arm was the remainder of her clothing, which she added to the pile next to her open suitcase.

"What do you think you're doing, girl?" Julie asked with stunned dismay.

"I'm getting myself and my daughter out of here,

162

Aunt Julie," Amanda responded in an unemotional monotone before turning toward the chest to remove her lingerie and night clothes. "We can't stay here now."

"And just where will you go?" Julie moved into the room and lowered herself onto the edge of the bed while she watched Amanda fold and toss her things into the suitcase.

"Back to civilization, where I belong. I should never have come here. I can see that now. It's my fault as much as yours. Charity always makes a poor solution."

Julie didn't respond to that, but her eyes narrowed slightly as Amanda bustled about the room, the tightly coiled tension and anger in her niece obvious in her movements.

"What are you planning on telling little Sarey about this sudden urge to move?"

Amanda stopped just short of her dressing table, going completely rigid and still.

"That's something you might have considered before you brought us into this situation without a single word of warning, Auntie. What I tell Sarah is my own problem, though it won't be easy. She's learned to love the TJ and the people living here. Uprooting her again makes me physically ill when I think . . ." Amanda drew in a shaky breath, her shoulders quaking slightly from the emotions threatening to spill over in a torrent. "Her safety is more important," she finished, and continued to the dresser, nearly losing her control once again when her eyes rested upon the jar of sweetly scented cream.

Julie was beginning to feel a little sick herself. She

163

might have handled Amanda's anger, or hurt tears. But this aloof composure put her completely off balance. Leaving the bed, Julie stopped Amanda as she would have filled a hatbox with the contents of her dressing table. She spun the younger woman around, tired of looking at that stiff back. "You've got every right to be upset with us, Amanda Jean. It don't matter much now that we thought we were doing right by keeping the full story from you. Our hearts were in the right place, but it was wrong. I can see that now. But you've got to believe that I'd never have let you, or that child, step one foot in this town if I'd thought there was any danger."

"Well, Auntie, you were mistaken. After today, there's little doubt those people will stop at nothing to get what they want." Amanda's tone was sharper than she'd intended, and she flinched inside at the hurt she witnessed in those weary brown eyes.

"Amanda, you don't understand the half of what is happening here. That's our fault, I know," she interjected quickly. "But you've got the wrong idea over what happened with them Granger boys this morning. Honey, it wouldn't have made the slightest difference to Jack and Billy if the TJ was solid as a rock and nobody'd ever heard the name Brinkman. They would have come after Jase for the pure hell of it. I'd hoped those two would have left their school-yard bullying behind now they're grown men with families of their own. Guess there's some folks who never grow up. For heaven's sake, don't judge everyone in Stockton by their low standard. Oh, there are some who will shoot off their mouths, sign petitions, and be general pains in the butt. Still I can't—won't—believe there's a single one of them who would do me, or mine, any real harm."

Amanda swallowed hard. She couldn't break down now, couldn't let her aunt sway the decision she'd made. "I believe you believe that, Auntie. Unfortunately, you weren't there so you can't possibly know the malice and the hatred I felt from those men. I can't live like that, and I won't have Sarah subjected to that kind of viciousness. *We have to leave!*" Breaking away from her aunt's hold, Amanda tossed jars and bottles carelessly into the box. When she finished, one container remained—the one she wouldn't take with her, because it would remind her of the man she knew she'd not be able to forget this time.

"You're really set on this, then?" Julie asked, growing truly alarmed. "You won't even give me a chance to explain what's really going on here? Amanda, I can't let that man steal my land. Maybe I don't have a chance in hell of beating Brinkman, but I owe it to Todd's memory to at least try . . ."

"Auntie, please," Amanda cut in. "You don't owe me explanations or reasons. Though I wish I'd been apprised of the real facts before coming out here, I'll acknowledge they were never any of my business. I can understand and accept that. You thought you were helping me. I don't doubt your motives for a minute. I'm grateful. Really I am." She was precariously close to bawling like a baby, so she hurriedly rushed through this prepared little speech. "Don't you worry about Sarah and me. I've enough money for train fare and friends who will take us in temporarily until I can find work of some sort. It's what we would have done had your invitation not arrived. We'll be fine . . . really."

Julie Danfield listened quietly while Amanda spouted her reassurances and absolutions of guilt. With her hands on her hips she eyed her niece up and down. "That's the biggest bunch of hogwash I've ever heard all of a single piece, Amanda Jean. You're madder than blue blazes 'cause Jase and I kept you in the dark, and you've got justification. Plenty of it. But I'm not going to let you go taking off out'a here in a huff. We were wrong in what we did. Still, you owe me at least the courtesy of a fair hearing. Give yourself the next twenty-four hours to think this through. We can talk again tomorrow. Then, if you are still determined to go back to Kansas City, I'll tell Jason to drive you to the station. Will you do that much for me, Amanda?"

The tears she'd held back for so long were now streaking down her cheeks. Amanda nodded her agreement, though she doubted anything would change her mind now. When Julie came up to hug her, Amanda put her arms around the older woman's shoulders, returning the affection and comfort. She wished today had never happened, but it had.

"That's my girl," the older woman praised in a voice husky with emotion. "We'll work this out, I promise. And remember, I can always sign this place over to Brinkman. Then we could all climb on that train for the big city. Now, dry your tears and promise me you won't upset Sarah with any of this just yet."

"I promise," Amanda croaked, gladly jumping at the chance to put off breaking her little girl's heart again. "Why didn't you tell me, Auntie?" She finally said the words which had been hounding her since Stockton. "You should have told me."

Jason wasn't at all surprised when Julie knocked on the bunkhouse door an hour after they'd all shared a very strained, too-polite supper. In fact, he was ready for her, immediately pouring out a glass of Todd Danfield's home brew, which she accepted with a grateful smile. When she'd finished coughing and choking her way past the first sip, Jason led her to the sofa, where she sank down onto the cushions. "From the way things were at supper, and since you took that drink so readily, I'd say your conversation with Amanda didn't go well."

"Shoot," she managed, still gasping slightly. "I'd say it went very well, considering I caught her packing up her things, hell-bent on leaving with the first train out of here." She looked up at him over the rim of her glass, noting how his entire body grew taut at this information. "I managed to convince her she needed another day to give leaving some thought. Promised you'd drive her to the station if she still felt the same the day after tomorrow."

Jason walked to the window, saying nothing for quite a while. "Well, I hope you don't expect me to abide by that promise, Julie. Amanda isn't going anywhere. Not now. Not ever. Or at least, not without me."

"Rather figured you might say something like that. But unless we can convince her she *wants* to stand with us and battle this thing out, we've got no right to play God with her and that child's life. Today flat scared the hell out of her, Jase. And I can't say I blame her for what she's thinking and feeling. Or for her anger."

He turned back to her. "How did she react when you told her how Brinkman has manipulated the TJ's downfall."

"Didn't tell her," Julie said flatly, her mouth drawing down. "To tell you the truth, I don't think Amanda's much interested in the whys or the wherefores. She only sees the trouble and wants to get her child away from it—far and fast." Taking another bracing sip of the potent liquor, Julie appeared to lose herself in thought. "Jason, if she can't be talked out of leaving, I'm going to agree to sign those papers. My conscience couldn't live with sending Amanda and Sarah back into that life they were living before. I'd rather give it all up. This ranch isn't worth that much grief." She began to cry softly.

Jason came to her immediately, pulling her close. "Hush now, old girl. The TJ isn't worth a single one of your tears, either. Trust me to handle Amanda. I don't doubt she's alarmed by what happened today. She probably also feels as if we've betrayed her trust—which we have in a way. But I don't believe she really wants to leave."

Julie sniffed and wiped her eyes. "Jase, maybe she doesn't have the grit for this kind of life. Even in the best of times, it sometimes gets harder than some folks can bear in the way of work and heartache."

"Are you trying to tell me the woman who took on both Granger brothers lacks courage? She's leery of cows, but every morning she's up at dawn, her hands beneath Bess, and dodging hard swipes of that cranky animal's tail. She'd much rather walk five miles than ride one. Still, she swallowed her apprehension and is learning to ride. If that's not grit, then how would you define the word?"

"Guess you've got a point there. Doesn't mean she likes what she's doing, though." Julie pulled away from him slightly and grabbed his chin, clucking her tongue when her eyes settled on his puffy lip. "Why in the name of heaven would you be so damned determined to sink your roots in a place where folks toss insults and their fists at your head like it was their God-given right? Jase, if we prove Brinkman for the crook he is, that doesn't mean people will start looking at you kindly. We both know they don't need a Brinkman to feed their grudge against you. I always did say your mama could have saved you, and this town, a good deal of trouble by naming your papa before she died giving you birth."

Jason's features tautened, but this time he didn't back away from the truth. "How could she?" he replied with only a trace of the old bitterness. "There were too damned many candidates for the title. It would seem my mother wasn't starving for lack of customers. So, you see before you the child who belongs to all, and can be claimed by none."

"And they've been punishing you for their own sins these past thirty years," she stated. "Can you really live with more of the same for the next thirty or more?"

He shrugged slightly as if the problem she posed was of little account. "The circumstances of my existence can't be changed or resolved, Julie. I'm a living, breathing fact. Hopefully, without the good Reverend to whip them into a frenzy of guilt and self-condemnation every Sunday, a few might have learned a little tolerance—for themselves and for me."

"Well, for a man who just recently had his face pounded to pulp by two of those tolerant citizens, I'd say you're being mighty optimistic."

"Not the same thing," Jason said with conviction. "You simply don't understand my relationship with the Grangers. I doubt very much if Jack or Billy gives a hoot who my pa might be. I learned very young those two enjoy a good scrap more than just about anything. And I've always made a point of giving them one whale of a good scrap. Crazy as it might sound, I truly believe they see Jason Thorne as a worthy adversary."

"Well, that's a real comfort," she snipped sarcastically. "The next time I see your face in the dust, with Jack or Billy's foot across your neck, I'll remind myself you're eating dirt because they hold you in such high esteem."

Jason roared with laughter, giving her a hearty squeeze. "I told you it sounded crazy. Now, let's get back to the subject of keeping Amanda home where she belongs. She's given you twenty-four hours. I want free rein, with no interference, for that same amount of time."

"I don't know about this, Jase," she hedged, not caring too much for the peculiar look in his eye.

"Do you trust me, Julie?"

"Well . . . I . . ."

"Surely you know I'd rather die than hurt her. Tell you what, if she's still determined to leave after tomorrow, I'll see that she and Sarah are safely delivered to the Peabody train station when I drive over for the wire." He was lying through his teeth and suspected Julie Danfield knew it as well.

"Just exactly what are you planning?"

"Whatever it takes, Julie . . ."

Treading carefully, Jason entered Amanda's room just as the rooster was crowing the dawn. Beneath the light covering of a sheet, she slept on her back, her arms flung over her head. His eyes were drawn to her high firm breasts, and he felt a stirring in his loins as those firm mounds rose and fell with the rhythmic breathing of her slumber. Stamping desire down, Jason placed his hand on one of those out-flung arms.

"Amanda," he said softly. "Wake up." When she didn't even stir, Jason let his fingers trail up and down the silken exposed flesh, tickling the tender underside of her elbow.

She frowned in her sleep and rolled to her side away from him. Settling himself on the edge of the mattress, Jason leaned across her. "Amanda, unless you wake up right now, I'm going to strip off my clothes and crawl in there with you. I guarantee you won't be sleeping through what will happen after that."

Her eyes popped open, and she flipped to her back. "Get off my bed, and out of my room!" she said on a strangled gasp, struggling to pull the sheet up to her chin, finding it trapped beneath his weight. When his eyes laughed at her efforts, she attempted to push him off the mattress. "I'll scream for Aunt Julie this time. I swear I will, Jason."

"No you won't," he said with confidence. "But it won't be necessary in any case. Tempting though it might be to put it to the test, we've got fence posts to reset. Or have you forgotten?"

Flat on her back with Jason looming above her, Amanda felt entirely too vulnerable. His gaze seemed to dwell on her breasts beneath the thin cotton of her nightgown. She tugged at the sheet, but could not dislodge it from beneath his hips. She felt the taut muscle of his thigh against her side and feared he was right when he claimed there would be no screaming should he press the issue. How could she want him, and know him for the deceitful, untrustworthy manipulator he was? "Get off this bed . . . please."

He shocked her by immediately complying with her request. It was necessary to leave her now, or he'd not leave at all. "Get dressed, Amanda. We've got work waiting."

She'd sat up and had the sheet beneath her chin before his backside had barely cleared the mattress. "Hasn't something slipped your mind, Jason? There won't be any wire to string to those fence posts. Not that it would make any difference. My days as a volunteer slave are over."

"Is that so?" he drawled. "Well, unfortunately, I'm in no frame of mind to accept your resignation. And there will be wire, Amanda. Make no mistake about that. So drag that pretty fanny out of bed and get dressed. The coolest part of the day is already going to waste."

"Go to hell, Jason," she seethed.

With lightning quickness he'd snatched the sheet,

ripping it from her. "I'll give you fifteen minutes. If you're not outside in that allotted time, on the wagon and ready for work, I'm coming back." He went to the wardrobe and pulled out her clothing, tossing the shirt and trousers across the foot of the bed. "Put these on, and make it snappy, or I'll be back to see to the task myself. Of course, we might get a little sidetracked in the process. . . ."

Amanda watched him swagger to the door in stunned silence. The look in his eyes when he glanced back convinced her completely he had meant every word.

"Fifteen minutes," he reminded, closing the door softly behind him.

"Amanda! I could use some water. *Now* if you don't mind!"

Oh, but she did mind, she railed silently, heaping curses upon his head even as she snatched up the bucket. She minded every minute of this grueling heat. She was beginning to despise the sound of Jason's voice as he played his foreman role to the hilt. She was also furious with herself for not calling his bluff this morning. He wouldn't have dared carry through on his threat, she now realized. Not with Aunt Julie and Sarah sleeping along the same hallway. Idiot, she called herself. Fool, she repeated.

While the water slowly trickled into the bucket, Amanda's attention wandered toward the surrounding landscape. Once it had seemed to represent hope and peace with its wild beauty. Now there was only the harsh, forbidding reality surrounding her. Grasses, once so lush and green, filled with a profusion of wildflowers, had turned the color of ocher beneath a punishing sun. The very earth was being sucked dry of moisture in this unrelenting heat. There wasn't even the promise of rain in the cloudless blue sky. It was ugly and unforgiving. And her soul was as dry of hope as the land.

I have to get away from here, she cried in silent panic.

Growing frustrated with the waiting, Jason tossed his shovel aside and walked over to the wagon. Letting his eyes rake over a woman daydreaming off into the distance, he cleared his throat loudly.

"Amanda," he said slowly, deliberately, "at this pace it will probably be Christmas before these posts are ready for wire."

"Good," she snapped, looking at him with eyes the color of the grass and dangerously close to igniting into a full-blown wildfire. "I should miss that particular chore." The bucket had finally filled, and she grunted a little when she heaved it out of the barrel. Amanda let it drop down onto the bed of the wagon. It landed with a dull thud, water sloshing up over the sides. "Your water, Boss."

The belligerent tone, and her lack of cooperation while she dragged her feet through an entire morning, finally snapped Jason's control. He moved as if to take the bucket, but took Amanda instead, grabbing her waist to haul her down.

"Get this straight, woman," he spat between clenched teeth. "Before this wagon heads back to the house, should that be midnight, Christmas, or sometime next year, this particular fence line will be ready for wire. You can, of course, start back any time your feet feel inclined to travel. The house, Mrs. Ames, is approximately five miles due southwest, give or take a hill or two. And you might as well accustom yourself to walking . . . because that's the only way you'll be leaving this ranch."

She broke away from the hands gripping her ribs. "What do you mean by that is the only way I'll be leaving?" It was impossible for his features to be any harder, the dark eyes more threatening. Still she didn't fear him. She was too angry to be afraid. Not even when he swore at her viciously and he began to advance. "I asked what you meant by that, Jason," she demanded even as her better instincts were telling her she should back away.

"Exactly what I said, Amanda. The first night you arrived I warned you there would come a time when you would want to hightail it back to the city. And I also stated the day would come when it would be necessary to remind you of what you said that night. You promised me an extra pair of hands, lady. I intend to hold you—willing or unwilling—to that pledge."

Her spine stiffened. "You misrepresented the circumstances. I was intentionally misled, which should release me from any promise solicited under false pretenses."

Jason stopped cold, unable to entirely deny her charge. "We never lied to you, Amanda. You just didn't care enough to learn the truth, even though it was staring you in the face every hour of every day. In fact, I'd lay down good money to wager you've never bothered to ask Julie how she managed to lose forty pounds, ten ranch hands, her friends, and

nearly her home all in the space of a single year? Did
you give her half a chance to explain yesterday? Are
you even interested now?" His eyes raked over her,
and they were overflowing with scorn. "Tell me
something—were you always a self-centered bitch,
or has life warped you that way?"

Chapter Eleven

AMANDA WAS AFTER JASON BEFORE HE COULD TAKE three full steps away, grabbing his arm to spin him around with a strength that surprised them both. "How dare you speak to me like that!" she exclaimed, her face flooding with the heat of her fury. "Did it ever occur to you that I never thought to question, because I trusted both my aunt . . . and you . . . implicitly? How could I have dreamed the two of you would withhold vital information in allowing me to make an intelligent decision before coming out here? Instead, I received a letter of invitation chock full of praise for the TJ's miracle-working foreman: the man who would save the ranch, and make life simply wonderful again for us all." She took a short gasp of hot air, which only served to fuel an already raging inferno of temper. "My aunt might have a penchant for finding rainbows and silver linings in the clouds, but I can't believe she'd be that self-deceiving. How much of that hopeful gullibility are you responsible for planting, Jason? How many lies did you have to spin to gain Aunt Julie's foolish faith?"

Jason stared at her in total amazement before he laughed outright. "Jesus, talk about someone with a gift for self-deception. Your aunt and I wrote that letter together, and the only reference she made to my opinion on the future of the TJ was to say I hoped we could turn things around soon. That was true then, and it's still true today. But how you managed to get *wonderful* out of that statement, or any other made in that letter, is beyond me." Some of the fire went out of her eyes, and he sensed another one of her emotional retreats. This time it was Jason's turn to jerk her back when she would have walked away.

"You don't like hearing the bald truth, do you, Amanda? Don't you realize what you've done yet? You'd been having one hell of a hard time because of that old man you married. So you ignored the obvious, rewrote that letter to your liking, and decided not to acknowledge anything that threatened your need to feel safe and secure."

"That's not true," she rasped. "Do you really believe I was so desperate I would have brought my own daughter smack into the middle of a potential war?"

"Yes," Jason returned softly. "The woman who

was sending an average of one letter a week, each one more desperate than the last, would have grabbed at any solution. Should we have brushed you aside because we had problems of our own? At least, here you were guaranteed food, shelter, and the company of people who loved you. Would you have fared better in Kansas City?"

"From the frying pan into the fire . . ." she retorted, yanking free of his restraining grasp. His harsh judgments of her character had cut deeply with an uncanny precision and perception. She wanted to go off and lick the raw wounds he'd inflicted before he went on to strip her bare. But her pride wouldn't allow her to run away this time. She stood her ground, unaware of the pain shadowing her tawny eyes. "How glibly you shift responsibility, Jason. You accuse me of being a self-centered bitch." Amanda got a little of her own back by hurling his own words at him. He winced visibly. "Are your motives so pure they can stand close scrutiny? What is your expected gain in this? Have you nominated yourself for sainthood? Or do you see yourself as the hero of some silly melodrama where you protect two hapless widows and a child from the greedy clutches of the evil Mr. Brinkman? And all out of the goodness of your heart. Or isn't it more logical that you've finally discovered a way to pay a few people back for all those years they treated you like dirt?"

Jason didn't react at all the way she'd anticipated. She saw it first in his eyes, and then it spread to his mouth in that singularly stunning Pan-like grin.

"Tit for tat," he said, reaching out to grab the thick braid hanging down her back, sweeping the hat from her head with his free hand. "By golly, Amanda," he said huskily, giving a sharp tug on her hair so that she could not avoid the probing of his eyes. "I do believe there's hope for you yet."

With her hair captured, Amanda was completely vulnerable to the descent of his mouth. His lips settled softly upon hers with an undemanding tenderness which swiftly defeated any will to protest. The hands she had instinctively raised to his chest to push him away were now clutching fistfulls of his shirt. His mouth cajoled while his tongue teased until she wanted more, forgetting entirely her new determination to despise this man. She forgot everything but the heady feeling he aroused within her, the musky aroma of his damp skin, and the hard flesh beneath her palms. This was unlike any kiss they'd shared before, long past or recent past. Every cell in her body was awakening. This was a communication so elemental that her mind was unable to accept the message singing through her blood. At that moment Jason lifted his head.

"Why did you do that?" she asked, breathless with confusion.

"Mandy, if a man is to be judged, it might as well be for a sinner as a saint." He kissed her again, hard and quick. "That will have to hold you for a while. If I keep on kissing you, Christmas will come and go before I remember there's work to be done." His eyes dropped to where her hands still clung to his shirt. "You'd better let me go, woman. I could get the idea you want me to make love to you nearly as bad as I want to do the loving."

She uncurled her fingers and her hands dropped to

her sides. "You are still the most arrogant, cocksure man I've ever known."

He chuckled, but made no comment, going after the bucket he'd left in the wagon. When the contents had been dumped, Jason tossed the empty container her direction. "One more should do it for this hole."

The full moon was rising when the wagon lumbered back through the gate. Amanda was exhausted, though she wasn't suffering the physical distress of the last time. She climbed down off the wagon unassisted, very glad this day was done.

Jason came around the wagon too late to help her. "Should I fill the tub for you tonight?"

He'd asked the question casually, but Amanda felt her face suffuse with heat at the memory of her last bath and the subsequent events.

"No," she responded curtly. "I won't need it. I'll wash in the basin."

"I'm glad to hear you aren't in any pain tonight," Jason continued in the same light manner, already moving to unload the wagon. "Carry this into the barn for me, will you?" The request was politely made; however, Jason didn't bother with Amanda's consent. He just shoved the heavy shovel into her hands. "Put it down beneath the loft overhang nearest this door."

It was less taxing simply to put the tool away than argue over his high-handed ordering again. Amanda walked into the barn's dim interior. Fortunately, the roof had enough gaping holes to allow some filtering of the bright moonlight. But beneath the shadowy overhang it was still very dark. She felt for and located the wall, propping the shovel against it. When she turned to leave, Amanda walked smack into an obstacle which hadn't been there moments before. And when that dark shape reached out and grabbed her, she let out a startled yelp. "Jason?"

"And who else would it be?" he answered with a chuckle, steadying her trembling shoulders.

His husky voice, this intimate darkness, and senses too poignantly haunted by a kiss still shatteringly vivid brought a rush of desire within Amanda. It was swift and strong, alarming her with its force. She sought to escape it, stepping back quickly, only to encounter the blade of the shovel. Her heel came down on metal and she lost her balance. The shovel went crashing to the floor and Amanda hit the wall hard. Only Jason's quick reflexes prevented her from landing on the sharp edge of the metal tool as she slid down the rough wood.

"Whoa," Jason uttered, hoisting her upright so that she was braced between him and the wall. "Are you all right?"

Amanda had been momentarily stunned by the force of her contact with the wall. She drew her breath in sharply, expanding her lungs to take in the air which had been forced out of them only moments ago. It was then that she became aware of his thumbs pressing against the outer swell of her breasts, and the spread of fingers just below her armpits. The ability to breathe at all became hampered when he accidentally—or purposely?—moved his thumbs.

Jason was keenly aware of her quivering softness. Her small gasp when he rotated his thumbs slightly told him she was not oblivious or unmoved by his touch. Was she frightened? Or did she want to be caressed, stroked? Oh God, he wanted so badly to fill his palms with her fullness. He knew her skin was softer than the finest silk, and more wonderful to touch because it was warm and alive and could pulse and tremble beneath his hands . . . and mouth.

For Amanda time hung suspended. The scent of hay was strong within her nostrils, and she closed her eyes against the flash of memory. The scene would not be banished, and she could again feel Jason's eyes on her naked flesh, knew the gentle caress of his hands as they had discovered her aching nipples so long ago.

She shuddered and felt the tips of her breasts harden. Still his hands didn't move, so near, yet so far from what now ached to know the splendor once again. She was going insane with the feelings quickly running out of control. Her protective instincts screamed that she not give in to these driving urges, demanding she put an end to this torment now, while she still could. "J-Jason . . ." Amanda had meant to plead for her release, but when his name left her lips she knew it had become an entreaty.

"Oh, God . . ." he groaned deep in his throat as he slid his hands over the soft mounds, cupping them, discovering the ripeness of her maturity, and the eagerness within her. There was no need to coax her nipples to life. They were already hard against his palms. His fingers found the buttons of her blouse. He flicked the top one open, and then the second. Any minute he expected to hear her reject his intent, so he moved swiftly, folding back the fabric until all that remained between them was the thin cotton of her camisole. The pads of his fingers traced the edges of the garment, nudging it aside.

Amanda was swirling in a world of pure sensation. His touch was so light it was as if butterflies were dancing across the surface of her skin. They fluttered over her straining nipples and a soft sigh escaped from her throat.

Jason slid his thumbs back and forth over the velvet tips, pushing the fabric farther down. "Soft," he muttered, pressing his lips to the hollow of her throat. "I have to taste you, Amanda," he whispered there.

A warm wetness replaced the ethereal caresses, and Amanda's knees buckled. A hard thigh stopped her descent, pressing her upward, giving ease to a new wild throbbing. She felt as if she might shatter into a million pieces. Nearly did shatter when a piercing voice exploded into her surreal, dreamlike state.

"What is taking the two of you so long out there!" Julie Danfield called out. "I've had supper on the table for ten minutes, and it's getting cold as ice!"

Jason moaned against Amanda's breast just as every muscle in her body went from fluid giving to rigid denial. He brushed his lips across the tender sweetness which had so fleetingly been his, bidding it a temporary farewell. He pulled himself away, rearranging her camisole in the process. Jason didn't need to see her face to know that her expression was one of horror and shame over the passion she'd allowed herself to experience. "Amanda," he said anxiously, "I want—"

"Yes, I know very well what you want," she rasped while her trembling fingers fumbled to button her shirt. "Well, it's not going to happen. This was a terrible mistake. I—I don't know what madness possessed me. . . ."

"The hell you don't!" he grated, capturing those flying hands and holding them firmly at her side. "Christ, but you act more the frightened virgin now than when you were sixteen and had the claim to that shrinking innocence. But back then it was all I could do to keep your hands off *me*." He felt her flinch at the truth and knew he'd wounded her with his thoughtless phrasing. Regret filled his voice. "I didn't mean that the way it came out. You were the most wonderfully responsive girl I've ever known, Amanda. You still are. Why do you throw up walls between us? Every time I tear down one, you throw up another. Each time you lower the barrier just enough to let me glimpse that spirit and warmth you once were so filled with—"

"Don't!" she cried out. "Please don't say any more."

"What are you afraid of? Me? My God, you must surely know I'd rather die than hurt you."

"Oh, yes, Jason," she snipped. "You're undoubtedly the most selfless person I've ever known. That's why you're encouraging an old woman to hold on to a bankrupt ranch and take on an entire town in the process!"

"You don't know what the hell you're talking about," he shot back. "And you don't particularly want to know, do you? Tell me, do you have all the facts to make an informed decision on your future? Hell, no!" He yanked her away from the wall. "You only want to run away and hide. Well, you started running long before yesterday. Jack and Billy merely gave you the excuse you'd been searching for. This Brinkman business is only a smoke screen, a straw to grasp which will enable you to put as much distance between us as possible. That's why you refuse to ask questions, demand answers. You're scared to death what you learn won't be the horrible disaster you want to imagine, and then you'll have to stand and face what really terrifies you. And that, Amanda, is what you feel for me." His voice was raw with the ache of his own pain.

"Why?" he asked roughly. "Was the hurt so terrible that you won't allow yourself to remember how good it was between us? Are you afraid if you let down your guard, you'll have to accept that what we shared was too strong to die?" His hands dropped away from her shoulders and he left the shadowy darkness of the overhang. A shaft of moonlight fell softly across his face, letting her see the wretchedness there. Her heart twisted for his pain.

"What do you want of me, Jason?" she cried in a small, choked voice.

There was a long, pregnant pause before Jason responded. "I want you to stand still long enough to find out. Stop spinning away from us . . . from me. Will you do that for all our sakes?"

It wasn't too much to ask, and it was something she could grant without committing herself. "Yes," she told him. "For a few days, anyway."

Jason didn't much care for the qualifier, but made no comment. He was too damned relieved she agreed to anything.

"Come on, then," he said, holding out his hand to

her. "Let's go in to supper." The length of time that she took before he felt her palm slip into his told him this simple gesture of trust had been difficult. But it had been given. He allowed himself to take heart, giving her fingers a gentle squeeze as they walked hand in hand toward the house.

Chapter Twelve

It had been more months than Julie Danfield cared to count since company, other than Grant Winston, had presented themselves at the TJ. Consequently, she was shocked, and a little bit leery, when she found Bert Taylor on her front doorstep before they had finished breakfast.

"Why, Bert," she greeted him with a reserved friendliness. "What brings you all the way out here? And on horseback, I see. I was beginning to think those animals had lost their usefulness as transportation these days." She looked pointedly at the machine taking up a fair part of her lawn.

"Don't say something like that to my father, Mrs.

Danfield. Just the sight of an automobile is enough to send him into a six-hour rage."

Some of her suspiciousness faded at his genuine attempt to break some of the coolness with a reference to his family. "I guess he would at that," she agreed with a chuckle. "Since he makes his living on horseflesh, those contraptions can't please him much."

"No, ma'am, they sure don't."

"Good heavens!" Julie cried. "Where are my manners to let you stand there on the front stoop. Why don't you take your horse on over to the barn, and then come back by way of the kitchen. You can join us for some flapjacks and ham."

Bert seemed to sag with relief. "I thank you, but I already had breakfast at home. I'd enjoy some coffee, though . . . if you've got it made."

"A whole pot," she told him, stepping back into the house. When he disappeared around the corner, Julie's brows drew together. "I wonder what Bert Taylor could want with us?" she muttered as she headed back toward the kitchen. It seemed to Julie that she remembered that Taylor had once been pretty thick with the Granger brothers.

Amanda was washing Sarah's face free of syrup when her aunt returned. "Who was it?"

"Real company," Julie told her, getting out a clean cup and saucer. "Or so it would seem. He'll be around in a minute after he takes care of his horse. Bert is the son of a rancher who has a spread about five miles the other side of town. The Taylors have always supplied folks around here, and most of the county, with their horseflesh."

"What does he want?" Amanda couldn't help the

nervousness at any thought of spending time with people outside this ranch. She instinctively drew Sarah closer.

Julie saw the anxiety leap into her niece's eyes, and her heart twisted when Amanda pulled the little girl into a protective embrace. "Honey, Bert Taylor is a good boy from a fine family. He's got a wife and two little boys. When he was younger he ran a little wild, but then our own Jason was never a saint, if you'll remember."

Amanda flushed at her aunt's reference to Jason's youth. No, he'd certainly not been a saint. Neither had she. "I'll take Sarah to her room and keep her entertained." She didn't get far. Julie grabbed her skirt and pulled her back.

"Let Sarah entertain herself. Whatever the reason for Bert Taylor's visit, there aren't going to be any more secrets in this house. Besides, if there's trouble, from what I hear, you're right handy to have around." She gave Amanda's cheek a pat.

Sarah wasn't altogether happy about being left out of things. Amanda soothed her by promising they would have a picnic lunch later in the meadow. When she walked into the dining room, she could hear a pleasant male voice. She stopped, took a deep breath, and entered the kitchen with a smile on her face. It was a shock to come face to face with one of the men who had been present in Hardy's store. At least this one had left, so perhaps he was not a threat.

When the introductions were made, neither Amanda nor Bert made any reference to their brief, hardly formal meeting in the store. When he smiled at her warmly, Amanda relaxed a little more and refilled her coffee cup.

"As I was saying, Mrs. Danfield," Bert continued where he had left off when Amanda arrived. "I was hoping to talk with Jason and you both. It's about Brinkman."

"Well," Julie told him, "I don't know exactly when Jase will be back. He rode out pretty early to check on the cattle. That storm the other night took out a large section of fence. So far, in this heat, the cattle have been too lazy to move very far from the pond. But if he has to go chasing cows, it could be a while before he rides back in."

"I understand. I guess it doesn't matter. There was just something else I wanted to clear up with him." Bert looked down into his cup for a few minutes. "Brinkman has made my Pa an offer for the ranch."

Julie felt hope rising like a geyser, but was almost afraid to let it surface. "So?"

Bert Taylor colored, feeling a twinge of shame, knowing he'd come here to ask for help, when all these months this woman had received not an ounce of support from people just like his own folks.

"Pa is against it." He stroked his mustache. "We haven't been able to sell a single horse since that Winston fellow first talked to us. Of course, Pa immediately blamed those new"—he grinned slightly—"infernal machines, as he calls them. But when the fire department purchased new animals from a rancher over in Peabody, and Gil Morgan refused to accept the colt sired from his own stud, we began to realize our troubles might be more serious in nature. Last week Clyde Hardy informed my wife our business would be on a cash-only basis from now on. Mrs. Danfield, I've never been slack on paying our bills. I'm not really even associated with the ranch. It's my older brother who's inherited Pa's knack with the horses. I only ride them to and from the station every day."

"Are you feeling pressured, Bert? Do you feel all that money and power breathing down your neck?"

Bert Taylor didn't flinch away from Julie Danfield's clearly aimed thrust. "Yes, ma'am. And I imagine you've had more than your share of that feeling these past months. It was my thought that maybe we might put our heads together and see what might be done about it."

Julie squealed with delight and jumped up out of her chair and practically buried Bert in an embrace of pure joy. "God bless you, boy. And I thank Him for sending you to us." She released the embarrassed Bert and whirled to Amanda, treating her niece to the same exuberant affection. "We've just been given that fighting chance I've been praying for, Amanda. If it wasn't so early in the day, I'd break out one of Todd's jugs."

When Julie had calmed down a little, Bert added another bit of heartening information. "I think we might also have a pretty strong ally in the mayor. Miles Davis came by the station to talk with me the other day. Winston had Sunday dinner at his home not long ago and suggested Brinkman might be interested in buying the bank. Miles is worried. If Brinkman gets control of the bank and makes our loans, then he'll put shackles on the entire town."

"Hot damn!" Julie hollered, smacking her hands

atop the table. "If we have the mayor with us, we've got better than a fighting chance. I can't wait to tell Jase—"

"Tell Jase what?" the man himself asked as he stepped into the house. His dark green eyes slid over Bert Taylor, but they were not unwelcoming. "'Lo, Bert."

Julie couldn't wait for polite exchanges of greeting. She was on Jason, breaking his ribs, before he could hang his hat. She rattled off the highlights of why Bert was there. "You were right on the money, Jase. It's all starting to happen just like you said it would." She turned to Amanda. "Jason believed from the beginning that Brinkman had his sights set on more than the TJ, but we couldn't prove anything. We couldn't even prove it was Winston, or men he hired, who kept scattering our animals. I thought we had solid proof when somebody took a sledgehammer to the windmill shaft. But like Jase pointed out, it could have just been some young boys up to no good. So we just stayed quiet out here, praying Brinkman would make a mistake folks couldn't ignore." She grinned up at Jason. "And, by golly, I believe he's finally done that."

Jason's return smile was reserved, and in her joy, Julie missed the dark concern in his eyes. "Old girl, I don't want to throw a cloud over your sunny face, but we're a long way from seeing that man out of Stockton. The majority of people in town still see him as their golden god of prosperity. Convincing them otherwise won't be easy, even with the Taylors to back us up."

"We can do it, can't we Bert?"

The mustached man was less cynical than Jason.

Of course, this was a new fight for him, not one he'd been battling for months. "If we can get enough people together, and if they'll listen for five minutes, I believe we'll gain allies."

Julie scowled as she moved away from Jason to fetch him a cup of coffee. "Winston has turned this town against me. I wonder if I'd get two words out of my mouth before doors started slamming in my face."

Again it was Bert Taylor who offered a possible solution. "Founder's Day is this coming Saturday. Everyone will be gathered. Between my family and yours, I imagine we'll be able to corner quite a few into hearing what we have to say."

"Get out your glad rags!" Julie whooped, and began dancing around the kitchen with the spryness of a young girl. "We're going to a party!"

Only Jason saw Amanda stiffen with apprehension at the thought of subjecting herself to Stockton and its possible threat once again. He leaned close and spoke to her softly. "Attending this celebration is strictly voluntary," he assured her. "We'll work something out if you don't feel comfortable about going."

For the next fifteen minutes they organized their course of action. Finally Bert Taylor rose from the table. "Jason, I'd like to speak with you privately for a moment," he requested, looking a little uneasy. "My horse is in the barn. Would you walk out with me? I've got to be getting home anyway."

The two men left together, and Amanda was forced to stall her questions when Sarah yelled from the bedroom. She went to see what the little girl wanted.

When Jason returned alone, Julie immediately started firing questions. "What was that private meeting all about?"

"Nosy, aren't you?" Jason teased. "Mostly it was some old business we needed to resolve. He also wanted to tell me that he'd heard of our need for wire. It seems his pa overestimated his order on fencing last year. They just happen to have several spools of Glidden double-strand stocked in their barn. Bert said we'd be doing them a favor by taking it off their hands. He and his brother Ken will be bringing it out in the morning. They volunteered to help string it as well—since they'll be out here anyway."

Julie stared at Jason in wide-eyed wonder for a long time. Then, without warning, she burst into tears. She sobbed for all those lonely, hopeless months of isolation, being friendless and alone in a community she and Todd had helped found. And she also was weeping for joy, giving free vent to the gladness of renewed hope.

Jason understood her garbled mutterings and let her bawl without interference. She had earned a good cry and more important, needed the release from old anxieties. Julie would have to find renewed strength for what was yet to come.

God, he hated to be the bearer of bad tidings. Especially now, when a small ray of sunshine had finally broken through. Damn Brinkman! he railed silently. Damn Winston and all those other unscrupulous, greedy men populating the earth.

"Julie," he started when she began to sniff and wipe away the tears.

"Goodness," she said unevenly, dabbing at his

wet shirtfront with her apron. "I've soaked you to the skin."

"Julie," he tried once again, "I . . ."

Her smile, and the happiness radiating from her sweet old face, nearly defeated him. How could he tell her, destroy this rare moment? He couldn't, he realized. Not now. Maybe later. Certainly he would have to tell her about the bull soon, and then he'd be forced to watch her reaction, the fear and fury return.

He'd discovered the animal was missing this morning when he made his customary check on the herd. It was unlike the lazy old Angus to wander far from his harem. He'd finally located the animal two hours later, miles from the herd, lying dead only a few feet away from the reservoir next to the windmill. And floating atop those few inches of stagnant water left in the tank were birds, poisoned by the same substance that had killed the bull. Brinkman—or Winston acting in his stead—had delivered a clear-cut warning. Their patience was at an end.

"Jase?" Julie asked, finally seeing the distress she'd missed earlier. "Is something wrong?"

He opened his mouth to tell her and get it over with, but the words clogged in his throat when Amanda reentered the room. "I just wanted to caution you not to expect too much Saturday."

"I'm not looking for miracles; I just want to make a few folks squirm, and maybe tickle their consciences a bit. I've got a whole year of grievances stored up. Matter of fact, the two of you had better keep me under a close watch. I'm liable to take a notion to bust somebody."

Jason had to grin at that. "Well, that might

depend on just who it is you intend to wallop. I might cheer you on." He turned his attention toward Amanda. "Where's our pickle this morning? I haven't seen much of her lately."

The caressing sweep of his eyes and the husky rasp of his voice did strange things in the deep pit of her stomach, making it difficult for her to speak. "She . . . she's in her room, and a little put out with us. Sarah doesn't understand why she was banished from the table while Mr. Taylor was here."

"Well, I'll go see if I can cheer her up," Jason said.

"That would be very nice of you, Jason. She's very fond of you and has missed the time the two of you used to spend together."

"I've missed her, too," Jason said quietly. "She's a very special little girl. Reminds me of her mother," he added as he passed by Amanda, his shoulder brushing lightly with her own when he exited the kitchen.

With Jason out of the room, Julie turned to Amanda with a tender smile. "Now, there goes a truly good man. How he managed to turn out so fine is truly a miracle; probably the only one Reverend Thorne is ever likely to claim. I wonder if that old bastard is still preaching." She seemed to shudder slightly, not seeing Amanda's similar reaction to the subject of Reverend Thorne. "I pity any community saddled with that crazy fanatic. It was justice, pure and simple, when folks turned on him and that cold-fish wife of his. Henry Blane—drunkard and useless excuse for a man that he was—needed someone to blame for what he considered Lucy's shame. Of course, if it hadn't been for Henry's big mouth, nobody would have known for certain she was in the family way before she and Jase eloped. Since he didn't have Jason around to flog, he turned on the Reverend. Henry claimed it was Reverend Thorne who had kept and sheltered the bad seed of the whore's spawn. Which was true enough, but not because that supposed minister of God had any compassion or charity in his hard heart.

"He sheltered Jason for one reason, and one reason only. Thorne took that innocent infant before he was even an hour old; probably before that unfortunate woman took her last breath. She either couldn't, or wouldn't, name Jason's father; a fact which must have pleased the Reverend to no end. He then proceeded to use that child—blameless for his parent's sins—and commenced to blackmail every man in this town who'd ever paid a visit to that small shack where Jase's mother had set up business. And there must have been quite a few, considering Reverend Thorne's success."

"Blackmail?" Amanda gasped. "Surely not!"

Julie's expression was grim. "Not for money. He wanted to insure his position. Since he was the last person to see Jason's mother alive, few were willing to take the risk she might have revealed a name. They were terrified of having their names blasted out from the pulpit some Sunday. Todd and me just quit going to church. I realize now we did wrong. We might have been able to help Jason, stop that old lunatic from tossing the boy at his congregation's heads week after week. It's no wonder folks started hating the sight of him. . . ."

Julie's voice trailed off while Amanda's skin tingled with gooseflesh. Never would she forget those burning black eyes, the booming voice condemning—

"Goodness," Julie uttered. "How'd I get on that subject? Oh, yes, I was saying what a wonder it is Jason turned out so fine. One of these days, Amanda, some lucky female is going to reap the benefits of all the loving Jason has stored up inside. Whoo'ee!" she hollered, giving her niece a bold wink.

Amanda's face flamed hot as she glanced away. "Auntie, I—I'd very much like to know about the TJ's troubles sometime soon."

"No time like the present," Julie said affably. "But let's get these dishes soaking while we talk. This molasses is getting rock hard."

While the kettle was boiling, Julie told Amanda of the foreman she'd trusted. "Stoney was a good man, and I needed someone who could walk into saloons and cattlemen's clubs, where a woman would cause a fuss, if not raise a few roofs." She went on to explain how Stoney Markum had carried her power of attorney, in order that contracts could be made on the spot, rather than waiting for her permission.

"Stoney had a good head on his shoulders. A bit too good, I discovered after he met up with Brinkman. Anyway, we'd had a few rough years after Todd died. Part of that was my fault. I just lost heart for a while without him. But last year was going to make up for the past five. We'd had a mild winter, and an even better spring and summer. The herd was fat, healthy, and the market was ripe. Stoney took off for the Kansas City Cattlemen's Meeting like he did every year. I'll swear to my dying day he didn't leave this ranch with the idea of robbing me blind.

That got planted when he met Brinkman. I'm sure of it.

"I'd say Mr. Brinkman must have convinced Stoney he'd been wasting his time and breaking his back all these years, and was nearly fifty years old with nothing to show for all that effort. The long and the short of this, Amanda, is that Stoney Markum sold Brinkman the entire herd. Then he collected his traitor's fee and took off for parts unknown to retire in style."

Amanda was watching Julie's face so closely her fingers were nearly scalded by the boiling water Julie was pouring into the dishpan. The shock and pain of that betrayal had not faded for Julie. Neither had the fury which could still blaze strong in those brown eyes more accustomed to loving and laughter. "Wasn't there anything the police could do?" A crime had been committed. Had nothing been done to catch the criminal?

"Oh, the Kansas City police sniffed around some. But I've never believed they put too much effort into locating Stoney. I would imagine Brinkman has a few influential friends in the city government. The sheriff here was helpless to do anything. It was out of his jurisdiction.

"So, about three weeks after Stoney disappeared, I was forced to stand by and watch forty years of careful breeding being driven off the TJ range to be slaughtered. And it was also the first and only time I met Mr. Brinkman himself. I suspect the man came to gloat. Stood there and smirked at me the entire day. Amanda, I've never had the urge to shoot somebody before, but—" Her dark expression lingered for a few minutes, then brightened into a smile of wry humor. "You should have seen his face after he discovered Stoney had miscounted the herd. The sheriff was here keeping things legal, so there wasn't anything that bastard could do while I took my time picking out the finest fifty."

Julie seemed to savor the memory. Amanda didn't push her to continue. The dishes were put in to soak and the table cleared and washed of crumbs before Julie went on with her story.

"Without cattle to run there wasn't any reason to keep the hands on. Most of them left right away, a few stayed on for a while. But after I'd cleared up all the expenses for the previous year, I could see they'd have to go as well. So before they rode out, I stocked up on supplies for the winter and got ready to hibernate. It was a bad time, Amanda. A very bad time. I'd never been alone in my entire life, and all of a sudden the only company I had was the sound of the winter wind screaming in through the windows. And when it wasn't blowing, this place was silent as a grave. Sometimes I thought I'd go plumb batty. . . ."

When her aunt's voice broke entirely, Amanda led her to a chair and urged her to sit down. She pulled a hankie from the pocket of her skirt. "Here, use this instead of your apron."

Julie managed to snort out a small chuckle and blew her nose with enthusiasm. "My mama would have had a fit if she'd seen me wiping my face with an apron. You know, at one time I was a city prissy just like you, Amanda Jean. So there is hope for you. Look how well I turned out."

Amanda couldn't entirely share Julie's lightness. "Auntie, why did you never write and tell me what had happened? Did you think I cared so little?"

"Lordy no, child. You'd just buried your husband not long before, and I knew you had enough on your mind. Besides, admitting I'd been hoodwinked stuck in my throat. I wasn't having much to do with anybody. Maybe that's one of the reasons my friends turned away. Could be I turned my back on them first. Anyway, it didn't appear I was going to make a go of this place on my own. Selling out to Brinkman seemed the only solution. The lonelier I got, the better Grant Winston and that stingy contract he carried in his pocket started to look."

"Where does Jason come into this?" Outside she could hear Sarah's laughter blending with his. It was a good sound.

"Well, I'd say that's another miracle for the books. He claims he was passing through Kansas on his way to Denver, and just stopped by to say hello."

"Don't you believe him?"

Julie grinned a little strangely. "Honey, at the time, I was too sick to question anything. I had the fever and Jase moved in bag and baggage. First thing he did was tell Winston where hell could be located. Then, when I could stand on my feet again, he contacted the Pinkerton Agency to locate Stoney and investigate Brinkman. The rest I think you know."

No, Amanda didn't know. Not nearly enough. The questions began pouring out of her like a flood, especially ones concerning Jason. Julie answered one or two, and then begged off. "Honey, my throat is raw from talking so much. Let's get these dishes out of the way. I've let so much bottled-up emotion fly this morning, it's plumb taken the wind out of me."

On the blanket they'd spread over the dry grass of the meadow, Sarah pretended to feed one of her dolls part of her sandwich. Sarah's entire collection of dolls had come out to participate in their picnic. There were blondes, brunettes, redheads, and a few bald dollies from a younger age.

On her small corner, Amanda watched as Jason came toward them. Her expression was one of bemusement after witnessing that agile vault over the fence, which had lost little spring or height in twelve years.

"May I join you, ladies?" he asked, removing his hat, running his fingers through the raven thickness of his hair.

"If you can find a spot to sit down," Amanda said with an amused smile as her eyes swept the doll-laden blanket.

Sarah immediately went about solving the problem. "Oh, Mabel can sit over here with Georgia, and Kathleen can move next to Joanna . . ." And so it went until adequate space had been cleared.

Amanda passed him the picnic basket. "We don't have much to offer. There is some chicken left, and part of a ham sandwich. If we'd known you'd be joining us, we wouldn't have been quite so gluttonous."

"It won't kill me to cut back on one meal," he said, patting a stomach that didn't carry a single inch of flab, drawing Amanda's attention to his lean, and sinewy form. How many other times, she wondered, had they sat together in this very spot, on days exactly like this one? A lump rose in her throat, and she washed it down with a sip of tepid tea.

Examining the mason jar she was using for a glass, Amanda said, "When I first arrived here, I missed so many conveniences. Plumbing headed my list. Now I believe I could live quite happily without hot running water, telephones, and electric lighting, if I only had ice for my tea."

"Maybe someday the TJ will have all those things," he offered.

"Maybe," she agreed. "Jason, I want to thank you for—" she looked down into her lap, smoothing her skirt over her knees, "for many things. But most of all for being here when Aunt Julie—"

"Don't," he said abruptly, uncomfortable with her uneasy gratitude.

Amanda was afraid her stiff manner would be misconstrued as insincere. But with Sarah present it was impossible to speak freely.

"Who is this pretty thing?" Jason asked, picking up the doll closest to his right hip in an effort to ease the strain.

"That's Mary," Sarah answered. "She's four years old now. And she's not very pretty anymore. See those scratches on her face? I didn't used to be very careful. Her hair's nearly all gone, too. But I think I love Mary best."

Amanda had to smile at that. At one time or another Sarah loved each and every one of her dolls the very best. Jason was watching that smile, and the love behind it. It caused an ache inside of him, a longing to see that tenderness upon her face when she looked at him. He let his gaze slide over this woman he loved so badly it hurt. She wore her hair in a high, feminine pompadour today. Tendrils curled at her temples and behind her ears, and the silky locks seemed to radiate with the heat he knew was also in her passion. The blouse she wore was simple, unadorned with laces or frills, but the way it flowed over her breasts—

When he felt that hot stab of desire, Jason pulled his gaze away. "Tell me about some of your other friends, Pickle."

"Oh, dear, you'll regret this," Amanda said in a low undertone.

Ten minutes later Jason knew only the surface had been scratched, and still the history of the dolls went on. Sarah had concocted elaborate backgrounds for each and every one of her dolls, and would expand on the stories whenever inspired. But when Amanda would have come to his rescue, he wouldn't allow it, insisting, "I *did* ask for this." After another ten minutes or so, he was looking at Amanda and fairly pleading for the reprieve he'd previously refused. She smiled and let him suffer.

Eventually Sarah ran out of dolls. Amanda quickly encouraged her daughter to pack her things away. "Honey, why don't you start taking things back to the house. We have a lot to carry back. It will probably take two trips or more."

When Sarah was reluctantly carrying the first armload of her toys across the meadow, Amanda began to wonder if sending the little girl away had been wise. Jason was watching her closely, and she felt her skin heating beneath his intent regard.

"Jason, what are our actual chances with Stockton and Brinkman?"

A single eyebrow lifted. "Our?" he drawled. "Are you including yourself in this fight, Amanda?"

Her lowered chin snapped up, and the golden eyes flared hotly. "You would not accept my gratitude, and prevented the apology I had intended to follow. Consequently, I refuse to be subjected to your sarcasm now."

She felt badly enough about her childish behavior of late. But he didn't have to continue flogging her with it unnecessarily. She rose to her knees and began packing their lunch away with furious movements.

"You've a short fuse, Pepper," Jason told her as he took her by the shoulders and forced her to sit back down. "That was pleasure you heard in my voice, not sarcasm." He lowered his lean body onto the blanket, reclining on his side to prop his head on his hand. "If there are any apologies forthcoming, I'm the one who should be making the speeches. I hurled a lot of hard things at you yesterday. Some were fair. Some weren't. And I've been thinking about your leaving. Maybe you should go away someplace until this is settled. Not that I believe there is any danger of violence. It's just that things might get really unpleasant and tense."

"You *want* me to leave?"

"Don't be unnecessarily stupid, Mandy. You know better," he said with husky suggestiveness. "It would only be temporary. A week or so over in Peabody until we know how folks are going to respond on Founder's Day. They have a decent hotel. You and Sarah would be very comfortable."

While Amanda was contemplating Jason's sudden shift in attitude, he was going over the reasons that had spurred him to reconsider their safety. Finding the dead bull this morning had alarmed Jason. He'd always been so positive Brinkman was a man who preferred using subtle methods of persuasion, tactics requiring subterfuge and finesse which were impossible to prove. Until today Brinkman had followed that type of program, using propaganda, and occasional harmless sabotage. Dead bulls and contaminated water, however, constituted a real crime and left indisputable evidence behind. It also spoke of a rash, desperate carelessness, as did this unnecessarily premature attempt to ruin the Taylors. Why, after months of exhibiting the kind of patience required for hell to freeze over, would Brinkman now start making stupid mistakes?

Julie, who'd been madder than a wet hen over the loss of her prized bull, had ventured an opinion. She believed Winston might be calling his own shots. Since the TJ obviously wasn't foundering, nor did starvation of its occupants seem imminent, perhaps Winston feared the loss of his position with Brinkman. If Julie was correct, Jason had every reason to be worried. Winston was an ass—an incompetent, bungling, dangerous ass.

"Jason," Amanda said sharply after several futile attempts to break through his distracted state. "Is something wrong? You look very disturbed."

His eyes refocused and moved over her face, lingering on every feature. "I guess you caught me wool-gathering," he evaded with a smile. It was his own decision not to tell Amanda about this most recent incident. At least not for the time being. "Have you decided?"

"I'll go to Peabody," she conceded. "But please

understand it's primarily for Sarah's sake. I must consider her welfare first and foremost."

"I'm not going to argue that point, Amanda. I love her, too."

Amanda felt a sudden, poignant ache to hear those words of love spoken man to woman. She shifted her gaze away. "What are the honest odds of convincing Stockton that Brinkman has evil purposes?"

"They're certainly better than they were yesterday now that the Taylors are in this as well. But they're a stubborn, pigheaded lot. They won't be easily swayed from their dreams of new wealth."

"How is it that you were able to see through Brinkman so clearly?"

He rolled to his back and pillowed his head upon folded arms, squinting as the sun fell full upon his face. "Most have never traveled more than fifty miles from here. They're innocents in a way. They don't know the Brinkmans of the world, haven't met them in every town and city from the Appalachians to the Rockies, and on to the Pacific. North, south, east, and west, men exist with their lust for power, their greed to possess and control. The money and profit they hope to gain are secondary. Their egos demand they own everything in sight and dominate absolutely."

She heard no rancor in his tone, only pragmatic certainty. "If you've made the acquaintance of so many, you must have traveled a great deal."

"I have," he said simply.

Seeing that he wasn't going to offer any information, she hesitated to probe further. Yesterday, she would have let this subject drop. Today she desperately wanted to know more about the years gone by. "Doing what?"

Shielding his eyes with his hand, he studied her long and hard, not really certain he wanted to pursue this topic quite yet, and definitely not in any great detail right now. Still, he'd walked right into this.

"Blowing things up mostly," he finally said. "It's my specialty."

"I don't understand," she said, truly confused.

"Explosives," he clarified without embellishment.

"Isn't that rather dangerous?" Her voice was suddenly tight with fear.

"It has its moments," he said lightly. "I'm very good, Amanda. I'm also very, very cautious. And, as you can see, I'm still all of a piece." He flexed his arms and lifted his legs. "There are no parts missing or nonfunctional."

The slow grin caused her paling face to heat. For different reasons, both adults were very glad when Sarah came skipping back for the rest of her dolls. Jason rose immediately and offered to help the little girl carry her things back. "I'd better stop lazing around and start rigging a crosspole for the wagon. Thank you for sharing your lunch with me."

"It wasn't much," Amanda apologized.

His gaze lingered upon her upturned face, on the slightly parted lips. "On the contrary, Amanda. It was a great deal."

As they walked across the meadow, Amanda heard Jason teasing Sarah. "Pickle, some of your friends weigh a ton. You'd better keep them away from the pastries and cakes."

"You're silly, Jason," Sarah said, giggling.

And also very tender and kind, loving a little girl who needs his affection, Amanda acknowledged. She watched as he vaulted easily back over the fence and then retrieved the dolls he'd handed to Sarah. Very gently he placed them upon the ground and reached for the little girl. When he swung her up and over the high rails, Sarah clung to him, receiving a big hug and a kiss before he put her down and went on about his own business.

There had once been another young girl who had also known the gentle strength in him when climbing fences to reach or leave this meadow.

Was the hurt so terrible . . .?

Chapter Thirteen

AMANDA TRIED TO PUSH THAT QUESTION AWAY. IT would not be banished.

"Was the hurt so terrible?" she asked herself, sitting back on the blanket to gaze out across this meadow, remembering all the times she'd shared the sunsets with Jason in this place; recalling a sudden summer squall, and a girl's first kiss.

The talk of Founder's Day, Reverend Thorne, and Lucy Blane had brought all those old memories very close to the surface. They seemed to clamor to be set free, released from the darkness where she'd locked them away.

Was it time to take them out, let them loose where they might wreck havoc with her emotions? Or wasn't it possible that, when examined rationally, they would cease to badger and haunt, and could be put to rest?

Amanda held very, very still. She weighed all the consequences—or so she thought. How could a memory bring harm? It had been so very many years ago, and she'd been so foolishly young and unsophisticated. Ignorant, actually. Not so much in age, but in her level of maturity. A late bloomer, they'd called her, slow to flower into her womanhood.

She'd been *too* innocent. Much like an infant just learning to explore the world around him and grabbing at anything capturing his fancy; not realizing the shiny object he coveted was a kettle, or that the stove beneath his desire was dangerously hot.

Jason had been Amanda's kettle, and she'd reached for him with both hands, without a single thought to the pain of being burned. . . .

Amanda slept lightly, restlessly. The faint tapping on the window awakened her instantly. She was out of bed and on her knees before the open window in seconds. "Where have you been?" she whispered. "I've been so worried!" Seeing Jason's face eased some of her frantic anxiety, but his wretched expression brought it all back in a hurry. "What's wrong?" she exclaimed.

"Hush," he told her in a low growl. "Meet me in the barn. I have to see you."

"Now?"

"Please, Mandy," he pleaded urgently. Not waiting for her response, he whirled away and loped out of sight.

Without a single thought to her robe and slippers, Amanda tiptoed through the house, sneaking carefully past her aunt and uncle's room, pausing briefly to hear the reassuring sound of Uncle Todd's snores. Aunt Julie, she knew well, slept like the dead.

The bunkhouse was dark, and it seemed even the night creatures were unusually silent. Outside the barn she looked around her, a little hesitant to step inside that pitch blackness alone.

"Jason?" she called softly.

"Here," he answered, pushing the door open just enough to pull her inside. The lantern glowed softly, casting shadows on his grim face. She didn't hesitate, flinging herself into his arms, hugging his neck so tightly that he groaned softly in pain.

"Oh, Jason, your foster father is a horrible man. After you ran away, he grabbed me and wouldn't let go. He said awful things about hell and the devil."

"Damn him," Jason said vehemently, holding her closer. "May God damn him to hell for that. Why didn't you run like I told you?"

She sniffed and wiped her eyes on the sleeve of her nightgown. "I kicked him," she told him a little sheepishly. "Hard," she added.

"Good," he spat. "I hope you broke his leg. What exactly did he say?"

Amanda pulled back a little so she could look at him.

"Crazy things. He was all wild and raving like a madman. I was really scared, Jason. He didn't make any sense at all."

Jason was gently smoothing her hair. But his eyes were so haunted they frightened her more than Reverend Thorne. "What's wrong? Why are you looking at me like that?"

"Why did this happen now?" he said more to himself than to her. "It wouldn't have mattered before. I wouldn't have known the difference. God!" he cried, pressing his face to her hair, his hands roaming across her back. "Why now?"

His voice had become a harsh croak. Amanda felt the pain and despair in him, though she could not fathom the cause. Her instincts were to offer comfort, and she stroked his trembling shoulders, moved her hands over the tensed muscles of his back.

When his mouth sought hers in a bruising kiss, she never thought to complain about the punishing force. Nor did she question the heated urgency within him as he cupped her hips and brought her hard against him and she felt his body changing through the thin fabric of her gown. Then it seemed as if his hands were everywhere, heating her flesh, sometimes hurting the tender budding of her breasts. Something deep inside her began to ache.

"Jason, I feel funny," she said, pulling away from his embrace. "I hurt way down here." She spread her fingers low on her belly, and saw him shudder and swallow hard.

"I want to look at you, Mandy. Would you let me look at you?"

She didn't understand the strained tension, or the husky fervor of his request. "You *are* looking at me, silly."

"No," he rasped. "I mean with your nightgown off."

Her eyes flew wide, and instinctively she clutched the high buttons on her gown. "Off? You mean look at me . . . naked?" she squeaked. Amanda couldn't remember the last time she'd stood naked, even before her own mother. The changes in her body this last year made her uncomfortable with herself. She didn't think she wanted to do this. Not even for Jason.

As if he read her answer in her eyes, Jason made a deep, gut-ripping sound in his throat. "I—I'm sorry. Forget I asked that. . . ." He spun on his heel and marched toward the back of the barn, his hands stuffed deep into his pockets.

She could barely see him in the thick shadows, but the strange choked sounds coming from him were awful. Never had she heard a man cry. Or maybe he was laughing? It could have been one or the other. Somehow she couldn't think it was amusement. Jason wouldn't laugh at her silliness. He would yell, or glower, but never would he make fun of her. But why would he cry?

"Jason, are you mad at me?"

"No," she heard him say gruffly, adding, "it's all right, Mandy. I shouldn't have asked. I had no right, no damned right at all. Jesus, I'm as foul as he said to ask that of you."

"You are not!" she breathed vehemently. Almost of their own volition, her fingers undid the buttons at her throat, and grasped the hem of her gown. She had it yanked over her head before her mind could muster a second thought.

From the darkness came the most vicious, ugly curse she'd ever heard. It didn't take a great deal of sophistication to recognize the foulness, even if she hadn't the slightest idea to the meaning. Her entire body quaked with shame. She snatched up her gown and held it before her, covering herself, wanting to die because he'd found her so ugly. Tears ran down her cheeks, blinding her, and then a soft, muted wail erupted from her heaving chest. Then Jason's arms were around her, and his hands were smoothing over her shoulders. He was whispering things about her skin, praising what he'd seen so briefly. She didn't believe a single word.

"Don't pity me!" she snapped, jerking away from him. "I know my body is ugly. I'm not like the other girls at school. They make fun of me—"

"You're perfect," he insisted, yanking on the cloth she held tight against her chest. "Let go, Mandy. I want to see."

He asked so sweetly, with such tender reverence, she let him draw the nightgown from her hands. "Beautiful," he said with emotion. "Small and perfect."

He began to caress her so gently that she hardly felt his fingers as they traced and explored almost every inch of her naked skin. "This is wrong, Amanda," he said, even as his caresses grew bolder, more tangible, bringing back that strange aching.

"Oh, I feel funny again. What is it, Jason? What causes my belly to feel so empty and full all at once?"

"Here?" he asked, sliding his palm down over her stomach, going lower and lower until she gasped and her knees buckled.

"Yes . . . right there. What are you doing?"

Jason drew her toward a bed of loose hay, gently

urging her down. When he'd taken his fingers away, Amanda knew a conflict never before felt.

"Why did you stop?" From the look on his face, he seemed to be struggling with his own tumult.

"Do you trust me?" he whispered, looking down into her face. "I swear I won't hurt you, but I need to touch you so badly I'm dying inside. You're so sweet and giving, Mandy. I . . . I have to know . . . need just once . . . ." His eyes closed on a shuddering breath. "But I won't if you're afraid, or if you don't want me to."

"I'm not afraid, Jason," she said softly, touching his arm. "It's just that when you . . . did that, I felt . . . *strange*."

He'd shifted to lie beside her, his fingers gently tracing over her face. "I'd die before hurting you, Mandy. Maybe you'd better put your gown back on. I'm afraid I won't be able to stop when I should. I don't know if I could."

"It didn't exactly hurt, Jason," she explained, not wanting him to think he'd caused her pain. He hadn't. Not really. "It only ached funny."

"Like this," he whispered against her mouth as his hands began to stroke her flesh again, and he kissed her deeply, letting his tongue explore the soft recesses of her mouth. "And like this?" His head dipped and she felt a wetness on her breast which heightened the feeling beneath that other caress.

"Ohhh," she cried softly when she felt his mouth close over her nipple. The rhythmic tugging there, coupled with the fever rising beneath his fingers made her entire body arch up off the hay. "Jaaa . . . son!"

Deep inside little tremors grew to throbs until it seemed all the blood in her body had centered in that place between her thighs. It grew hot, and then little explosions went off inside, and she felt as if the heat were spreading outward. When the pulses stilled and her flesh had cooled, Amanda saw that he was watching her. His dark eyes were passion-filled, and his voice was raw with emotion when he spoke. "You are so beautiful. I'll never forget . . ." He rolled to his feet, but was back seconds later with her gown, pulling her boneless body off the hay to pull the concealing cotton over her head. "When you've decided to hate me I want you to remember two things." He took her hand and pressed it against the fly of his trousers, molding her palm to the rigid swelling there, his features going taut when her curiosity had her exploring the length and breadth of this wondrous discovery.

"Enough," he finally grated harshly. "It's enough for you to remember. Someday you'll understand. . . ."

With his arm around her waist, he led her out of the barn. In the moonlight she thought she saw tears on his cheeks before he hugged her fiercely. "Remember that it was never a lie with you, Mandy. Try to forgive me if you can."

"I don't understand—"

"I love you, Mandy. Remember that always. . . ."

So many years, a lifetime ago. Amanda dashed her fingers at the wetness streaking down her face in a flood, but she couldn't stem the tide. Until six weeks ago she'd never seen Jason again. By the next dawn he'd been gone, eloping with the girl who was going to bear him a child, though it would be many years before this particular aspect was fully comprehended.

Had the hurt been so terrible?

Yes . . . and no.

It had been agony to know Jason was gone from her forever, torture to hear he had taken a wife, because marriage was for a lifetime. Yet, all the while, Amanda had clung desperately to Jason's parting words, her youthful naïveté allowing her to believe absolutely what logic and reason would later tell her simply could not be.

It had been the last summer of her childhood, and the dawning of the woman she'd finally become.

Jason had been put away in a most secret, guarded part of her being until eventually his memory had become much like a sweet dream which, upon awakening, drifts softly from recall.

The Taylor brothers arrived at the crack of dawn to wolf down the huge breakfast Julie and Amanda had prepared. Ken Taylor was several years older than his brother, and not at all the dapper image Bert projected. He was tall and lanky, his raw-boned features showing a serious nature. But he smiled easily enough when Julie Danfield teased him about the impossible amount of food he could put away and then take seconds.

The men were sent off with mounds of sandwiches while Julie fretted there wouldn't be enough for them to eat if Ken was along. The day was long, and Amanda discovered she was restless, bored with the routine of ordinary chores. Inwardly she laughed at herself for feeling jealous of the men who were stringing wire to posts she'd helped set. But somehow she felt as if she'd had the cake without the icing in not seeing the entire job through.

The moon was already rising by the time the wagon came back in. Amanda followed Julie outside. Sarah hung back near the door, developing a sudden shyness of strangers, peeking around the corner of the house while Bert Taylor teased her with silly faces.

"The wife is expecting another one in the fall," he informed Amanda with pride. "With the two boys, we're really hoping for a girl. I'd be tickled to death with something as sweet and pretty as that little thing over there."

Amanda heard almost nothing of Bert's attempts at conversation. Jason had turned around for Julie, showing the back of a shirt dark with dried blood. Amanda's sharp indrawn breath, stifled Bert's ramblings.

"It's not as bad as it looks, Mrs. Ames. A staple didn't hold and the wire backlashed just as he was moving away. Are you all right, ma'am? You look a little pale."

"Fine," she said absently, walking toward the injured man, reaching him in time to hear Ken Taylor tell Julie, "I doused it with iodine when it happened. You might have a look at it later. Could have been worse. I once saw a man lose an eye—"

"Ken," Jason cautioned swiftly. "I don't think the ladies need to hear that." Neither Julie nor Amanda appeared to have much color, but the younger woman appeared near tears. It puzzled him.

Julie recovered quickly. "Anybody else hurt?"

"Just the usual pricks and scratches," Ken Taylor assured her. "Well, let's get this wagon unloaded and the horses unhitched so we can get ourselves home. Mrs. Danfield, we discussed tomorrow and decided to meet at our place about ten o'clock. We all agreed that presenting a united front right off would make folks take some notice." He didn't add that there was a certain safety in numbers, but it hung there unspoken between them all.

In a short time the Taylors were on their way to Fairmont. The minute they were out of sight, Julie turned her mother-hen eye on Jason. "You get to the bunkhouse and start filling a tub," she ordered. "I want your back whistle clean. And if you can't reach to scrub it good yourself, I'll be washing it for you."

Jason glanced at Amanda, who was already returning to the house. A twinkle ignited in his eyes. "I'll manage, but I'd appreciate not having to come to the table for supper. Do you think you could arrange to bring my meal with the iodine?"

Julie followed that telling stare. "I suppose you'd rather have something more appealing than my old mug come with your supper, too?" The grin that spread across his face was absolutely wicked, causing Julie to blush as she hadn't done in years. "You'd best not be thinking of being too rambunctious with that hurt back. Besides, early as it is, I imagine Sarah is still fidgety enough to go roaming."

The smile faded to a glower, and Julie was chuckling when she walked off.

Jason was stretched out on his belly across his bed when the knock came.

"Come in," he hollered sleepily, his eyelids growing heavy. The warm bath and the mattress felt too good, and Jason was already half asleep. He really wasn't expecting Amanda. It had been wishful thinking since the first. She would find some way to avoid being alone with him.

His eyes opened wide when a slender form passed his bed and placed a basket on the table. "I'll be damned . . ." he mumbled beneath his breath, seeing but not believing. Not once did she glance his way as she unpacked the contents of the basket, and then went in search of his few pieces of silver and china. In minutes his meal was waiting for him, hot and steaming, and Amanda was calling him to the table. He hadn't thought she realized he was even in the room.

The lady in question was anything but oblivious. In fact, if he'd seen her face when she'd entered and discovered him sprawled across the bed, his darkly tanned skin contrasting sharply with the white bed linens, Jason would have taken heart that the time for his patience was nearly at an end.

Amanda's instincts, from the first, had warned her to leave the past alone, keep it buried deep. For a very long time she'd let those inherently wise impulses protect her fairly well. Then yesterday she'd sent them packing, deciding to take the rational approach. Now her emotions were running willynilly and out of control. She hadn't even enough common sense left to have flatly refused her aunt's request she play nursemaid to Jason's injured back.

He'd been so still, Amanda had almost decided he was sleeping until she turned toward that big brass bed to find him watching her.

"Your supper is ready," she said in a small,

strained voice. If he responded verbally, Amanda didn't hear. She was being drawn into the depths of those forest-green eyes, being called by powers beyond herself to become lost and be glad for it. "Aren't you hungry?" she asked again when he didn't immediately rise.

"Famished," he said, pushing himself up off the bed, and quickly approached the table. But Jason's gaze was not on the food as he stood before her, wondering if his thundering heart was visible as it slammed against the naked wall of his chest.

Amanda averted her eyes from his smooth, glorious skin. She reached into the pocket of her apron and pulled out a bottle of iodine and a folded pad of linen. "Turn around," she requested. "I'll put some of this on your back."

Despite her stiff tone, Jason sensed the change in her and he couldn't quite take it in. He didn't dare put too much faith in his own intuition right now. His emotions and needs were too powerful and might color his judgment. The wrong thing done or said might tear apart that fragile bridge he'd felt between them these past two days. Getting a strong grip on his desires, Jason gave Amanda an easy smile.

"That's a good way to spoil a man's appetite, Amanda," he said, taking the antiseptic from her fingers, putting it aside. "If you don't mind, I'll postpone the torture until after I've eaten."

"Oh, of course," she said in a rush. "I'll come back later, then."

He touched her shoulder lightly when she would have turned toward the door. "Don't," he said almost too urgently, quickly attempting to cover his mistake with a slight cough. "Please stay and keep me company. I'm too accustomed to conversation being served along with my meals. I doubt I could eat alone now."

After that pleasantly phrased appeal, Amanda knew she'd appear ridiculous if she ran out now. But, dear Lord, how was she going to survive looking at his half-naked body and not reveal how it affected her?

"All right," she finally agreed.

"Good," he said congenially as he threw his leg over the chair and sat down at the table in a single fluid motion. "It appears there's enough tea for two here. In fact, there's enough food for six. Help yourself to a plate and a glass and join me if you want."

"Thank you, but I've already had supper. I might have some tea, though."

She didn't really want the beverage. However, fetching herself a glass was a way to distract herself from the man who disturbed her more by the minute. She spent an inordinately ridiculous length of time looking over the shelves in this small kitchen area of the bunkhouse. "You've arranged this room very efficiently," she commented, pushing cups and saucers around on the shelf. "How do you find the time to keep everything so neatly placed and clean?"

Jason speared a forkful of Julie's snap beans. "For one, I don't spend enough time in here to dirty the place usually. Most of the time it's pretty cluttered, but I gave the place a fair cleaning last night."

"I wouldn't have thought you would have had the energy after struggling with rigging that crosspole all afternoon and long after dark yesterday." She had turned back around, but chose to keep this short distance between them for now.

"Some nights I don't sleep very well. It helps to keep busy," he said with a casual shrug, wondering if she would guess it was thoughts of her that kept him awake. And unless he turned his thoughts right now, she'd see the source of his discomfort the minute he stood up from the table.

Amanda finally brought her glass and joined him at the table. Adding several spoonfuls of sugar, she stirred the amber beverage until not a crystal of the sweetener remained to cloud the liquid. Beneath the concealing drape of her lashes, she was surreptitiously letting her eyes roam over his chest and shoulders. His skin appeared as smooth and lustrous as rich satin in the glow of the overhead lantern. He was a man beautifully made.

"Did I hear Ken Taylor say you finished stringing the entire line today?" she asked quickly when he caught her looking at him.

The fork paused midway to his mouth, and the corners of his lips quirked. "Three experienced men can do a lot in a short time. But listen to you. Just then you sounded the experienced old rancher's wife. Where has the city girl gone?"

"Oh, she's still around to plague me." She laughed. "She made an appearance this afternoon when Aunt Julie sent me out for that chicken on your plate. I doubt I'll ever accustom myself to neck-wringing."

He looked down at the golden-brown delight on his plate and gave a small shudder. "I might do a little cringing at that myself, Mrs. Ames. Lady, you've got grit."

The quiver of his muscles made her mouth go dry. "Not really. I do it because it's necessary, not because it gets any easier with practice."

"As I said, you've got grit. Courage is looking what we fear or despise in the face, and going ahead with it anyway. You don't lack courage, Amanda."

"Maybe," she said with a shrug. "Were you afraid when you were handling dynamite and blowing things up?"

"Always," he said flatly. "Fear is one of the first things I was taught when I went into the trade. A wise man warned me that the day you stop being afraid, then life has lost its meaning and you're a dead man anyway."

"Are you saying fear is healthy?"

"In the proper perspective. Strong emotions remind you you're alive. When you can't feel them, or won't allow yourself to feel them, then you are not really living. Fear, hate, and love are a part of life. Anything that holds those feelings in check is a living death. But any one of those three can overwhelm and conquer the others."

"What happens then?" she asked softly.

His eyes were deeply intense upon her face. "We either find heaven, or make our lives hell on earth. So there you have the Thorne philosophy on life. Does it make any sense?"

"No," she admitted on a short chuckle. "I believe the world is a bit more complicated. But since it's *your* philosophy, my comprehension isn't really required."

"I wouldn't say that," he drawled, then braced himself for the question it was time to pose. "Are you ready for your stay in Peabody?"

Amanda looked down and fingered her glass. "I've already packed a few things for Sarah and myself, if you're still willing to drive us to Peabody, that is." When he didn't respond immediately, her eyes returned to his impassive face. "Jason, if it weren't for Sarah—"

"I understand," he told her, and he meant it, too. Amanda was doing what she felt was right for herself and her child. He had no call to feel this plunging disappointment. He smiled at her gently and was glad to see the apologetic guilt fade from her golden eyes. He then pushed away from the table. "I guess it's time to take my medicine like a man," he said, and handed her the bottle of iodine. "Do your worst, woman. Just be merciful and quick about it."

When he presented his back, Amanda's breath caught sharply at the sight of those long scratches and deep punctures running in a narrow, uneven line across the entire width of his back. "My God," she gasped.

Her breathy invocation brought his head back around. "That bad, is it? Christ, Amanda, if Ken had looked like that when it happened, they'd have carried me back in flat on my face."

"I'm sorry," she said, giving herself a hard mental shake. "It's just that I've never seen wounds like these. Normally I'm not the least bit squeamish." She left the chair. "Bend over a little."

He did as she requested, supporting his upper body by placing his hands on his knees. The low slung trousers he wore rode down even lower on his narrow hips, revealing a thin band of paler skin just above the swell of his buttocks. Without the knowing probe of his eyes, Amanda looked at the sleek length of his torso, the wide spread of shoulder, and muscles which bunched and tensed there as he mentally prepared himself for the sting of antiseptic.

"Jason, I do believe you're dreading this."

"Damn right," he muttered. "Remember I've already experienced this once today. It burned like fire."

"Well, you have my permission to holler if you like. Sarah always does, so I've grown immune to the wails."

"Hard-hearted, you mean," he shot back, and then hissed audibly when he felt the iodine against the raw and open wounds. "Jesus—" he spat, and very nearly did holler like a kid.

"Sorry," she whispered on a wince, spreading the antiseptic quickly, feeling his pain as if it were her own. Never had she felt such a bonding with anyone other than Sarah. She believed with her whole heart that some mystical bonding did truly exist between mother and infant long after the cord of life had been severed. But what could bind her so completely with this man?

Suddenly she felt compelled to wrap her arms around his waist, press her cheek against his bare back, and hold on tightly to him as if there would be no tomorrow. But fear was overwhelming love. She stepped back and recorked the bottle.

"All finished," she murmured.

"Oh, no, you're not," he complained. "I've seen you with Sarah and you always kiss and make it better." Twisting his arm around behind him, Jason tapped the area just above the punctures. "Right here should be close enough to do some good."

He was teasing her, falling back on the suggestive

word play that kept the tension high between them and slowly broke down barriers. It was also a guaranteed method to send her out of here in a little huff. In another minute he was afraid he'd be dragging her over to his bed. He didn't dare look at her for the same reason, which was why, when he felt her cool mouth press and move over his spine, Jason nearly left his boots and shot clear through the roof. Only the weight of a fierce and violent erection kept him anchored to the floor while his head was spinning out of control.

When the crazy tilt of his world righted once again, he was alone with his agonizing arousal, and the echo of the screened door as it slapped shut behind her.

Chapter Fourteen

AMANDA SCRUBBED KITCHEN COUNTERS THAT WERE already spotlessly clean. When that was done, she took the broom to the floor with a vengeance, sweeping furiously with little results. This chore, too, had been done earlier, but unless she kept her mutinous body active, she knew she would be overcome by the passions that had been stirred to life when she'd felt Jason's smooth skin beneath her lips. She could taste him still.

Amanda groaned and involuntarily clenched the muscles of her thighs. It only made that pulsing ache more acute. She couldn't shut out the vision of his hard muscled chest and back. Beneath his trousers she knew his legs would be lean and sinewed. His buttocks were tight, and—

An old memory caused her stomach to feel as if it were falling, dropping down to that throbbing, now liquid center of her being. He was magnificent there as well.

"Stop this," she ordered her mutinous body, forcing her mind to consider safer topics.

She went over a list of items she had packed for herself and Sarah, mentally checking them off while wondering if they would be adequate. She had no idea how long they would be away. Jason had indicated it would be at least a week, possibly longer depending upon how soon the TJ's future was resolved.

And what was the future? Julie had firmly stated that unless they found sufficient support to challenge Brinkman's intended takeover, she would sell. Staying in the face of such opposition would make their lives here impossible. They'd make a new life elsewhere.

Not once had Jason been included in that new beginning. Would he pack up, bid them all a fond farewell, and go back to blowing things up? Would he someday lose his fear and become one of those technically dead souls marking time until death became a violent reality?

She shuddered and made a strangled sound deep in her throat. Once she had been afraid of the old wounds her memories might open. She now realized nothing could be worse than the thought of losing him again. Would she never know the strength of his passion, or feel the smooth satin of his naked skin against her own, his mouth and hands showing her the glory of his loving?

Along with a fresh wave of desire which raced through her veins came an anger directed solely at herself. What in the name of God was the point of trying to save herself from the hurt of losing him again if she was going to drive herself stark raving batty in the process?

Stripping off her apron, Amanda purposefully stepped out into the moonlit night. There was another who was having difficulty sleeping. She could hear the soft strains of his gramaphone as they drifted out to her, calling for her to share the company of the bunkhouse and learn the passion of a man's body, discover if the vow of an always love had been more than a boy's salving of his conscience.

She very nearly made it all the way. She had gotten as far as the pump outside his door when the old fears caused her to pause, and then freeze where she stood. For Amanda, taking risks had become a lost art. Allowing herself to walk into the bunkhouse, and accept whatever fate dealt to them thereafter, was a greater risk than any she had ever known.

Stifling a sob behind her hand, Amanda began to run blindly. By the time she reached the gate, she was crying so hard she didn't hear the rusty hinges groan as she passed through. The thick grass of the meadow muffled the sound of her feet as she continued to run, until her legs were trembling, and her lungs felt as if they would burst. Her knees gave out and she went down on them, folding over until her head practically touched the ground. Her chest hurt from the sobs and the inability to take in enough air. Blood pounded in her ears, drowning out the heavier footfalls of the man who had pursued her.

"Oh, Mandy!" Jason exclaimed tenderly when he found her slumped over and crying miserably, tearing out his heart with those awful sounds. Sitting down next to her, he pulled her against his chest and held her tightly against him.

Amanda's arms went around him and she was holding on for dear life, her tear-streaked cheek stroking over his hard chest. He felt so good against her, warm and strong, yet tender in the hands stroking her back. Her own palms pressed him closer. This was Jason, her first love, and her last love. She realized now that he had been her only love, and the years between had been the dream from which she had finally awakened.

Jason was afraid that Amanda might crack his ribs, she held him with such fierce strength. But it would be a glorious pain, he decided. Perhaps he should be trying to determine the source of her feverish distress, but he was too content to hold her in his arms. He forced himself to ignore the rapid rise and fall of her soft breasts against his belly, forget for a moment his own urgent needs. Taking a quick shuddering breath, Jason looked up into the face of the moon. It mocked him. As well it should. Beneath the slight weight of her hips he could feel himself growing hard and full and ready with his love for this woman. There wasn't even shame for his body's reactions. If anything, he was slightly chagrined by his inability to control this response. Hell, he'd had more command over himself at eighteen.

It was his undemanding silence and the unquestioning comfort being given that brought an end to Amanda's tears. When she quieted she accepted the peace that followed. Here, with Jason's arms wrapped around her, Amanda felt no fear, only joy. She sighed softly, her breath wafting over his flesh.

"Hey," he whispered against her brow, touching his lips there. "You wouldn't be falling asleep on me would you?"

Her answer was to move her mouth over his chest, searching and tasting every inch within her reach, dipping her tongue into the pulsing hollow at the base of his throat.

Jason moaned and his arms tightened convulsively when he felt that wet, gliding caress. He shifted, moving them both until she was lying half beneath him upon the thick grass. Staring down at her, Jason was unable to entirely believe what he read in her warm, glowing eyes.

Amanda touched his cheek, pressing her palm there. "I've remembered, Jason," she told him with eloquent simplicity.

His heart stopped and then started again. He moved her hand to his chest, pressing her palm against the galloping heartbeat there.

"All of it?" He wanted to be absolutely certain. If he had misunderstood, he was afraid it might tear him to pieces. "Have you truly remembered how it was?"

"Yes," she breathed on a gentle smile. "Every moment and every second."

"Then tell me," he prompted softly. "Two things . . ."

Unhesitatingly her hand slid down over his belly,

showing him in gesture, as well as in word, how very clearly she remembered.

"This," she said, covering him with her palm. "You gave without taking. Wanting me then, as you do now, you denied yourself for my sake." Her voice was slightly husky as she explored how much he needed her.

"God," Jason breathed, closing his eyes on a convulsive shudder. She'd been a bold girl in her curiosity. Now it was with a woman's experience that she stroked him to even greater urgency.

For Amanda this was a discovery; not the act, but the pleasure she derived from it. What once had been a duty, a necessity to arouse an older man's desires, became a glory. She felt her breath quicken. The cloth that strained beneath her fingers became a frustration, and she began to work the buttons on his fly.

Jason, too, wanted to feel her touch without restrictions, but was afraid he wouldn't be able to contain himself if he allowed this.

"Soon," he promised, gently forcing her away even as he was finding his way beneath her skirts. Slowly he let his hand glide up the entire length of her long, beautiful leg until he reached the lacy edge of her short drawers. Then he slipped beneath the fabric to find the woman. "Oh, yes," he whispered when he found her dewy readiness.

Their mouths met and clung, savored delicately for a time. But it was not enough. Beneath the light strokes of Jason's fingers Amanda's dormant passion was awakening in a hot burst. She pressed herself hard against his hand, and then cried softly when it was withdrawn. Jason soothed her disappointment with the strokes of his tongue inside her mouth. There would be no one-sided loving this night. When she reached her pleasure, he wanted to feel it with every fiber of his being, buried deep and full, Amanda closing around him.

Their kisses grew more desperate, deeper, wildly stirring. Amanda grew bolder, returning his intimate kiss, letting Jason draw her inside his mouth. Both were breathing raggedly when Jason lifted his head and pulled Amanda into a sitting position.

His hands were shaking and he had difficulty with the small buttons down the back of her dress, but finally he was drawing the garment off her body. The skirts and petticoats were also tossed aside. Shoes were removed, stockings lovingly rolled down, with kisses planted along the way. Then, when she was only in her camisole and drawers, Jason sat back on his heels and waited.

Amanda was uncertain, but too hungry for him to care. Crossing her arms she drew the camisole over her head, proud in her mature nakedness, her breasts full and aching for his caresses. Still he didn't move, and she didn't understand until he said, "Touch me now, Amanda."

She moved to her knees and eagerly let her hands roam freely over his body. She heard his breath catch when the first button on his trousers was released, and then the second. A sudden shyness overtook her, and she looked up into his dark, unfathomable eyes and saw the corners crinkle up slightly as he smiled his encouragement.

To help her, Jason cupped her breasts and teased

the tips with his calloused thumbs. Amanda was trembling when she released him and encircled the enormity of his need for her. Again desire surged too hotly, and he rasped, "Enough," as he'd done so many years ago.

"Never have I forgotten how you taste," he said, dipping his head, supporting her back with his arm while his tongue swirled and lapped over her hard nipples. First one and then the other received his homage until she was crying out, tunneling her fingers through his hair. Jason drew her into his mouth. Amanda's head fell back and she arched, offering herself up to him, feeling as if she'd been created only for this sweet pleasure. Her desires started to spiral with every loving tug of his lips and tongue. "J—Jason . . . please," she begged, falling back and taking her with him, the movements of her hips and legs an eloquent imploring.

He drew off her drawers and tasted the tender inner flesh of her thigh with his teeth, nipping gently. He would have liked to linger there, but remembered his earlier resolve to take them on this journey together. He kissed her briefly in promise of another time, and then moved up over her body while her lithe legs were trapping him in that cradle where he longed to be rocked. He kissed her hungrily with an unbridled passion that was beginning to consume them both. They were flesh to flesh, man to woman, and there was no more waiting for either of them.

Amanda sobbed when he searched and found, adjusting herself slightly to make him more welcome.

Jason watched her eyes glaze over as he slowly

penetrated her tight velvet warmth. He felt as if he'd come home at last. When she would have moved beneath him, he held her hips still, savoring this moment.

"Two things, Mandy," he said against her mouth. "I charged you to remember two things. Tell me the second one."

She was nearly out of her mind with the feel of him so deep inside, really a part of her now, in body as well as in soul.

"Tell me, Mandy," he urged.

She saw his need in the tight strain upon his face, but knew this man's stubbornness. For so many years she'd sealed it away, keeping it inviolate and fresh in the deepest reaches of her heart. "You said you loved me," she answered, never doubting that it had been the absolute truth.

"Always," he finished, kissing her again as he began to move within her body. "And God help you, Amanda, but you're about to discover just how much. . . ."

Amanda was stretched out atop Jason's length, her head pillowed against his chest. He was pulling the pins from her hair one by one, putting them aside, and spreading her thick, unruly tresses over his neck and shoulders. She lifted her cheek and turned to look at him.

"Why are you doing that?"

He smiled. "Because I forgot to do it earlier, and there's something about making love to a woman with her hair up that's a little wild and wicked. Besides, your hair betrays you, sweet Mandy. Try as you might, you can't control or confine it's vibrancy, or hide its fire. It's always springing free on you at the damnedest times."

Her throat clogged with tears when she saw again the love in his face. How could she have been so blind all this time? But who could have believed a summer romance between two very young people, at the very worst times in their lives, could have been so deep and true that it had survived time, other marriages, and life in general. Loving him was unbelievable. What she'd felt only a few moments ago when he'd taken her beyond herself in a passionate fulfillment never before experienced was unbelievable. But then when he smiled at her just that way, she could easily believe him to be a mythical creature, her Pan of the meadows and forests.

"Jason, I've been such a silly fool—"

"Shhh," he hushed, pulling her up so he could find her mouth, nibbling there until she felt as if all the bones in her body had melted down to molten liquid. "Tonight is only for loving. We'll save the verbal flogging—mine included—for another time. It doesn't matter, Amanda," he whispered fiercely. "Nothing matters, but this . . ." He lifted her so that he could lave her breasts with his tongue and nip gently at the sensitive peaks. She trembled anew when he worked his hand between their bodies to cup the soft mound of her womanhood with his palm. Gently he began to probe there, rekindling the fires. She could feel his desire building, growing hard beneath her thighs.

When Jason began to guide her hips, silently telling her what he wanted, Amanda's eyes flew wide with surprise. "Can we—I mean, is it possible?"

Jason thought he would shout with joy at the

discovery that her beautiful innocence was not entirely gone. "Oh, sweet, you have much to learn. And I've twelve years of the most erotic fantasies of you to satisfy." His voice grew strained when she took all of him. He saw the response of her passion in the way she threw her head slightly back, and that fire-silk hair was tossed with an almost wild abandon. He guided her motion with his hands until she caught the rhythm and took command. Then his hands were free to caress her breasts, to pull her beautiful face down to his so their lips could touch and their tongues taste.

A fine sheen of perspiration was caught by the moon, making her skin luminescent. Jason felt he could watch her like this forever. This was his wildly passionate Mandy, the girl who gave without qualification. She was magnificent.

When he felt those hard internal pulses caressing him, Jason clenched his teeth, prolonging the moment until he was on the thin edge of sanity, watching her ecstasy as he'd done so many years ago, loving her beyond reason or time. Then, with a shout, he let himself join her in glory, filling her with the very essence of himself.

The night seemed to explode all around them.

Without a single twinge of guilt, Amanda decided she looked positively splendid. This dress had always been flattering—one of the few of Harry's lavish gifts that had not been returned. The pale peach color was perfect for her complexion and did not clash with her hair. It was fashioned of the finest lawn, and the fabric was softly feminine. The bell skirt draped gently over her slender hips and seemed to open like a flower at the hem. The bodice, with its lace V insert running up into the high ruffled collar, drooped over a tight satin waist sash.

Her slender, long-waisted figure was perfect for this fashion, even if the dress was a few years out of style. She chuckled at this twinge of worry over fashion. Amanda quite imagined the ladies of Stockton would consider last year's hobble skirt the height of absurdity—which, of course, it was.

Her hair had been more trouble than it was worth, but the high pompadour was finally anchored to the pads with borrowed pins. Her own had been strangely misplaced, lost in the high grass of the meadow.

Just the thought of those hours beneath the moon made Amanda's body tingle and her spirit sing with the joy of Jason's lovemaking. Leaving him for her own lonely bed had been difficult, for both of them. When he'd said good night at the kitchen door in the wee hours of the morning, Amanda had felt as if he was taking the greatest part of herself along with him.

Some of the gladness faded when a twinge of the old fear returned. Should Jason leave her, really leave her, she didn't know how she would bear it. She thrust the idea aside, refusing to allow it to cloud this wonderful morning.

Amanda was just reaching for her flowery hat when Jason knocked on the frame of the open door and came striding into her room. His arms were around her and his mouth was slowly moving over her own before she could give him the speech she'd planned.

"God, you're beautiful," he said earnestly when he stepped back, his eyes warm as they looked her over.

"I might say the same of you, Mr. Thorne," Amanda told him, trying very hard to sound casual and blithely unsurprised by the expert tailoring and fine cloth of his vested, dark gray suit. This was not the old broadcloth sack suit customary among men outside the city. It was the kind worn by men of wealth and position, by men of power. It didn't fit with her image of the man usually dressed in dark chinos and cotton shirts. Did one need suits of this caliber to blow up things?

"Where are your bags? We'd better be on our way, if we're detouring by way of Peabody. The Pickle is already in the automobile, so excited she can hardly contain herself. You did tell her she wasn't attending the Founder's Day celebration, didn't you."

"No, I did not."

"Don't you think you should have?"

"No," she repeated flatly.

"Amanda, she's not going to be very happy about this."

"On the contrary, she'll be delighted with the Founder's Day celebration."

Surprise flickered over Jason's face.

"What did you say?"

Amanda closed the distance between them, sliding her arms around his neck, molding her body to his. "We're not going to Peabody, Jason. I unpacked our things this morning."

The hands at her waist tightened. "I don't want to be apart from you either, Amanda. But essentially

242

nothing has changed. Honey, it won't be that long . . ."

"It would be eternity, Mr. Arrogance. However, being separated from you is not the only reason behind my change in plans. Jason, I want—*need*—to be part of this battle against Brinkman. And I thought that's what you wanted as well. Surely you can't have objections?"

"I can think of dozens," he told her, his expression warning he was deadly earnest. "Amanda, I blame myself. I've said some harsh, unfair things which have probably put this wild notion into your lovely head. Sweet love, you don't have to prove anything to me."

"I know that," she returned softly. "This is for myself, Jason. It's very important to me."

His brow furrowed. "Then you should have all the facts. I've kept something else from you because I believed you and Sarah would be safe, away from here." He then told her about the poisoned water reservoir, emphasizing the magnitude of this newest act of sabotage.

Amanda listened intently, weighing carefully the import of his warnings. "I understand fully, Jason. But it hasn't changed my mind. I'm going with you to Stockton today."

"You are not."

"Oh, yes I am."

"Amanda . . ." he grated warningly.

"What, Jason?" she returned, her arms sliding around his neck.

Chapter Fifteen

THE COURTHOUSE LAWN WAS A SCENE OF GAITY. Though all the adults were dressed in their Sunday best, the children were blissfully unconcerned about the grass stains and dirt dotting their clothing as they participated in games for prizes. Right now a three-legged race was just ending with the two Taylor boys taking the blue ribbon.

Standing next to Amanda, their mother clapped and shouted, waving her arms at her sons' victory. It was such an entirely normal scene, Amanda could almost convince herself that undercurrent of tension did not exist. Unfortunately, it was all too apparent on many faces in the crowd. She'd been introduced to a great many people by her aunt. Their reserve had often hit her like ice water in the heat of a July day. Julie Danfield, though, seemed oblivious to her cold reception. She gushed at each and every one as if they were her dearest friends, asking about their families, children, grandchildren, the state of their health, with such genuine warmth, most could not look her directly in the eye for long. Which, of course, was the response she intended. Julie Danfield was shaming these people, reminding them of things more comfortable to forget—the years of friendship and good times.

Neither did she hesitate to remind them of the bad times. Like now. Julie had cornered one of the farmers who had refused her a contract for this year's crop of hay. Amanda cocked her ear and listened.

"You know I'll never forget that awful winter when your Mattie—God rest her—was down with a broken leg. Remember, she slipped on the ice when she was coming in one morning from the barn." The man next to Julie nodded, looking acutely uncomfortable while Julie continued to talk. "What a pickle that was. There you were with them four little kids, all of them half sick with a fever, and a wife who couldn't get out of her bed. It's a good thing Todd found that cow of yours wandering on the road. By the time I got there to take over, you looked like a man who'd been beat to death, George. Never saw a human being so frazzled in my entire life. Mattie was in pain, and every one of those children were squalling at the top of their lungs. Do you remember what you said to me?"

She eyed him pointedly, and his head dropped to his chest. "You looked at me and you said, 'Thank God for you, Julie Danfield.'"

"Poor Mr. Franklin," said Alva Taylor. "Julie's really spreading it heavy with him, but he deserves it. I fully expect him to go skulking off, whimpering like a kicked puppy any minute. But then, the Taylors deserve their fair share of being slapped in the face with our sins. Todd and Julie Danfield were good neighbors, always there in an emergency, ready to offer a helping hand. Usually were the first to a party as well when good fortune needed celebrating. We should all hang our heads for the way we've turned our backs on that good woman." Tears sparkled in Alva Taylor's eyes. "Isn't that right, Ma."

Her mother-in-law nodded. "I purely don't know what gets into folks. Guess it's the devil." She chuckled. "Though we ain't seen much of Lucifer since old Hell-fire and Damnation left town."

Amanda cocked a questioning eyebrow at the older woman standing next to her very pregnant daughter-in-law. "Reverend Thorne, girl. But I guess you wouldn't know much about him, except that he was Jason's foster father."

"All I want or need to know," she told Moria Taylor.

Julie returned to the small group of women. There was a broad smile on her face. "George Franklin has agreed to attend the meeting and give us a listen. Says it's the first he's heard of possible trouble. Can you believe that?"

"Could be he didn't want to listen, Julie," Moria observed. "Maybe none of us did."

Julie narrowed her eyes at her old friend. "Moria, I'm getting plumb sick and tired of listening to you flog yourself. Now, if you want on my list, I'll be happy to oblige. Otherwise—"

The two older women laughed when Moria vehemently denied any interest in subjecting herself to Julie Danfield's particular brand of punishment. "There's some sins I'd just as soon not be reminded of, Julie. So I'll just leave off counting my own, and you won't have to worry about digging under my skin."

Amanda, too, was glad she wasn't on Julie's list, though she deserved top billing in her own mind. Julie had opened her home and her heart. What Amanda had given in return was blind panic, and shrieking hysteria at the first hint of trouble. It was not going to be one of her more cherished memories of herself.

"Here come the men," Alva said.

Amanda had already spotted Jason. He was impossibly handsome. Few women could let him pass without surreptitious second looks. They might spit on his feet, but they'd take an eyeful survey in the process, Amanda thought with disgust.

When they drew near, Amanda saw the hard look in his eyes, which softened the minute his gaze rested upon her face. He came directly to her side, taking her hand and squeezing it fiercely, not letting her go while Julie solicited reports from the Taylor men.

"We aren't having much luck," Bert told her. "Half the time folks won't stop long enough to listen."

"You've got to *make* them listen, Bert," Julie said emphatically. "Use what they owe you against them if you have to. I don't necessarily mean money. We've all pitched in and helped one another through the years. Remind them of that. Hit 'em low in their gut where it hurts and make them squirm inside."

"Julie, I don't feel right about throwing my own good deeds in my friend's faces," said Harvey Taylor, the patriarch of this family. "It don't seem right somehow."

Julie turned on him. "Does it seem right to you that you'll soon be forced off your land? Is it going to be right when these people are next in line? Harvey, Brinkman has been fighting dirty, using low-down tricks just shy of illegal. Sometimes you've got to fight fire with fire."

When they were all properly chastened and sent back out on their missions, Jason remained at Amanda's side. "I think they'll accomplish more if I'm not around," he said with a rueful smile. Amanda made no comment. She simply let her fingers caress his. He would claim not to care. She knew better.

"Where's the Pickle?" Jason asked when the silence grew too telling.

Amanda nodded toward a huge maple tree nearby. Seated beneath the sprawling branches were two little girls, one fair, one dark. Both had their stockinged legs stretched out before them. They were chatting nonstop, and every so often one, or both, would nearly fold over in uproarious laughter. "She's made a fast friend."

"So I see," he said smiling. "Who does she belong to?"

"You won't believe me when I tell you."

"Try me," Jason prompted.

She turned to him. "That is Miss Nancy Granger, Jack Granger's oldest daughter." When he frowned, she immediately went on to explain. "It's all right, Jason. Her father knows very well who his daughter is keeping company with. Alva Taylor introduced us, quite formal and properly, to Jack and his wife. I couldn't believe it was the same man from the store. He actually took my hand and told me he was *right proud* to make my acquaintance." She shook her head slightly. "Jason, I really believe he meant that."

"I'm not surprised. Jack has always been fond of a good scrap, and fonder still of anyone who will give him a worthwhile challenge. You earned his respect, Amanda."

"So have you," she said softly.

Jason's hand slid up her arm. "Do you know how much I need to kiss you?" His head tipped closer, and his voice became very low and deep. "More than that, I'd like to have you naked beneath me, your eyes clouded with passion while you writhe—"

"Jason!" She looked around to see if anyone else had heard him. Her cheeks were flaming. And deep inside desire was building.

His eyes were dark and burning with his own response to the images his words had created. Very lightly he let his fingers stroke over her warm cheek. "Woman, you're so hot you burn me up."

Julie Danfield stopped a few feet away and watched these two people she loved eat each other up with their eyes. It was rare when she couldn't sleep, but last night had been one of those exceptions. She'd heard Amanda pacing in the kitchen long after bedtime, and she'd known when she left the house. It had worried her when the young woman didn't return, so Julie had gone looking. She'd hesitated approaching that brightly lit bunkhouse. Hearing no sound, she had eventually worked up the nerve to knock on the door. There hadn't been anybody there. A check of the grounds and a holler into the barn also turned up no sign of Jason or Amanda. With both of them missing she didn't worry quite so much, and had gone back to her bed. Still it had nagged at her. Uncertain just how far Brinkman would go, afraid he'd gotten wind of their plans somehow, Julie had not spent an entirely peaceful two hours waiting until they returned. Which they had, cozy as you please, setting the back of the house on fire with those long, long kisses. She'd felt a little warm herself when she'd tiptoed back to her room.

She walked up to them now. "Let's fetch our Sarey and find us the food table," she suggested. "The two of you look hungry enough to start nibbling on each other."

All in all it had been a successful day, Julie Danfield decided, very satisfied with the results. Twenty men and women had agreed to meet the next afternoon. Of course, it helped when Miles Davis offered his house for the gathering. Having their elected mayor questioning Brinkman's tactics was nearly as effective as being shamed into opening their closed minds.

Julie smothered a yawn behind her hand. The sun was setting, and she admitted her day was about done as well.

"Tired, old girl?" Jason said, giving her a quick hug.

"Didn't sleep well last night," she informed him with a sidelong glance. "Had some restless critters about the place keeping me awake and worrying."

"Really," he said uneasily, surprising himself by being embarrassed by her knowing look. "Julie, I—"

"They won't keep me awake tonight. That's for certain. Nope. Now that I know those critters are two-legged, and not prowling around to make trouble, I'll sleep like a baby." She yawned again. "Jase, do you think Amanda would be very disappointed if we headed on home soon? I'm dead on my feet. Sarah's starting to look a bit droopy as well. There's really nothing more we can accomplish here, and with the sun going down the men are liable to start drinking heavier. Some have been at the kegs most of the afternoon."

"I'll go find her," Jason told Julie, knowing her worries were primarily for his sake. He was no coward, but dynamite was safer than this particular crowd, especially liquored up with false courage. Julie and the Taylors had hit some of them pretty hard. A few would try to drown guilty consciences with whiskey. Jason had no illusion about the target they would pick to let some of that emotion fly.

"She's with Alva Taylor still. Sarah's over there by the Granger family. You bring Amanda, and I'll get our girl."

Amanda was decidedly uneasy while she strolled across the courthouse lawn on Grant Winston's arm.

She knew he was the enemy but had found it impossible to deny his humbly phrased request for these few private moments of her time. She owed him something for his timely interference in Hardy's store.

"So you see, Mrs. Ames," he was saying, "Mr. Brinkman is not the evil machinator I've heard him presented as today. His interest in this town is only for the good of the majority. Unfortunately, there will be the few who will be hurt by his plans. That is only business, nothing personal I can assure you.

"Every year young people leave communities such as this one by the droves. The world is changing, growing, discovering wonders every day. Stockton, and towns like it, simply aren't keeping pace with that progress. Surely, just recently from the city yourself, you can see how simple things are here. Many things haven't changed since this town was founded. The younger generation is growing discontent. They want the good things the modern world can give them. Soon this town will only be inhabited by old people. Then it will die with them."

"Perhaps," Amanda hedged, conceding privately he had a solid argument. "But surely you aren't saying that Mr. Brinkman's interest is purly benevolent?"

"Good heavens, no," he admitted with a laugh. "He's a man of business, first and foremost. My client sees a profit here. Otherwise, he wouldn't bother."

She appreciated his candor. "And what of you, Mr. Winston? What is your advantage in this?"

"A very large commission, Mrs. Ames. I've never denied that fact. I'm also just as I've represented myself, an attorney working in his client's behalf. No more, and no less."

He was simply too smooth, Amanda decided. His answers were too pat, as if they'd been said a thousand times before. She was beginning to see why Jason detested his slick manner and glib tongue.

"I'm sure," she returned flatly. "However, the TJ is my home now. It distresses me to consider having it taken over by anyone. So I'm afraid I won't be of much help in convincing my aunt it would be wise to reconsider her stubborn position." She felt him tense as she turned to him, her eyes snapping. "That is what you wanted, isn't it? Didn't you hope that I'd be favorable to reason, and would apply a little pressure on Mrs. Danfield?"

"Yes," he admitted frankly. "She's causing quite an unnecessary stir. You must be practical about this, Mrs. Ames. Although I admire your loyalty, I'm afraid you are letting it color good judgment. The TJ, as it stands, is financially destroyed. She has no cattle to market this season, and won't the next either. Without a source of income to rebuild and restock, the future is hopeless. I'm very concerned about you, Mrs. Ames. Things will get terribly difficult very fast this winter. How will you manage? Forget about Mr. Brinkman or his more expansive plans. Are you willing to face starvation and poverty for a principle?"

Amanda felt a stab of the old panic, the sensation of the very air being squeezed from her lungs. She took in a deep breath and gave him a level look. "You may be right, Mr. Winston. However, despite everything, I will not turn my back on my aunt when she needs me. Nor will I betray her. You see, I've discovered starvation to be preferable to choking to death on my own conscience and shame." She disengaged her hand from his arm. "Good evening, Mr. Winston."

A strong arm sliding around her shoulder prevented her haughty withdrawal. She glanced up into his face, her temper taking fire, when she saw that he was looking over her head with the strangest expression on his face. Turning her head, she saw Jason standing close by, his thumbs thrust deep into the pockets of his expensively tailored trousers. On his face she saw bitterness and jealousy. In his eyes there was also confusion, which grew to blazing fury when he finally realized she was being held against her will.

"I suggest you let go of me immediately, Mr. Winston."

"No," he hissed. "You'll not put yourself in jeopardy for that bastard's sake this time, dear lady."

"What do you mean? What jeopardy?" Jason was alone except for a single old man who was approaching on his left.

But behind the old man, who leaned heavily upon his cane as he walked, people seemed to appear from out of nowhere, some of them coming at a run. Jason appeared unaware of it all. He was looking only at Grant Winston with murder in his dark eyes.

When he saw Amanda trying to struggle free of an unwanted embrace, Jason knew he was going to beat the shit out of that dandified, troublemaking, son-of-a-bitch attorney. His black rage blinded him to the horde at his back. Neither did he see that cane lift high. But he heard it whistle through the air before it

landed hard across his shoulders. Pain exploded
inside his brain, and he nearly dropped to his knees.
The second blow caused him to stagger as he whirled
to defend himself. Somewhere, far behind him, he
heard Amanda cry out. But the tongues of fire that
licked across his back caused a roaring in his ears
when he faced his attacker.

Readying himself to deliver another brutal whack,
the old man lifted the cane again. His white hair
stood up in clumps all over his head, and his glazed
eyes were half mad. Jason dodged the descending
cane, but made no attempt to launch a counterattack
against his former father-in-law.

Helpless, Amanda watched the crowd close
around Jason and that insane old man, forming a
protective circle as if this were part of the day's
entertainment. She fought desperately to free herself from Grant Winston's impossibly strong hold.

Winston was not escaping entirely unscathed.
Sharp elbows gouged his belly. Nails raked his hands
and would have taken out his eyes if he hadn't
captured her wrists. She was like trying to tame a
wildcat. "Mrs. Ames. Please attempt to control
yourself. I'm only holding you for your own safety."

The heel of her shoe drove back against his shin,
and Amanda knew a momentary satisfaction when
he grunted with pain. "I'll kill you for this, Winston!" she screamed at him. "*Let me go!*"

Jason could not maneuver away from that whipping rod of wood. He was surrounded by a solid wall
of human flesh. If he managed to escape one of
Henry Blane's wild thrusts, they would push him
back toward the crazed old man, shouting their
encouragement all the while. Henry's breath was

wheezing in and out, strong with the smell of whis-
key. He was weakening on each attack, too sick and
old and drunk to maintain his earlier brutal force.
And, despite the crowd, Jason managed to evade
Henry more times than not. The pain was minimal.
He'd been smacked this hard by a cranky cow.

"Ah, Henry, you gotta do better than that. The
bastard's still on his feet!"

The humiliation of being flogged before the entire
town, Amanda, and friends newly acquired stripped
Jason of dignity. It reduced him to a boy again,
skulking around corners, walking with his head
down, his hands thrust deep in his pockets, terrified
someone would recognize and stop him. He was in
front of the church again, his insides churning while
his bastardy was announced week after week from
the pulpit, the finger pointing at *his head,* not out at
the congregation. The blame was on Jason Thorne
for being born, for existing.

His dreams were going up in smoke along with his
pride. There was no place in Stockton for Jason
Thorne. There never had been, nor would it ever
change. This is what Amanda would live with, if he
was fool enough to stay here.

Amanda was sobbing, the tears blinding her. She
no longer struggled. Dear God, she hated this town
for what they could do to him. She felt sickened by
them all. Her head snapped up when she heard a
collective groan. Bert and Ken Taylor were attempting to shove their way through the crowd, but were
having little success while they were constantly
pushed back. Then two more men joined the effort,
only these two applied less polite methods. They

gouged and punched, and tossed men out of their way as if they weighed little.

Thinking these two men meant harm, not good, Amanda screamed as Jack and Billy Granger reached the center of the tight circle.

Jason heard the whistle of the cane again. It landed across the back of his neck. Henry must be getting his second wind he thought as he went down, catching himself on his hands and knees. Just where they always had wanted him. Crawling before them like an animal.

"Goddamn, Henry! You're sotted again."

The voice was too familiar for Jason not to recognize. He lifted his head, and looked up just as Jack Granger sent Henry Blane's cane flying over the heads of the dispersing crowd. If that wasn't unbelievable enough, Jack Granger extended a hand and pulled Jason to his feet. Then Bert Taylor was at his side. "Are you all right, Jason?"

"Oh, I'm dandy," Jason drawled sarcastically, rubbing his neck, feeling the welt that was beginning to rise.

"That bastard raped my little girl," Blane sobbed. "He molested my baby, and never paid a day for the crime. Then he took her away and murdered her in some godforsaken wilderness. Raped her, I tell you!" The old man's voice had risen on every accusation.

"Sure, Henry. We've heard it all a thousand times when you start talking out of the bottom of a whiskey bottle," Jack said with irritation. "But that don't make it true, except in your own soaked brain. The truth is you were always a no-good drunk.

Shoot, I wouldn't be a bit surprised if Lucy didn't seduce Jason here just to get away—"

Jack was lifted clear off the ground by a man three inches shorter and filled with the strength of his fury.

"Careful, Jack, you go too far. *Lucy was my wife.*" Each word was clearly enunciated as Jason let the bigger man down slowly. "I thank you for your assistance, but if you speak her name in less than complimentary terms again, I'll wrap your teeth around your eyeballs."

Jack Granger's eyes glinted with excitement. "We'd both enjoy that. But now's not the time. Besides, I meant no offense against Lucy, and I'll apologize for it."

"Apology accepted," Jason said dully. In other circumstances hearing Jack Granger back down on anything would have brought shock. Being rescued by the Grangers should have struck him dead with surprise. All Jason wanted was to get the hell away from this town. He glanced over his shoulder to Amanda, still in Grant Winston's embrace. He was no longer holding her by force. She was standing rigidly still and tears were streaking down her cheeks. The pain in her eyes nearly killed him.

His jaw was working vigorously when he turned to Bert Taylor.

"Would you and your family look after my women; see that they get home safely?"

What Jason was feeling was written all over his face. Bert Taylor understood. Jason had been stripped bare of his pride. Being fussed over by females was the last thing he needed right now. Any man would want to go off and toss a few down.

"Be glad to, Jason," he said simply, without

hesitation. "Just don't go off too far yet. There's things about what happened just now you need to know and understand."

"Do I?"

Jason Thorne walked away, and he didn't look back.

Chapter Sixteen

WHEN THE TAYLOR WAGON TURNED OFF THE MAIN road and started down the lane to the TJ, Amanda began to tremble, clutching herself tightly against the icy grip of fear on this sweltering summer night.

Julie saw her niece shudder and reached over to pat her arm.

"He'll be there, honey. Jase wouldn't run out on us now, no matter how good his reasons."

Amanda wanted so desperately to believe her aunt. If only she could stop seeing those desolate eyes as they'd rested upon her so briefly before he'd walked away.

"Oh, Auntie, I'll die if he's gone."

One night. She couldn't live the rest of her life with only one night to give meaning to her existence. She hadn't even told him how much she loved him.

"Amanda," Julie said sternly. "That man has a love so powerful for you it's been painful to watch at times. He'll be there waiting, and he's going to need you to be strong for him. Don't you give him less than he deserves, and has earned. Do you hear me, Amanda Jean?"

"Yes," Amanda sobbed. "Oh, God, I hope you're right."

Julie settled back against the flat rails of the wagon. "I'm right," she said with absolute conviction, shifting the little girl asleep on her lap. "So you just stop shivering and shaking. What happened to the woman who walloped the daylights out of Grant Winston for not letting her brawl with half the population of Stockton?"

"She nearly broke her hand on his rock-hard head," Amanda stated as she flexed her aching fingers.

Julie chuckled. "Lordy, I bet that man's ears are still ringing. Where did you ever hear language like that, Amanda? I was downright shocked."

A small smile broke through. "I lost my temper. When that happens, I rarely remember anything I've said or done afterward."

"Well, that's convenient."

"Yes, I think so." The smile faded, and she tensed when the wagon made that last circular turn. She closed her eyes and she prayed nonstop that Jason would be there. She felt Julie's hand grasp her own, and her heart pounded until she heard her aunt say, "I can see the moon glinting off his machine from here. It's parked where it always is."

Amanda's breath came out in a rush. She hadn't realized she'd been holding it.

"Thank God," she whispered.

By the time Ken Taylor pulled the horses to a stop in front of the house, Amanda could both see and hear evidence of Jason's presence. The bunkhouse was flooded with light, and the strains of a Sousa march were blessedly loud in the air. She hopped off the back of the wagon and reached for Sarah, who was groggily coming awake with Julie's gentle nudging.

"Come on, sweetheart," Amanda encouraged. "You're too heavy for Auntie to lift." With little grunts of complaint, Sarah scooted into her mother's arms. Amanda held her high and close, carrying her to the house.

"I'd carry her for you, Amanda," Ken offered. "If you think she'd let me."

"Let's not risk it tonight, Ken. Personally, I've had enough chaos for one day."

"Ain't it so," he said pleasantly, opening the door for her. "Excuse me if I'm speaking out of turn, but if I were in Jason's shoes, I doubt I'd appreciate too much fussing. When a man's feeling strong and full of his own worth, then a little coddling can be appreciated, even enjoyed. But times like this, the best medicine is good liquor and a bad—" His jaw clamped shut when he realized what he'd almost said. He ducked his head and pulled his nose. "Uh—well—" He grinned sheepishly. "Never mind.

If you don't need me for anything, I'll head on home."

"Thank you so much, Ken. For everything."

"Glad to help out, Amanda."

"Oh, you have," she assured him. More than you'll ever realize, she added privately. So, Jason needed good liquor and a bad woman, did he? She wasn't certain about the first, but she had no doubts he would have plenty of the second.

Together Amanda and Julie put Sarah to bed. She fell asleep almost immediately, one of her "most favorite" dolls tucked securely beneath her arm. When the door closed behind the two women, Amanda turned and hugged her aunt tightly. "I'm so grateful you kept Sarah away from that horrible scene today. That, at least, Jason won't have to add to his distress."

"It's for certain he'd be sick if Sarah was upset in any way. What are you going to do, honey?"

Amanda averted her eyes briefly. "Auntie, I'll do anything . . ."

"No, don't tell me," Julie said quickly. "I'm going to bed. Which is where little children and old women belong at this time of the night. In bed . . . asleep. *Sound asleep*," she emphasized as she went off down the hall. "Good luck, honey," Julie added before the door shut on a soft thud.

Amanda stood out in the hallway for several minutes, pondering on the behavior of a bad woman. Her lips quirked at the realization most would already think her morals quite beyond redemption. Still she couldn't go to him like this, wearing her very pretty, so proper high-necked dress. Whether she was good, or bad, Amanda did not want him indifferent.

Taking a deep breath and letting it out slowly, she walked into her own room. After finding the night-gown she'd worn the night of the storm, she removed her clothing. In the process she caught a glimpse of her own reflection in the mirror as she passed by. Backing up, she scrutinized the picture she made in her good underthings, and a very slow smile began to spread across her face. The camisole was modest, but so thin and fine in texture her nipples were clearly evident. The lacy-edged short drawers drew the eye to her sleek thighs. And with her stockings and slippers the entire effect was quite naughty. No, he'd not be indifferent.

If he wasn't dead drunk, that is.

Amanda grabbed her wrapper, grumbling because it was cotton, not silk or satin, and pulled it on before she could change her mind, then belted it loosely. When she walked, an enticing length of leg was revealed. Then she raced straight out of the house before her courage failed.

Seated on the sofa, staring into the empty hearth, Jason heard the screened door open and close. He didn't look back. If his guest was female, under the age of thirty, and past childhood, he was in no particular hurry to face her. God, how he dreaded seeing that pinched expression, the fear back in those lovely eyes. With his head resting against the back of the sofa, Jason closed his eyes and let the strains of *Semper Fidelis* pulse inside his head. Between his feet was one of Todd's jugs, but it was tightly corked, unopened, and he was stone-cold sober. Which was unfortunate, he realized too late.

He still didn't open his eyes when the music stopped abruptly, but the rustling of cloth caused them to drift open. Before the fireplace, Amanda was posing and posturing, trying to drape her body in impossible positions. Finally she found one that was not only satisfactory to her, but reasonably plausible for the human form. Then she turned her head slowly toward him and fixed her mouth in what he assumed she considered a seductive smile. Their eyes locked, and he saw a flicker of flustered apprehension before her long eyelashes began to bat at him with the velocity of a hummingbird's wings.

Jason leaned forward and rested his elbows on his knees, propping his chin in his hands. He was tempted to see how long she could maintain this very interesting rendition of a tart, but when she began to teeter, he gave up on the idea.

"Just what, in the hell, if I might ask, do you think you're doing?" he drawled.

Amanda struck a less precarious pose. "I'm the second part of your cure." She whipped her wrapper away from her legs. One foot was arched, the knee bent for effect as she waved it at him from beneath the slit in her robe.

"My what?" Jason asked with a little shake of his head.

"Well, I have it on good authority that when a man is feeling miserable and low"—she made her voice as breathy as possible—"good liquor and a bad woman can cure what ails him."

Jason sat back and continued to look at her, the expression on his face and in his eyes unreadable. Then he crooked a single finger at her. "Come here," he said in tone that told her his impassive demeanor was a façade. She hesitated. "Come here," he said again in a more commanding manner.

It wasn't the command which had her flying onto his lap, but the arms he extended and folded around her when she pressed close to him. His face was buried against her shoulder, and she could feel the tremors in his body, which grew alarmingly until she was being jostled by them. "Oh, Jas—"

Her wail of concern changed to a cry of pique. This high emotion which was tossing her about on his lap wasn't the extreme wretchedness she'd thought. He was laughing, and the moisture collecting at the corners of his eyes were tears of mirth.

"God, you're really something, woman," he finally managed to say. "Part of my cure, huh? You know, with you at my side, I could almost believe myself capable of conquering anything . . . even the citizens of Stockton." He sobered and the smile faded. "Almost," he added in a subdued tone.

Amanda plowed her fingers through his hair, pushing his head back against the sofa cushions, holding him there. "Listen to me, Jason Thorne. Bert Taylor tried to tell you something about that attack this evening and you refused to hear him out. Well, you're going to hear me, mister, so listen up good. Are you paying attention? Or, more to the point, are you sober enough to comprehend?"

Jason stared at her, wondering what one good thing he'd done in his life to deserve this woman.

"I never uncorked the jug. So be warned, I'm counting on you to make up the difference in relieving my misery." To emphasize his point, Jason's hand caressed her thigh, and her little catch of breath nearly brought another smile. "Well, are you going to talk? You most definitely have my attention." He shifted his hips slightly, letting her feel just how attentive he truly was.

"Stop trying to distract me," she snapped, tossing his caressing hand off her leg.

"Is that what I'm doing? Am I distracting you?" He found her thigh again, only this time a little higher than before.

"You're trying very hard to avoid this conversation," she whispered, pressing her forehead to his. "Jason, the other day you made me hear some pretty hard things about myself. I didn't particularly want to listen, either."

"Amanda, don't you realize that whatever you've got to say won't alter a damn thing. I was clubbed in the courthouse square by a sick, drunk, hate-crazy old man, and I couldn't—wouldn't—lift a single finger in my own defense. I owed that old man every one of those licks, and took my punishment. Unfortunately, my flogging was accomplished in public, which is like declaring open season on my hide. They'll all be wanting a piece of me now. It's finished here."

"Then you aren't particularly interested in hearing that Grant Winston whipped that group into a mob after he'd spent the afternoon plying them with liquor and dragging out the past. He was quite creative on the present as well, so I heard. Wouldn't you—"

"No, I wouldn't," he said more harshly than he'd intended. "Amanda," he said more gently, "there is nothing you can tell me about Winston, or this town, that would come as any particular surprise. Deep down in my gut, I think I always knew it would never change."

"Why did you come back here, then?"

The hand that had been resting on her leg lifted to stroke her cheek.

"Primarily for you," he said, brushing his fingers across her lips. "I began corresponding with Julie after Lucy and Susan died. When I learned your husband had passed away, I nearly killed myself finishing up the job I was working on to get here before some other fellow snapped you up again. I would have come straight to Kansas City, if not for the fear you might have already remarried or moved away. Julie was my link to you. When I got here, she was in a hell of a mess, and I got detoured from my purpose temporarily. However, we were keeping close checks on you. If you'd been honest with your aunt from the beginning, we'd never have let you battle that alone so long." He kissed her lightly, hushing her when she would have spoken.

"But it's this land as well, Amanda. There's something about these hills that latches on to a man. Put simply, it's home. There's a beauty that few can see at first glance. It isn't like the mountains, or the ocean. One look and their majesty inspires poets. Here, you have to stop and take your time. You have to watch the seasons, because it's never the same way twice. With every sunrise and sunset, there's something discovered that you didn't see the day before. I've missed it, and didn't even know it all these years." His voice grew softer on every word, his touch more tender upon her face, and his eyes more loving than she'd ever seen them.

"I wanted to come home, Amanda. That's what the TJ always represented to me. From the time I was fourteen, the summers here were the best part of my life. Todd would take me aside and patiently show me how this or that should be done. When I did well, he praised my efforts. When I screwed up, he sent me back to start again. He *never* made me feel less than a man. And there was Julie with her excuses to get me into the kitchen where she could feed me. Do you know she gave me the first caress of my entire life? One day she put her arm across my shoulders and gave me a squeeze. I nearly killed myself getting out of the kitchen before I hid out in the barn and blubbered like a baby. And when I left, you had become part of that picture. When I thought of you, dreamed of you, it was always here. . . ."

Both had tears in their eyes when his voice trailed off.

"I love you very much, Jason Thorne. You know that, don't you?"

"Yes," he croaked. "And it's a good thing, woman. Because you're all that's left of my dream now."

They held each other for a very long time. Finally Amanda lifted her head from his shoulder.

"What now, Jason?" She would not try to convince him to stay in this place. They would destroy him in time.

"I don't know. I haven't allowed myself to think that far ahead yet. But I don't want you to worry. I've done pretty well for myself over the years. We'll manage fine. One thing for certain, I won't leave

Julie until this business is settled. Then . . . well, then we can decide."

"Will you go back to your old occupation?"

He heard the fear in her voice. Lucy had always sounded slightly anxious, her face set much like Amanda's when she asked him about the next job, not even able to breathe safely when the current one was done.

"I don't think so. You see, I'd started losing my fear. I was taking on the jobs no sane man would tackle, thumbing my nose at fate. Life means too much to me now." He reached up and began pulling pins from her hair, unrolling the pads supporting her elegant style. "I know you need security, Amanda. You'll have it, I swear—"

She kissed him hard. "I need *you*."

He tousled her vibrant tresses. "One of these days soon I want you to confide in me about Sarah's father. But not tonight. Tonight we have more important things to accomplish."

"Such as?"

His lips curved upward in a mischievous smile. "First of all, if you're to be my bad woman, then you've a few things to learn. You can start by standing up and slipping off that modest wrapper."

She did, letting it fall at her feet.

"Now shake out your hair and toss it back."

Again Amanda followed his instructions.

"Very good," he praised softly, feeling the muscles of his stomach contract when she stood there tousled and incredibly seductive in her skimpy, soft underwear. "At least you look more the part of the temptress."

"What now?" she asked, feeling decidedly uncomfortable beneath his hot gaze.

"Well, there is only one basic rule that a lady of questionable virtue needs remember. And that is that she never, never questions or denies any request her gentleman might make in the course of an evening. She is there to satisfy any pleasure and desire that might strike his fancy."

"Jason, I—I don't know . . . about this," Amanda gulped.

"You don't need to know, Mandy. I have all the knowledge either of us need to play this out. Just remember, this was your idea. You came to cheer me up, and I don't mind admitting I'm in dire need of cheering. Shall we go on?"

She nodded, not daring imagine how many women he'd known to allow him to gain such expertise in this game.

"Your seductive pose is all wrong. You're standing too stiffly. Here, let me show you what I mean."

He pushed off the sofa and breathed "relax" in her ear before he began to position her body as if he were a sculptor and she his living clay. He molded every inch of her body with his hands, moving her this way and that, all the while watching her face.

"There," he breathed finally, stepping back to admire his handiwork.

Her skin was flushed from head to toe, glowing with the dawn of her arousal. Her lips were slightly parted, and little panting breaths were being expelled. Jason let his gaze linger on his finest accomplishment, the eager thrusting tips of her breasts, pebble firm and trembling slightly with her respirations.

"Now wet your lips, Amanda." His own breathing wasn't any too steady as he watched her small tongue glide over the fullness of her mouth.

"Again," he rasped.

This time he was there to sip and partake of her sweetness. She was so innately sensual it was difficult not to take her there and then. With extreme effort, he stood back once again.

"Now undress me, Amanda."

Without hesitation she immediately went to do his bidding, totally involved in the game now. When she spread the edges of his shirt, she didn't need his voiced request to touch his beautiful chest, or to run her fingers over his nipples and delight in the response so similar to her own. On her own initiative she touched her tongue to one, and then the other, loving the way he shuddered beneath her. With his encouragement, and without, she slowly removed his clothing until he stood naked and splendid before her. His state of arousal made her weak and she drew her eyes upward.

"What now, Jason?"

What he was thinking would have made her swoon. Even bad girls, who were very, very good, needed to be led gently. "Take off everything but your stockings and shoes . . . slowly."

The camisole was drawn up inch by inch, crawling upward until he grew too impatient and urged her instead to hurry. Immediately he realized Amanda had not been trying to tease, but had felt shy about baring herself so boldly. He was rushing her into intimacies between them she wasn't ready for. Even knowing that, Jason couldn't stop it now. There were too many empty nights, filled only with dreams. Dreams of Amanda and moments such as this. He'd seen one dream taken from him tonight. He was too selfish to give up another. When she finally stepped out of her drawers, Jason smiled at her gently.

"You are so very beautiful. Just being able to look at you this way makes up for everything."

Her modesty faded, and she held herself erect and proud while he looked to his heart's content. When he began to explore her with his hands as well as his eyes, Amanda didn't think she'd ever known greater contentment. She let him lead her back to the sofa.

"Sit down, my love," he requested with a gentle push. He knelt before her, bracing his arms against the edge of the bottom cushion. Rocking forward, he kissed her with an unrestrained passion, working his lips over hers, pressing, and then easing back only to start the process all over again. He placed lingering kisses on her eyes, the tip of her nose, and touched his tongue to the freckles across her cheeks.

"I'd rather taste you than peppermint," he told her as his tongue dragged down her neck.

When he found her breasts her eyes closed as he alternately nibbled and suckled there, until she was certain no other woman on earth had ever been loved with such exquisite care. With every tug of his mouth fire shot to her loins, creating an inferno of need. She didn't even notice when he nudged her knees apart and wedged his body there. But she knew when his fingers found her liquid warmth and made her cry out from the delicate probing.

The sound she made nearly robbed Jason of his hard-fought control. He moved both hands over her hips, sliding them beneath her.

"Do you know how many nights, imagined moments such as this have robbed me of sleep, and nearly of my sanity?" As he talked he was edging her hips nearer the end of the cushion, dropping light kisses on her stomach and the tops of her thighs. "Remember now, no questions, and no denials. You're to allow me any pleasure I desire." He spread more kisses across her legs. "And also remember how much I love you."

His mouth began to work closer and closer to the apex of her thighs, his head dipping to kiss her softly, briefly, where she'd never before been kissed. Amanda gasped when she felt that faint touch again, wanting to protest vehemently. She held her tongue until he wedged his shoulders beneath her legs. "Jason!" she cried hoarsely. "You—you surely don't mean—"

"Hush," he insisted, letting his warm breath caress and fan across her delicate flesh.

"You wouldn't," she groaned, knowing it was exactly his intent.

"Ah, but I would," he told her with a nuzzle. "I am," he added.

Amanda's hips left the sofa with the shock of his mouth moving over her flesh. Her heart leapt up into her throat, and there were no more denials as he took his pleasure, and gave her even more with the tender forays of his lips and tongue. And when she could stand no more, Jason took her up and over the edge of the world.

Amanda awakened to the sunlight streaming in through the window of the bunkhouse and across

Jason's wonderful brass bed. She automatically reached for him, but he wasn't beside her. Her head came up off the pillow. He was sitting cross-legged and had been watching her sleep.

"I was just about to awaken you. It would probably be best if Sarah didn't find you here."

She sat up immediately, hearing him chuckle before he pulled her to him for a long kiss.

"My Lord, Mandy. You're blushing. After last night you're still blushing. You really are a wonder. Sensual, passionate"—he paused for effect—"imaginative, and yet still enough of a lady to blush crimson when caught naked in her lover's bed in the light of day. Do wives blush as prettily, I wonder?"

She scrambled off the bed, dragging the sheet with her and wrapping it around her nakedness. "I would imagine so, if they're married to you, Mr. Thorne. You have the most outrageous—"

"And you love it!" He shouted after her, leaving the bed unabashedly in his natural state to go in search of his trousers. "Will you?" he asked rather absently while stepping into his customary chinos.

"Will I what?" she responded equally vague as the camisole slithered down over her breasts, hiding her from his view.

Jason rounded the sofa and hooked an arm around her waist, pulling her hard against him.

"Will you blush when you're Mrs. Thorne?"

The soft embers which were always aglow in her golden eyes leapt to flame, but not the angry kind. This was the warm flame of the hearth, the soft flicker of a fire on a winter's evening, welcoming a man home.

"I'm certain of it," she said softly, her voice thick with love. "And you'll keep making up new fantasies to fulfill to keep me blushing, won't you?"

"Is that a rhetorical question, Amanda?"

"Yes, I suppose it is."

"When are you going to tell Sarah?" Julie was asking while she put another stitch in a tiny little dress.

"I don't know," Amanda answered honestly. "She was so devastated when Harry died. I know she worships Jason, but will she accept him as her father? Then, on top of that, we'll probably be leaving sometime not in the too distant future." Amanda's voice caught on the last. "I can't bear to think of leaving you, Auntie. Won't you even discuss—"

"Why don't we start taking one day at a time around here. First let's see what happens at the mayor's house this afternoon. Now that I've stirred up this hornet's nest, I can't very well just tell people like the Taylors that I've changed my mind."

"No, I guess you can't." Amanda looked out over the meadow. They'd brought the kitchen chairs outside and were sitting in the shade of the house where a cool breeze was coming in off the hills. "Auntie," Amanda said with a puzzled frown, rising slowly from her chair. "Do I see smoke over there? Or is it just my imagination?"

Julie dropped her sewing things and left her chair to walk briskly to the rail fence. Cupping her hands over her eyes she squinted off into the distance. Then she whirled around.

"Amanda, I want you to go and pack clothes for

the three of us. Just grab as much as you can and stuff them into the biggest suitcase you can find. I'm going to the bunkhouse and do the same for Jase. When you're done with that, come back out here. If Jason don't see that smoke and get himself back here, we're going to have to hitch the horses to the wagon."

"Why—What?" Amanda sputtered.

"Prairie fire, girl. And there's nothing that moves faster, or is more unpredictable under God's heavens. And, grab up as many matches as you can find and put them where they'll be handy." Again Amanda gave her aunt a dumb look. "Where do you think the expression fight fire with fire came from, girl? *Now, move your bustle!*"

Chapter Seventeen

AMANDA WAS LUGGING THE SUITCASE OUT INTO THE yard when Jason came riding back through the gate. He pulled the horse up and dismounted in the same motion, wasting no time as he began unsaddling the bay. Julie came out of the bunkhouse and tossed a carpetbag down near the suitcase.

"What have we got, Jase? Or can you tell?"

He tossed the saddle and tack carelessly into the barn.

"It's big and hot, and it's moving right this way. I've opened all the pasture gates. Are you ready?"

"Sarah's packing some of her dolls," Amanda told him.

He turned to her with regret in his eyes.

"Tell her to be very selective, Amanda. We'll be crowded in the automobile as it is."

She didn't question his judgment. "I'll go take care of it."

"How do you think it got started, Jase? I know it's been dry, but I thought we had a month or more before the grass turned to tinder, especially since it's cooled off some lately."

"Julie, *how* makes little difference. It's spreading and the wind is moving it along at a healthy clip. We've got to get into town and organize a brigade for firebreaks. Otherwise, we're ashes."

Within ten minutes they were all squeezed inside the cab of the automobile. Sarah was on Julie's lap since their luggage was stacked where she would customarily sit. Between Amanda's legs in the front were picks and shovels to dig trenches. The small box of Sarah's "most favorite" dolls rested between herself and Jason on the seat.

Amanda turned to her aunt and caught Julie hanging her head out, possibly taking one last look at her home. She whirled back around and tried to hide her own tears. When Jason's hand slipped into her own, she squeezed it tightly. Behind them, still in the distance, yet growing denser, thick clouds of smoke rose up to block the sun.

They made it into Stockton without incident, and Jason stopped the automobile near the courthouse square. Groups of people were moving about the street, shouting to one another, while wagons were pulled into the street and loaded with firefighting materials. When they emerged from the vehicle,

Jason directed the women toward the mayor's house.

"You'll be welcome there, and I'll know where to find you later."

"Where are you going?" Amanda pulled on his arm when he would have sprinted away.

"There's a fire to fight, Amanda. The sooner we get started, the better chance we have of keeping it contained." He read the fear and concern in her expressive eyes. "Honey, they're going to need every strong back they can get. My head will be safe." He gave her a quick grin. "At least until this is over. By then, there won't be man with enough energy left to crawl, let alone start up a brawl." He gave her a hard, quick kiss before moving to Julie and Sarah. They, too, were hugged before he went loping off with his tools to join the men.

It didn't take long for the Davis home to fill with women and children coming in from outlying farms and ranches. All were fearful and anxious for their homes and loved ones. It seemed the winds had shifted and were now blowing directly out of the west, which would bring the flames across the most heavily populated region in this area. It also meant that the town of Stockton lay directly in the fire's path, should the blaze reach this far before it was controlled. But the wind could be capricious and could turn without warning. Right now the TJ was safe from immediate danger. Right now they were all alive and safe.

When Doc Kelly came by the house to solicit volunteers for a first-aid camp and rest station for the firefighters, Amanda jumped forward to volunteer, only to be dragged forcibly into another room by her furious aunt.

"Have you lost your ever-lovin' mind, Amanda?" Julie ranted, throwing up her arms when her stubborn niece refused to relent. "That's a raging, maybe out of control, prairie fire out there. There isn't going to be no fire wagon to come rolling to the rescue, girl. Honey, I've seen walls of flame ten, twenty feet high. These fires can go for days, destroying hundreds of miles of grass and property. They twist and turn with the wind like a snake—over yonder one minute, heating your backside the next." She took Amanda firmly by the shoulders. "You just go out there and tell Doc Kelly you didn't know what you were letting yourself in for. He'll understand, with you being new to this kind of thing. They'll all understand."

"I can't, Auntie," Amanda said firmly. "Think about this for a minute. Only four other women volunteered. That means there will be ten or more men apiece for every woman going; possibly more if help from Peabody arrives. Do you believe if there's a choice between two injured men needing help, any one of them would choose Jason? They'd stop to wrap a stubbed toe while he bled to death and you know it!"

Julie's hands fell away. "I can't argue with you there, Amanda. Just keep your eyes open and do what they tell you. Don't try to be some silly heroine. You've got a little girl needing you. And, if something should happen to you, and I had to face Jason with it, honey—"

"Don't worry," Amanda breathed, giving her aunt a quick hug. Then she was running to join the others before they could leave her behind.

Amanda emptied a dipper of stew into a bowl and passed it to a weary, soot-stained man. She watched as he and several others gulped down this meager meal, drank as much water as they could get, and then headed back to the firebreaks. They came in shifts of no more than two or three at a time. The only other way they received any rest was when they were overcome by smoke and brought in over someone's shoulder for medical treatment. Even then, most went right back out there the minute they revived.

She looked over at the medical tent. Doc Kelly kept busy with burns and the men overcome by smoke. So far, there had been no serious injuries, for which they were all grateful.

From all reports the blaze was being contained at present. The wind was holding steady from out of the west, and if their luck held, the immediate danger would be over by midnight. But at all times they were ready to move swiftly should sudden gusts or shifts in the wind's direction put this camp in danger. The doctor had already said they were to jump in the wagon and leave everything behind on a single word.

Amanda had a moment to rest, and sat down away from the heat of the cooking fire, but not too far lest it should jump out of its confining stones. She'd learned a definite respect for fires and grass this day.

Sometimes the odor of burning grass and smoke

made her stomach turn, and she often wondered if some poor creature had been caught in the fire's path. As night fell, the leaping orange spikes of flame became more sharply defined, and somehow more ominous. The darkness seemed to intensify this terrible natural enemy. Yet, at times it could mesmerize . . .

Amanda shook herself. She was tired, but that was no excuse for sloughing off her duties. Fishing her small knife out of the bucket of water filled with recently peeled carrots, potatoes, and onions, Amanda began to slice them into the second pot simmering on yet another fire, adding the vegetables to the sparing slivers of meat. There was no salt, pepper, or other seasoning to make this bland meal palatable. But the men forked it down as if it were fare from the gods.

She'd just finished with the vegetables when three more men came in. Each time she scanned their faces for Jason. And each time she was disappointed. This, it would seem, would be no exception. She did, however, recognize Bert Taylor and Billy Granger in this group.

"Have you seen Jason?" she asked the two men as she filled their bowls and handed them spoons from the pocket of her apron.

"I did a while back," Billy answered. "He was digging like a madman, and looked to be fine."

"Thank you," she told him when he walked away. "Bert?"

"I'm sorry, Amanda. I haven't seen Jase for several hours. I'm sure he's all right, or somebody would have passed the word."

"Would they?" Amanda looked away. "Are you very certain they wouldn't leave him lying where he fell?"

Bert Taylor reached out and patted her shoulder. "He and Jack were together. They'll look out for each other. If you'll remember, it was Jack who put a stop to old man Blane."

Amanda snorted with humorless laughter. "I rather thought he did that to save Jason for himself."

Bert grinned and smoothed his mustache in an attempt to hide the smile he knew she wouldn't understand. "Well, that, too. But Jack's not a bad fellow. Billy, either. They just get a little rambunctious at times."

She felt guilty for keeping him from his rest period. "Go sit down, Bert. Alva will have my head if you're not taken care of properly."

Another hour passed with no sign of either Jason or Jack. Amanda peeled more potatoes and kept watch over the cook fires. When another man was brought in, this time with some fairly serious burns, she feared she would go insane if there wasn't any word or sign of Jason soon.

The woman who had been assigned to assist Doc Kelly came out to Amanda. "Mrs. Ames, the man they just brought in would like a word with you."

For a moment her heart stilled, and then she realized how foolish she was being. The injured man was twice Jason's age. While the other woman looked after the cook fires, Amanda raced over to the tent. And when she stood next to the cot where the man rested, she was glad she had a strong stomach. The right side of this poor man's face, neck, and upper body was a solid mass of oozing blisters.

"I'm Mrs. Ames. You wished to speak to me, sir?"

"Knew you were the lady in town with Thorne and Julie Danfield the other day. My name's George Franklin, ma'am. Thought you'd like to hear it was Thorne who pulled me out and carried me a half mile until he found somebody to bring me on in. He talked a lot about you during that mile." The old man tried to smile, and the pain brought a garbled moan.

"Don't try to talk any more, Mr. Franklin. I'm grateful to know he was still well when you last saw him. Can I get you anything?"

"No, I'm going to be fine. Just hurts like the dickens. But I've got a message for you. He said to tell you he'd heard you was here, and that you should expect him to—" The man looked embarrassed. "I apologize, ma'am, but he made me promise to repeat this just like he said it. He said to tell you that you should expect him to warm your backside till you can't sit for a month of Sundays."

A smile broke on Amanda's face, and relief sighed through her body. "He really is all right, then. Thank you, Mr. Franklin. I assure you I took no offense." Amanda thanked him again and turned to walk away.

"Ma'am," George Franklin called. "There's a good many fighting that fire out there who are startin' to say it's a pure blessing to have one of the devil's own out there with them. But no devil pulled me out of that brush and carried me out. I'd say maybe this town has a lot to atone for."

Amanda had to bite her tongue to stop from telling this injured man the town was a bit too late in having its eyes opened. However, that wasn't her place. Forgiveness or condemnation was Jason's.

She was folded over her knees, her eyes staring into the dwindling flame of her cook fire, when a voice brought her head snapping up.

"You're in a heap of trouble, woman," Jason growled.

"So I've heard," she informed him saucily, reaching for his hands and holding on tightly. He pulled her to her feet. She looked him over from head to toe, even to walking around him, before she was satisfied he was all in one piece. "You wouldn't do anything rash with all these people watching, would you, Jason?"

"Don't tempt me," he warned.

"Well, you'd better eat something first, then. Because you'll need your strength if you plan to tangle with me. Most anyone in this town can confirm that fact."

He took the bowl of stew she handed him and plopped down on the ground, pulling her down beside him. "You didn't tell how you'd handled Winston, Amanda. Jack hasn't stopped talking about you all day. It's a good thing I'm not sensitive about my manhood. Having a woman who wins battles, while I'm consistently picking myself up off the floor, could be a bit hard on a man's ego."

She rested her head against his shoulder. "Neither

your ego . . . or your manhood . . . has a thing to worry about, Jason. They're both quite well intact. Which I would gladly give testimony to should the need arise."

"There's only one need you have to worry about arising, Amanda," he whispered suggestively in her ear.

"Is it bad out there, Jason?" Amanda asked, changing the subject.

"I've seen worse. If this wind will hold soft like it is right now, we'll have this thing licked in another hour or two."

While he finished his stew, Amanda told him what was being said about him around this fire. In the men's voices had been a dawning of respect. He made no comment except to ask for more water when his cup was empty. When he'd drunk it, he came to his feet.

"If I don't see you again, I'll meet you back at the Davis house when we're through here. But don't worry if I don't show up until morning. Even when this fire is out, we'll be drawing lots to see which of us will post watch through the night."

On his way out Jason gave her a hard swat on the rear.

Amanda was stretched out on a quilt in the middle of the Davises' living room, sound asleep, when something prodded her awake. She opened her eyes to see Jason squatting down beside her.

"Is it over?" she asked with a yawn.

"We believe so," he whispered back. "Why are you sleeping on the floor?"

"Because there is no more room at the inn, so to speak."

"Let's go home, then," he said, lifting her right up off her pallet, standing her on her feet. "Where are Julie and Sarah?"

"Upstairs, sharing a bed." She was being swept along with him, her bare feet making no noise on the wooden floors. Jason, too, walked quietly. "Jason, won't they wonder where I've gone?" she asked in a slightly louder voice when they were outside the house.

"Do you really care?"

"Well, this really is highly improper. You know very well what people will think if I just go off with you in the middle of the night."

Jason put his arm around her waist as they walked. "I'll confess I abducted you and carried you off in a wild frenzy of uncontrollable lust. Then I'll offer to do right by you, we'll let Miles Davis marry us, and this town and their opinions can go suck an egg. How's that?"

"Impressive," she admitted with a chuckle.

She watched while he struggled to start the automobile, cussing a blue streak when it started and stopped several times. When he finally slid into the vehicle, he looked at her and growled, "Woman, you're going to learn to drive this contraption of mine. Because the next time I spend the entire day and most of the night fighting a prairie fire, I'm not going to be the one driving home."

"Yes, sir," she said meekly, settling back with a smile to watch him very closely all the way home, wishing that the TJ could always be home for them.

* * *

"Outrageous," she repeated again for at least the fifth time, shaking her head, unable to believe she'd been bullied into this.

Jason's eyes opened slowly and fixed on her warningly. "Say that one more time, and I'll do something that will make that word obsolete in your mind. You're also falling down on the job."

Amanda sluiced water over the chest she'd just scrubbed. One of his legs came up out of the bathwater and dropped down on her shoulder, nearly pushing her under the water they were sharing. "Jason, I believe you're trying to drown me."

His eyes were closed, but his lips moved in a twitch of a smile. She picked up the soap and began to lather that sinewy hair-roughened limb from his ankle as far as she could reach. Slick with soap, his leg slid over her skin until his knee was bent over her back. When she began to wash his thigh, she felt a slight flexing of his calf muscle, which tightened perceptibly when she started to move back, trapping her there. Irritated, she looked up at him to find a single green eye, with a decidedly wicked glint, watching her closely.

"Jason," she said with the most infinite patience. "You are too exhausted to be frisky, so please let's get on with this before we're both shriveled and prunish."

His leg slid off her back, and his wet hands captured the back of her neck, bringing her to him for a kiss. When he released her, his gaze was apologetic, even contrite as he lifted the other leg and cooperated until the job was done.

A short time later they were cuddled in the bed together, and Amanda had to smile when Jason apologized for not being able to make love to her tonight.

"Don't be unnecessarily stupid," she told him softly, playing with his hair, loving the way his head felt pillowed upon her breasts. He kissed her there lightly, and then he sighed deeply.

She thought he was asleep when he said, "Amanda, are you truly as unafraid now as you pretend to be?"

"No," she admitted. "But I *want* to be. Will that serve?"

"Mmmm," was his only answer.

Chapter Eighteen

AMANDA WAS KEEPING JASON'S BREAKFAST WARM.
He'd ridden out shortly after dawn to check the
stock and close all the pasture gates. Because the
wind had changed direction, carrying the fire away
from, instead of toward, the TJ, it was doubtful the
cattle had wandered very far. Since there had been
no major threat of fire or heavy smoke, the horses
had been content within the open barn. The only
animals known to be missing were the two fat dairy
cows, who had wandered off to explore the customarily forbidden grass elsewhere.

Dressed and ready to accompany Jason into
Stockton when he returned, Amanda grew restless.

With the meeting of the citizens postponed by the prairie fire, the future still loomed with a huge question mark. Brinkman's deadline on his offer for the TJ would run out at the end of this week. Would Julie be able to reorganize these people before that time? Wouldn't they be occupied in restoring routine after the chaos of the fire? Only one farm had been severely damaged, but fence posts were burned and charred, and animals freed from pasture gates so they could escape the path of the blaze would need to be rounded up. And the ones who had not escaped, and wandered injured, would have to be put to death or prepared for immediate slaughter.

No, Julie would likely not be able to gather the citizens together in her remaining time. What would happen now?

She moved through the empty house, looking for anything that would keep her occupied and her mind clear of the old habit of worry, but she could not keep her thoughts at bay for any length of time.

Amanda was primarily concerned for Aunt Julie. Should the Brinkman situation be resolved, the TJ's financial problems still existed. Amanda might not think highly of Grant Winston; however, she believed his assessment of this ranch's state of affairs had not been overexaggerated. Jason had said they wouldn't leave until Julie was back on her feet again. It could take months, even years, to slowly reestablish security. The thought, on one hand, made Amanda's spirits soar. On the other, they plummeted. What Jason might suffer to his spirit and pride in that time could alter their future in ways she was reluctant to contemplate. Would he grow bitter and morose? Could those who loved him not be lanced by that same two-sided blade of ugly hatred? And should a child be conceived and born in this hostile environment, would it not, too, bear the cross of its father's stigma?

If allowed, Amanda knew her very real concerns would eat away at her own determination to be strong for those who needed her strength. Right now she was holding up, putting on the happy face, hiding the fears of insecurity and uncertainty. She had not entirely fooled Jason, if his sleepy question last night was any indication. But, Amanda knew she must draw deeply upon her one certain strength. Her love for her aunt and daughter, and her total, abiding love for Jason Thorne, would have to be the glue that held her firm.

"Every cloud has a silver lining," she repeated over and over, wishing she had even the smallest measure of Julie's natural optimism.

"After the storm, comes a rainbow."

A great deal of problems might be solved by a decent cloudburst of rain, she grumbled silently.

The sound of the kitchen door opening took Amanda out of the parlor with its worn furnishings. No wonder Julie used it so seldom. It was positively gloomy.

Jason met her in the dining room, kissing her soundly before they went arm and arm into the kitchen, the room that was the very heartbeat of this ranch. Amanda took Jason's biscuits and ham from the warmer and put them before him on the table.

"Well, tell me what you found this morning," she asked somewhat impatiently.

"This will be a short tale. Did you know cows are basically stupid? I've rarely met creatures more dumb. Ours seem to be worse than the average. With the temptation of every pasture gate wide open, and smoke blowing across the field, I believe they moved all of thirty feet maybe."

Amanda laughed. "You shouldn't be complaining, but counting your blessings. The way you were grumbling this morning about chasing cows all over hell's acre, I'd think you would be grateful."

One of his brows lifted. "So you *were* awake and pretending to be asleep. I had my suspicions."

She gave him an impish grin. "I knew if you thought me awake, your day would begin far too late."

"You know me well," he observed before popping the last bit of biscuit into his mouth. "You're all ready to go into Stockton, I see."

The way his gaze swept over her when she left the chair to take his empty plate to the counter, caused a now familiar coiling deep within her belly. When she reached for the plate, Jason's hands captured her waist as he swiveled in his chair, pulling his legs out from beneath the table. She was drawn between his thighs and his nose nuzzled at her full and aching breasts.

"Jason," she said in an unsteady voice, "we've got to get into town. There isn't time. I—I'm all dressed."

"Won't muss a hair on your head," he mumbled against her, his fingers on the buttons of her dress, working his way from the waist up. "Let me show you," he urged, his voice thick and deep with need.

Amanda had no strength to deny him anything he asked, she'd learned. When he put his hands on her, she became a very willing slave to his whim.

He pushed the bodice of her dress off her shoulders. She helped him with the sleeves until the top of her dress lay around her waist. He then untied the ribbon at the gathered neckline of her camisole, and bared her beautiful creamy breasts.

"Unfasten my trousers, Amanda," he whispered against her skin, stroking her with his tongue. When she leaned over to do his bidding, her bounty swayed before him, and he filled his hands with the softness, using his fingers to stoke her fiery passion. When his own throbbing desire was released from the straining fabric, Jason went beneath her skirts and petticoats to draw off her drawers. Then he guided her to his lap, groaning harshly when they were merged as one. Their mouths met in a fiery kiss. Both were eager, hungry for the other, and their passion mounted quickly, fiercely, coming almost too soon to a shattering conclusion.

When Amanda was limp and languid against him, Jason told her, "Do you know how many mornings and nights I've sat right here through my meals so hard and full I could barely eat? And do you have any idea how close I've come to dragging you across me like this? God, this is one fantasy I never expected to have fulfilled. Sorry, my love, but I just couldn't resist—"

"Oh, don't apologize, Jason. For goodness' sake, don't apologize." She was trembling again as she felt him growing within her a second time.

When Jason helped Amanda alight from the automobile, he grinned when she took yet another survey of her appearance. "Narry a hair out of place, sweet Mandy. You look so prim and proper, not a soul would believe you'd just spent a good part of the morning wantonly loving your man smack in the middle of the kitchen."

"Shh," she hissed, her eyes darting to see if anyone was close enough to have heard him. "They've enough food for gossip as it is." Hearing the sharpness in her own tone brought Amanda up smartly. Her eyes were soft when they met his. "Please understand, for Sarah and Julie's sake, we must exercise discretion."

"No," he countered bluntly. "What we need is to be man and wife so it's legal for me to love you anytime and anywhere we choose. Give me the word, and I'll arrange it with Miles Davis right now."

"I want to. You know I do. Only, there's Sarah's feelings to consider. Jason, I want her to accept you completely."

"All right, little mother," he said tenderly. "I'll start charming your daughter until she's begging for me to become her new daddy."

Amanda gave a little laugh. "Well, since she already worships the ground you walk on, that shouldn't be particularly difficult. I just want to be very certain she's happy."

They were still discussing Sarah when they reached the mayor's house. The subject of their concern was playing tag with a half-dozen or more children on the front lawn and barely took time out from her game to wave. But as they approached the front door, Julie Danfield came rushing out.

"Jase," she said rather breathlessly, "I think you'd better make yourself scarce for a while. Fred Hopkins was out checking for any sparks or embers this morning and found a fuel can near where they suspect the fire got started. It's one of those containers you use for gasoline."

"And there's a group gathered inside who have decided arson should be added to the list of Jason Thorne's sins. Am I right?" Julie only nodded. "I appreciate the warning, old girl, but I've no intention of sprinting away like a guilty little boy. In fact, I'd very much like to answer those charges . . . face to face."

Amanda's fingers bit into Jason's arm when he made a move toward the house. But she released him when his eyes asked for her support, not her fear. Then he kissed her fingertips and turned to stride purposefully into the house. Amanda and Julie followed unobtrusively, taking up positions just outside the wide parlor doorway.

Seven unfriendly faces turned to greet him when he entered into this kangaroo court. One man sprung up out of his chair and hurled a metal cylinder across the room. Jason caught it deftly.

"You want to tell us what that is, Thorne?"

Jason carefully examined the scorched container, turning it this way and that in his hands, sniffing at the pour spout.

"It appears to be a gasoline container. I usually carry one much like it in my automobile when I'm traveling any distance."

The man who had elected himself spokesman for this motley group bristled at Jason's coolness.

"Well, then, maybe you'd like to start explaining why Fred Hopkins found that thing near where we figure the fire got started when he was out chasing his dairy cows this morning."

"If you're attempting to make a point here, Mr. Weir, I'm afraid you're not making yourself clear. Unless you men are accusing me of being responsible for yesterday's fire."

Several men leapt to their feet and began shouting just that accusation, and several more that were totally unrelated. Jason felt someone jostle him aside and wasn't surprised when Julie Danfield charged into the room.

"I don't think I've ever seen so many jackasses gathered in a single place in my entire life!" she railed at them. "Good Lord, use your heads— though I'm beginning to think there isn't much inside them thick skulls to use. Think! Before the wind changed, that blaze was heading straight for the TJ. And only a fool or a madman would put a torch to grass already tinder dry in a wind like that. Why would Jase want to destroy the TJ?"

She got an argument, and soon Julie was going nose to nose with half the male population of Stockton. Finally Jason inserted two fingers into his mouth and whistled shrilly. When the noise dropped off, he suggested, "Why don't we turn this over to the sheriff? And, while we're on the subject, has anyone thought to question Grant Winston on his gasoline supply, or what he was doing yesterday while the rest of us were getting the hair singed off our faces?"

"I talked to Winston myself this morning. He says he left early yesterday morning to drive over to Peabody, and that's why he wasn't here. You're just trying to shift blame, Thorne!"

"You've been lookin' for a way to get back at this town since you came back."

"Yeah, and it looks like he almost found it, too."

Amanda couldn't bear to hear anymore. She moved next to Jason and took the tightly clenched fist he held at his side within her hand, working his fingers apart to link them with her own. She flinched when she heard one man say, "We don't need no sheriff to take care of this bastard."

Again Julie tried for reason. "Miles Davis ordered you to keep a lid on your tempers until he could get back."

"Well, where the hell is he? He's been gone over an hour."

"What the devil was he thinking of doing anyway?"

One voice, silent until this moment, piped up and inserted some sense into this lynch-mob-style committee. Very slowly, and with pained effort, George Franklin rose to his feet. The burns he had suffered were livid and raw, but they also became his strongest weapon.

"The mayor told us to wait, and that's what we're going to do. Thorne pulled me from death last night. Now I'm askin' all of you to remember that fact, plus the risk he took upon himself to stand and battle those flames with us. If you all go off half-cocked and do something foolish, I'll see each of you answering for your actions in a court of law."

His quiet authority won out, though there was a low rumbling of dissatisfaction within the room.

The next half hour became the longest of Amanda's life, and she nearly bawled with relief when Miles Davis finally returned to his home. With him were the Taylor and Granger brothers, all four of whom immediately took their stand with Jason.

Soon after, the Sheriff arrived with the elegantly dressed Grant Winston at his side.

From his pleasant smile and manner, Amanda would have thought he was here to attend a dinner party if she'd not known better. He was every bit his customary charming self, greeting everyone by name, giving special attention to the ladies.

Only Jason noticed the careful way the man avoided shaking hands with those he greeted. Sheriff Bailey had taken command of this motley group and began to interrogate the attorney.

"You stated you were in Peabody all day yesterday. Can you verify that, Mr. Winston? Are there folks there who will back that up?"

"Of course," Winston said smoothly. "I spent quite a pleasant time with a lovely young woman and her mother. Though I was quite distressed when the news of the fire reached me there. I didn't drive back until early this morning for fear of being caught in the inferno. There was talk over there of sending a crew to give assistance, but before we could organize, word came you had things under control. From what I understand, you had luck with you last night. But, of course, I know very little about prairie fires."

Jason pushed away from where he'd been leaning indolently against the doorframe.

"Neither do you know much about gasoline, Winston," he said. "Otherwise you would have known that it explodes into flame, not at all like kerosene. You've probably never handled the fuel except to pour it into the tank of your automobile. Isn't that why you dropped this container"—Jason held up the can—"where Fred found it this morning? That was extremely careless of you, Winston. Otherwise, I doubt anyone would have questioned the fire was any more than a freak accident from a cigar or a carelessly dropped match."

"What would be my motive, Thorne? Why would I want to start such a disaster?"

"Ignorance, partly," Jason told him. "I doubt you realized the full potential of a raging prairie fire. Perhaps you only intended a few hours distraction to make certain the meeting scheduled here was disrupted. I don't think it was your intent to cause any destruction outside the boundaries of the TJ. Of course, you couldn't know the wind would change."

"There," Grant said smugly. "You lose your argument right there. Why would I want to destroy the very property my client wishes to purchase?"

Jason ignored the rumbles of accord within the room, wondering why they hadn't silenced him long ago.

"I said you were ignorant of the *full* dangers, Winston. That doesn't mean you are unaware of our practice of setting fires to burn off these grasses ourselves. Under controlled conditions, this is a beneficial rangeland practice, which produces a better, and stronger, yield of grass for our cattle. Nature taught this to the Indians long ago. They, in turn, used it as a weapon against early settlers. What had they to lose? I'll ask you the same question: What did you have to lose by setting fire to the TJ? Except for a small herd of black Angus cattle, I doubt your client views the humble dwellings and outbuildings of the ranch to be of any value. I don't think Mr. Brinkman would mourn an old ranch house and some tumbledown barns and buildings."

"You're reaching, Thorne. You want to shift suspicion away from yourself."

"No, Winston. I want to put suspicion on you, where it belongs. You had two motives. One was to make certain Julie Danfield was left little choice but to sell out. The second was to prevent these foolish people from hearing the truth about you and your less-than-sterling employer."

"You can't prove—why, it's absolutely ludicrous—"

"Winston, take your hands out of your pockets."

"Why?"

"Because I'm going to break your arm doing it for you, if you don't." Jason's expression was deadly earnest. He could see the indecision in the attorney's blue eyes and the temptation to force the challenge. He could also see the bigger man sizing him up. The minutes ticked away. Jason knew he would, and could, break this man's arm before anyone could blink. Perhaps it was the incontestable certainty within his own gaze that swayed the outcome.

Grant Winston slowly drew out his hands. The sheriff stepped closer. "Don't see no burns," the older man drawled.

"Neither do you see any hair, Sheriff," Jason pointed out. Grabbing Winston's right arm, he pushed the sleeve of his shirt and coat back to reveal skin as smooth and hairless as a baby's. "Have you taken to shaving your wrists, Winston? Or did you learn the hard way not to toss a match onto gasoline?" He let the man's hand fall. "I imagine if he's examined more closely you'll also find a blister here and there."

"By God, I believe you've got something,

Thorne," the sheriff was saying as Jason turned and walked back to Amanda. When he saw the pride in her eyes, he knew he truly did have something. More than he could ever possibly have dreamed.

Near the mayor's hearth, Jason watched those who would have accused him leave the room, one and two at a time, behind the sheriff. Grant Winston had been arrested on suspicion of arson. Jason doubted very much the man would actually pay for the crime, because proving his guilt in a court of law on such flimsy evidence was unlikely. However, in this town he was finished, and Brinkman along with him.

Had the past thirty minutes really happened?

He gave his head a disbelieving shake, wondering if he might have gone a little crazy. The men in this room, for the most part, had listened, giving his theories serious consideration. They'd heeded Jason Thorne, the half-breed, the bastard, and he wasn't certain what to make of that.

At the call of his name, Jason's attention was drawn to the parlor doorway, where Bert and Ken Taylor shouted a friendly farewell.

"Next time you're in town, Jase, stop by the station for a chat," Bert invited, and the genial expression on his face was genuine.

Jason felt certain this was a dream, and he was about to wake up, because reality, in the form of Jack Granger, was striding directly toward him.

Jack Granger stopped in front of Jason, and the mocking smile on the man's face was one familiar to the half-breed.

"Havin' you back in town seems to have its

advantages after all," Jack said in a tone just short of a jeer. "It's been hellishly dull since you've been gone, Thorne."

Jason watched Jack's hand extend, and hesitated only a fraction of a second before he gave this old enemy his own. There was the clench of muscle and bone as his fingers felt the gradual pressure increase. His own grasp tightened when the blood left his fingers. And so it went, this childish feud of superiority in the handshake that wasn't really a handshake, but one man's testing of the other man's mettle.

It ended in a draw, but Jason technically had the slight edge of victory. It was Jack who first took a gulp of air and expelled it slowly as his grip relaxed suddenly.

"Yep, hellishly dull," Jack repeated, the strain of the contest still on his face. However, the smile in his eyes was tinged with respect. "See you around, Thorne."

"I imagine you will, Jack," Jason returned.

The minute a foe, who might become a friend in time, left the room, Amanda came to his side, her eyes clouded with worry. When she looked directly at the hand he was flexing, Jason knew she'd been witness to some very silly behavior and grinned at her foolishly before slipping his tingling hand around her shoulder, drawing her close.

"Is everything all right?" she asked worriedly.

"Never better, sweet Mandy," he said, feeling contentment flow through him like a warm tide when he looked into her lovely face. With a motion of his free hand, he summoned Julie Danfield. "Well, old girl, it looks as if you're going to have to rebuild that bankrupt old ranch after all."

"Sure does look that way, Jase. Might be a bit difficult, since I'm flat broke."

Jason felt Amanda tense, and he soothed her with a gentle pat. "Well, I just might know a man who's awfully sick and tired of traveling hither and yon all over the continent, who might consider the investment."

"Takes a powerful lot of money to run a ranch, you know," Julie cautioned.

"Oh, he's got money to burn," Jason informed her. "What he doesn't have is a home and family, which by his standards are beyond price."

"Then that's just the kind of partner I could use," Julie said rather huskily, her eyes brimming with glad tears.

Jason opened his embrace and the old woman stepped into it as he drew them together, completing the circle.

Amanda felt him come up behind her, but didn't take her eyes off the brilliant sunset, even when his arms slid around her waist.

"You're upset with me for not telling you, aren't you?" he asked low in her ear.

"No," she responded, certain he would never understand, positive she could never really explain her ridiculous thoughts. He'd probably laugh himself silly if she told him she was upset because she had braced herself to face adversity and sacrifice and now would never have the opportunity. It was absolutely insane, this disappointment. She'd lost the chance to meet her fears head on and rise above herself with courage, fortitude, and love. Now she would never know if she was truly worthy of being Jason's wife.

"Talk to me, Amanda," Jason pleaded, fearful that this last secret kept from her had damaged the tenuous trust that had begun to bind them together.

She turned in his arms, smoothly, easily, seeing his fear and feeling instant remorse at being the cause.

"We're not poor," she stated. "We never actually were in any danger of starvation. You were supporting us all along."

"I told you I'd done well for myself," he said uneasily, watching the way the setting sun behind her seemed to get caught up in her hair and glow out of the warm embers of her eyes.

"Yes, you did, didn't you." Her arms draped over his shoulders. "However, you neglected one small detail. You might also have mentioned you owned the company that specializes in taking on impossible jobs, and that you've made yourself a small fortune blowing things up."

He grinned a little guiltily. "Well, if you'll remember, I was being somewhat distracted by this lady—and I use the term guardedly—who was doing her damnedest to seduce me at the time."

"That's no excuse at all, Mr. Thorne. You should have more control over yourself than that." Purposely, Amanda stepped between his legs, and did her damnedest to seduce him out of that control once again. Her success was immediate.

Jason drew in his breath sharply at the unsubtle

movement of her hips. "Do you want to hear this explanation or not, woman," he growled in her ear.

"Certainly," she responded, her own breathing none too steady as he backed her against the fence so that she could not mistake how little talking was on his mind. "But I think this conversation should be held in private; somewhere where we can work this problem out to our mutual satisfaction."

"Oh, I agree wholeheartedly. Can you suggest such a meeting place?" When her eyes shifted from his face, Jason looked back over his shoulder, following the direction of her gaze.

When he turned his head back, Amanda flushed hotly while that Pan-like grin spread and one brow lifted in roguish query. "Well, you're not the *only* one with fantasies, Mr. Thorne," she told him defensively. With a deep, husky chuckle, Jason was sweeping her up into his arms and sprinting that short distance toward the barn.

Tapestry

HISTORICAL ROMANCES

POCKET BOOKS

TAPESTRY ROMANCES